In Your Silence

Silence

Grace Lowrie

Published by Accent Press Ltd 2019
Octavo House
West Bute Street
Cardiff
CF10 5LJ

www.accentpress.co.uk

ISBN 9781786155313
eISBN 9781786155320

Printed and bound in Great Britain by Clays Ltd,
Elcograf S.p.A

Silence is more musical than any song.

– Christina Rossetti

Chapter One

She'd left me. My girlfriend of nearly six years just upped and left without warning. The first I knew of it was tripping over her house keys on the doormat and spotting an apologetic note stuck to the fridge. Which explained precisely nothing:

I'm sorry but it's over. I can't stay. Please don't try to find me.

It's not your fault, it's nothing you've done, it's just over, I'm sorry.

Goodbye, Cally.

Nonplussed I re-read it several times. Calm, practical Cally; this wasn't like her. We never fought, never argued; I thought we were happy; content.

Dumping my muddy boots at the back door I searched the rest of our terraced two-bed house, room by room, ducking my six-and-a-half foot frame, stepping crab-like through doorways and scanning the remaining space as if it was all a mistake, a game of hide and seek, or an elaborate joke – I certainly felt like a fool. But it was the second of April today – the deadline for pranks had passed. She'd taken all her clothes, most of her toiletries, her laptop, mobile, passport; even that big old stuffed bunny of hers.

Returning to the kitchen I dug my own phone out of my pocket and speed-dialled her number, but it went straight to voicemail and I suspected she had it switched off. Having left a brief message asking her to call me, I rang Cally's best friend, Marguerite. She was still at work in London and apparently surprised to hear from me. She claimed to have no knowledge of Cally's plans or whereabouts, but then, what had I expected her to say? She was loyal to Cally – she'd only say whatever Cally wanted her to say, and I didn't know Marguerite well enough to be sure she was lying.

Climbing into the van, I drove over to Marguerite's flat above the gift card shop. I listened at the door before hammering on it; but there were no signs of life from within. Should I call Cally's parents in Spain? Was that where she'd run off to? Did she just need a break; a holiday? Cally's mum and dad had seemed to 'approve' of me on the one and only occasion we'd met, but they were unlikely to help me against Cally's wishes. And anyway, I didn't have their number.

What to do? Returning home again I paced about in my socks, dried mud flaking off the knees of my trousers as I brushed past the furniture that we'd picked out as a couple – evidence of the life we shared. The framed black and white photograph above the fireplace caught my eye, showing the two of us side by side, and smiling.

This wasn't us – we didn't do drama and she knew I didn't like surprises. I had to find her; figure out what had gone wrong and fix it, so that the world could go back to normal.

My phone vibrated in my hand and I hoped it was Cally, but it was James. Muting the cheery ringtone I deliberated answering while his name flashed on the screen. He was my best mate; had been since school; ever since his mum died a few short years after my own. We never spoke about our grief, but it created a bond between us; a bond reinforced through playing rugby and helping each other survive our teens. Aside from a few years in which we'd attended different universities, we'd always kept in touch. And now that he'd moved back to Wildham our friendship was stronger than ever.

But I wasn't ready to share my 'news' yet; my increasing sense of shame. James would be occupied at the garden centre for the next few days – Easter weekend was always busy – and that gave me time to find my girlfriend and put things right before anyone found out.

She would change her mind and come back, I was sure of it; she had to; all she needed was time.

*

Eight weeks later I was sat in my local with my head in my hands.

'Orange juice or coke?' James said.

'I'll have a pint of lager.'

'Lager?' I met James's shocked expression with a standard blank one. 'But you don't drink.'

'I do today.'

He hovered uneasily by our table and I sighed.

'I'm teetotal by choice, not because I'm an alcoholic.'

'I know, but... Liam... you haven't had a drink for years, are you sure?'

'Yes. I'll buy it myself if it makes you feel better?'

'No, no, you deserve a drink and I'm happy to buy you one, only…'

'What?'

'Well, you've coped without her for two whole months… are you sure you want to do this to yourself now?'

He was right of course. I was feeling frustrated, foolish and sorry for myself, but I'd gotten this far; did I really want to make things worse…?

'Orange juice,' I grunted.

'Good choice.' He was clearly relieved as he headed for the bar.

Several pints later James was drunk on my behalf. We were debating rugby tactics, reminiscing about school days, and studiously avoiding the subject of our failed search for Cally. She'd ignored all my messages, made absolutely no attempt to contact me and if her friends knew her whereabouts, they were keeping it to themselves. Like a couple of amateur pseudo-detectives we'd spent our spare time searching for clues and chasing leads but we'd come up empty. She simply didn't want to be found. And if I was honest with myself, brutally honest, it wasn't so much her absence that hurt – it was my pride.

At closing I made my way to the door while James visited the men's room. Outside in the dark it was pissing with rain; it had been for days. I didn't mind it so much; it matched my mood. Before venturing out there I half-heartedly scanned the community noticeboard, crammed with colourful bits of paper. Between a leaflet promoting

4

a charity raffle and a depressing missing persons poster, my eyes alighted on a small, neatly-typed card:

WANTED: Qualified landscaper to renovate the dilapidated grounds of a local estate for a modest fee. Please enquire at the number below.

I snorted. The key phrase there was 'modest fee'. In my experience the more money a person had, the more reluctant they were to spend it. Even so, the position piqued my interest and might provide the distraction I needed. For the last ten years I'd been working for my brother, Lester; helping him build up his gardening business. It was now a great success – we had more than fifty maintenance contracts, both commercial and residential, which provided employment for six of us all year-round. Between us we'd built up a solid local reputation to be proud of, and being able to work outside suited me; I would never survive being stuck in an office day in, day out. But mowing the same lawns, trimming the same hedges, and mulching the same flower beds week after week wasn't enough for me.

At Cally's suggestion I'd taken evening classes in horticulture, planting design and hard landscaping. Maybe it was time to put those new skills to the test. Ripping the advert off the noticeboard I slipped it into my back pocket as James ambled towards me.

'D'you call a cab?'

'Nah, let's walk.' I slapped him on the back and his grimace made me smile as I stepped out into the cleansing rain.

Chapter Two

Outside it was another dreary damp squib of a day. I'd put on a dress this morning in defiance of the miserable weather, and now, at last, the rain had stopped. My work had taken longer than anticipated and the sun had dropped below the horizon, but I was still keen to escape the house. Before leaving I switched the chandelier on in the formal dining room so that light spilled out of the windows, illuminating a patch of dark terrace outside. Bypassing the kitchen I grabbed a coat from the boot room, made my way out through the laundry room, and then around to the south-facing side of the house.

It wasn't my coat – it was a heavy synthetic furry thing lined with silk, and it swamped my tiny frame, but I wore it often. The lining was starting to shred into ribbons and the once-white fur was now beige and caked with mud at the hem where it dragged behind my feet like a train. It was once Cornelia's.

I had no recollection of her wearing it, but then I had few memories of her at all. The ones I did have I suspect I'd concocted from photographs. Lifting one side of the collar I sniffed at it, but instead of her perfume I smelled only damp earth and mothballs.

Below the dining room windows I settled myself on the terrace, where the sturdy nineteenth century stonework was sheltered from the worst of the weather and it was drier beneath my bum. The moon was not yet visible from here, but the clouds were dissipating like fog and a few stars were starting to burn through the indigo blanket above.

A sharp cry made me jump and in the distance a fox trotted out of the shadowy undergrowth and across the scruffy field that was once a sweeping lawn. His sleek form and nimble trot were compelling to observe, but this was a dangerous place for him to be. Picking up a crumbling piece of paving and weighing it in my hand I chucked it in the direction of the wild animal in warning. The rock landed several metres short of him and he simply continued his unhurried progress with aloof disregard for me. Before long he had disappeared from view. Goodnight Mr Fox.

Sitting out in the evenings gave my eyes a rest from the computer screen, allowed my lungs to fill with fresh air and reminded me there was a whole world beyond my own. Which was good to know, even if I no longer explored far beyond the back door.

As a kid, back when the grounds were floriferous and neatly maintained, I would spend hours outside; reading books on the lawn, climbing trees, collecting blooms and bugs, riding my bicycle, or simply hiding under a bush. But the elderly couple who did all the gardening had retired several years previously, and since then the manicured gardens had become a sprawling wilderness. It was still my own private territory, a place to escape to if necessary, but nowadays, with the paths overgrown with nettles and riddled with potholes, it was too easy to get stung, twist an ankle, or fall in the lake and drown. And who would notice? Who would come to my aid? Absolutely no-one.

From the other side of the house came the creeping crunch of gravel beneath car tyres; signalling the approach of the black Mercedes which spent most of its life parked at the airport. My heart sank. He was back a day earlier than expected. Drawing my knees up I wrapped the fur coat tighter around me. It was getting late, maybe he wouldn't bother to come and find me. I should have left the lights off to make myself harder to locate.

After fifteen minutes or so I began to relax, serenaded by the haunting hoot of an owl. But his voice sliced through the hush.

'Beautiful night, isn't it?' Pungent cigar smoke preceded him, unfurling, and invading the still air. Not waiting for a reply, Gregory advanced across the terrace to the crumbling balustrade, his Italian leather shoes sharply accenting his footsteps and leaving a trail of crushed weeds in their wake. 'I think it's about time we got the grounds tidied up, don't you? It really is a jungle out here,' he added, taking another puff on his cigar.

A few moments ago I'd been lamenting the loss of the pretty landscape of my childhood, but now that he was suggesting reinstating it, I hated the idea.

'I can feel that look from here,' he said, turning back to me with a jarring smile. 'I know you don't like having workmen about the place, but the grounds are really letting this place down. And it would be far nicer to have tidy plants to look out at instead of this mess, wouldn't it?'

As he walked towards me, his suit jacket hanging open and one hand placed in his trouser pocket, I pressed my lips together. He stood over me and I refused to look at him. 'Come on, Melody, let's go inside.' He held one hand out to help me up and the whiskey on his breath made my stomach roll. Folding my arms across my chest I turned away. 'You can't stay out here all night. I'll carry you inside if I have to…' he warned.

Reluctantly I got to my feet, without his help, and ducked past him, but not fast enough. Grabbing my hand he halted me mid-step. The amused, glassy look in his eyes was one I recognised from previous occasions when he'd come home drunk. It made me uneasy.

'I wish you'd smile more,' he said softly. 'All I've ever asked for is your happiness… I… there are things I…' He hugged my hand to his chest, where his stale body heat leached through his silk shirt. Withholding the emotion from my face I stared blankly back at him and at length he released my hand with a defeated sigh. He didn't try to catch me as I fled back inside, coat billowing, and took the main stairs two at a time.

Chapter Three

The vast entrance gates to Wildham Hall were like something from a fairytale – an elaborate tangled briar of wrought iron, topped with ornate rose finials – Gothic and imposing.

I had driven past them countless times without ever catching a glimpsing of the property they guarded within. But now I was here by invitation, and despite the bright June sunshine and the birds singing in the trees, a shiver ran up my spine as the gates clanked slowly open before me.

The narrow drive was walled in with overgrown shrubs and roofed by woven tree branches, blocking out the sun and creating the impression of a long, winding tunnel. Beneath the tyres of my van the gravel was balding, potholed and lumpy, making for a slow and bumpy approach. Pruning back the trees and relaying the drive would be my first suggestion for improving this place, but I had a feeling the restoration list would grow and grow.

Where the trees cleared, the drive opened out before a large, elegant, stone-built house adorned with an array of tall bay windows, Gothic pinnacles and chimneys. Though weathered with age, the house appeared to have been well-maintained compared to the grounds; the woodwork freshly painted and the glazing reflecting the sky like mirrors.

As I parked up and headed for the front porch, a man in a tailored navy suit and a purple tie descended the steps towards me. His smile faltered slightly as he took in my size, but he politely extended a hand in welcome and I shook it.

'Mr Hunt?'

'Yes. Please call me Liam.'

'Welcome to Wildham Hall, Liam, I'm Gregory Sinclair – we spoke on the phone.'

He was about my age, though considerably smaller in stature; then again, so were most people. In a bid to minimise the height difference between us he had stopped on the lowest step, but from my vantage point it was still obvious that he used gel to try and disguise the thinning of his hair.

'Have you been in an accident?' he asked.

'Oh, no, excuse the state of me – I play rugby for the Wildham Warriors – we were practising yesterday and my face got in the way of another player's knee...'

'Ah, I see,' he said, relaxing slightly. 'Well, thank you for coming, shall I show you around and then you can ask me any questions as we go?'

'Great, thanks.'

'The Hall is Victorian, as you can see.' Sinclair set off across the drive. 'It was built in 1870 by my ancestors and has remained in the family ever since.'

I followed him around the side of the house to where a vast York stone terrace, in need of re-pointing, was edged with a crumbling, ornate balustrade. At intervals, wide, generous steps led down to the garden below, flanked by long parterres, over-run with weeds. The box-hedge borders were ballooning and in desperate need of clipping. Beyond these once-formal beds, a large, flat meadow of grass, which I was informed was once a manicured lawn, spread out like the skirt of a dress before the land dropped away. From that point a seemingly wild, rural landscape of lush fields and trees unfurled as far as the eye could see. By squinting I could picture the tidy parkland of yesteryear; sweeping grassland dotted with specimen trees, wild deer, and sinuously criss-crossed with compacted-gravel paths.

As we advanced across the terrace I sensed I was being watched from the upper windows of the house, but politely refrained from turning to check. I made copious notes and took pictures while Sinclair pointed out key features – a procession of blobby shrubs that were once identifiable topiary animals; a long avenue of unruly lime trees that marched away into the distance; a sunken area overwhelmed with brambles.

'This was originally a rose garden I believe…'

I had no ready reply for this and simply gazed in awe at the sheer scale, majesty, and potential of the place. It was a lot to get my head around and a huge project to quote for.

On the east side of the house, we came to an intricate iron gate set in a high brick wall, which led to an enclosed and abandoned kitchen garden, complete with a Victorian-style greenhouse; most of the panes were cracked or missing.

'I'd like everything reinstated; the glass house, the orchard, veg beds, fruit cages, herb garden…' Sinclair said, glancing up at me.

Nodding, I scribbled it down.

Beyond the walled garden was a stretch of woodland; about an acre, Sinclair estimated, as he led me along a muddy path. Despite having worn a collared shirt and my smartest suit jacket over my jeans and boots, I felt distinctly low-class and shabby next to the well-groomed owner of the estate. But at least my footwear was appropriate for the occasion. Mud splattered my host's expensive-looking shoes and soaked into the legs of his trousers, and I imagined his socks must be damp.

'This woodland will need attention, along with everything else; I believe some of the trees used to be coppiced regularly, but you're the expert; you'll have to let me know.'

I nodded as my eyes adjusted to the gloom and registered oak, beech, birch, hazel, hornbeam... mostly native, deciduous trees with the odd horse chestnut or sycamore thrown in for good measure. Set in a clearing was a roofless stone building clothed in ivy, and we stopped in front of its old wooden door.

'I believe this is a grotto; a fernery dating back to some time soon after the house was built,' Sinclair said. 'I think it was commissioned by an eccentric uncle but I've never been inside. It's completely overgrown and I was banned from playing in it as a child because it was considered too dangerous.'

'Dangerous?'

'Yes, I believe there's a natural spring, a well or something, inside... caves and boulders... I'm not too sure exactly; as I say I've never been in, but I think I've

13

got a key somewhere. If you're able to clear it out I'd be interested to see what it's like…'

'OK,' I shrugged. 'I'll add it to the list.'

I wasn't about to admit it, but I was desperate to get my hands on the grounds of Wildham Hall. It was a massive challenge; far larger and more complicated than any project I'd taken on before, but it was exactly the sort of work I'd always aspired to. The before and after photos would look stunning in my portfolio, and it would also keep my mind from thoughts of Cally.

Sinclair shifted uncomfortably. 'Right, if it's alright with you, I'll leave you to explore the rest of the twenty-five acres of the estate on your own. But I look forward to receiving your quotation in due course.'

'Great, thank you.'

He nodded. 'The gates will open automatically on your way out, and if I do decide to hire you I'll provide you with a fob so that you can open them from the outside.'

'Sounds good,' I said, as he turned and headed back towards the house without further hesitation.

With my skin still prickling from the sensation of being observed, I followed the great avenue of limes to its focal point – a classical domed folly with a marble seat inside – a Jane Austen type place in which to shelter on a rainy day. From there I travelled a ribbon of hoggin path along the bank of a stream. The water course appeared to be clogged with silt and plants, and the path had been completely destroyed. This, along with the mud and debris spread across the surrounding area, suggested the stream had burst its banks recently, probably more than once, which was something else I'd like to rectify given

14

half a chance. A small rusty iron bridge carried me safely across the stream to where it fed into a wide lake. This too was cluttered with reeds and rushes and in need of dredging, though the water looked surprisingly clean and clear. At the lake edge, a modest boathouse attached to a matching timber dock invited further investigation, but it was all locked up and I couldn't see much through the dusty windows.

By the time I'd made my way back up to the Gothic mansion and climbed into my van, the sun was high overhead, my notebook was full, and my stomach was rumbling. But I was hooked. Now that I'd seen the full scale and potential of this place, I'd be gutted if I didn't get the chance to restore it to its former glory.

As I turned down the dark tunnel driveway I checked my side mirror and glimpsed a slight, pale figure in a window of the house. I was too far away to tell if it was a man, woman, child, or ghost, but as I drove away I experienced the heavy weight of their gaze, long after the dense trees had shielded me from sight.

Chapter Four

Jeez Louise, bugger off already. Gone were the days when I would miss Gregory; yearn for him to return from his frequent business trips abroad; pine for his company and misbehave simply to get his attention. Lately I simply wanted him to go away and stay away. I'd rather have the big old house to myself – free to roam the rooms undisturbed, eat whatever, whenever and wherever I wanted, and play my music loud. His mere presence, with all his particular preferences and outmoded rules, put me on edge and made me irritable. Yes Gregory loved me; provided a roof over my head and food for my belly… but right now I wanted to be left alone.

It was Wednesday and he was still here. Thankfully he'd spent most of each day holed up working in the study, but I could smell him in every room. At meal times I had to sit and listen to the click and grind of his teeth as he carefully chewed each forkful of food, and endure his habit of dabbing at his mouth with a napkin after every other bite.

Between meals I focused on my own work. Three more manuscripts had arrived for me over the weekend, and proofreading always required an intense level of concentration – kept my brain occupied. I'd completed my work ahead of schedule, but I wasn't about to email the agency and let them know in case they increased my workload.

So now I was using new and creative methods to bypass the usage controls and content filters on my laptop so that I could browse the internet. It was ridiculous; I was a twenty-one year old woman and Gregory was still trying to preserve my so-called innocence. I let him believe his own delusions. With some covert help from a couple of hackers I'd met in an online chat room, I was navigating loopholes and virtually exploring the world for myself, regardless of Gregory's wishes. I happened to be browsing a website on Victorian pornography, of all things, when the entry system rang, and I crept along the landing to investigate.

The landscaper that Gregory had invited to come and take a look at the grounds was a hulking great brute of a man, unlike anyone I'd ever seen before. He'd turned up in a white van with 'Hunt Garden Services' in green letters down the side; his jacket straining across his massive back and shoulders as he climbed out. His denim-clad legs were the size of tree trunks and he looked capable of crushing a person's skull with his large hands. The purple bruising around his eyes and his crooked, almost-certainly broken, nose gave me the clear impression that he was violent and dangerous.

I couldn't hear what was being said, but instead of turning the stranger away, Gregory led him around the side of the house. Incredulous, and afraid to let them out of my sight, I rushed from window to window, leaving fingerprint smudges here and there as I pressed against the glass.

On the terrace below, the landscaper scribbled down notes with the worn stub of a pencil in a battered notebook, and held his phone aloft to take photographs while Gregory waffled on, presumably about the work he wanted doing. Surely he wasn't considering hiring this ugly oaf? Even his name – *Hunt* – it sounded so threatening! What about when Gregory went away again? What if he tried to force his way into the house and steal my virtue? I shivered.

Surreptitiously I tracked the man around the estate from all the bedroom windows and even from the tower room up on the second floor. But he did little other than gaze around, taking more pictures and writing in his book. Once he'd driven away and the gates had safely clanged shut behind him, I scrawled a message on my forearm and stomped downstairs.

Gregory was back in his study, seated behind his desk, carefully cleaning a hunting rifle with an array of small rags and brushes. The smell of the solvent tickled my nostrils as I glanced at the unlocked cabinet on the wall, which still contained his other four weapons, and back at the various dismantled pieces of gun laid out on the surface before him. He looked up at me as I approached with my arm stuck out before him.

'I don't like him,' he said, reading my words aloud. He sighed, weighing the barrel in his latex-gloved hands. 'Well I do. And if his quote is reasonable I'll be employing him, so you'd better get used to the idea.' Dismissively he returned his attention to his weaponry.

I crossed my arms and glared at him, but he wouldn't look at me, his mind was made up. Turning on my heel I stormed out of the room, slamming the door behind me. There was more than one way to skin a cat.

Chapter Five

'We're being watched,' Olly said, setting down a fresh bucket of mortar.

I didn't look up from the paving joint I was packing. 'Yeah, I noticed. Hey, careful where you're putting your feet.'

'Yeah, yeah, don't worry.' Olly stepped gingerly across the terrace, hunched down with his pointer and recommenced smoothing and finishing the cracks I'd filled. 'So, do you think she's the wife, the sister, the daughter, or what?'

I shrugged.

'She looks nearer my age than yours, but I dunno if she's too old to be the daughter...?'

I didn't comment. Mainly because I was a man of few words anyway, but also because that sort of speculation was unprofessional. Working with Oliver Dent made me even less inclined to speak; the lanky eighteen-year-old never shut up. Was it because he came from a large family that he felt compelled to voice every single thought that entered his head? Maybe it was the only way he could make himself heard over eight other siblings. Whatever the reason, he suffered from a chronic case of verbal diarrhoea – or rather he had it and *I* suffered.

But I wondered about her too; the mysterious girl observing us from the house. Almost three weeks had passed since Gregory Sinclair had given me the go ahead to restore the sprawling grounds of his mansion, and he'd been absent almost all of that time, working abroad. He'd left us with access to an outbuilding equipped with power sockets, a kettle, an outdoor tap and a flushing toilet; so that we would have no excuse to set a muddy boot inside the house. A cleaner – a stroppy, middle-aged, Irish woman with a sharp tongue – visited Wildham Hall three days a week, but otherwise no-one came or went except for the postman and the odd delivery driver.

I'd glimpsed the lady of the house a couple of times – she was petite, with jaw-length flame-red hair and a heart-shaped, elfin face. On both occasions she had immediately ducked out of sight, but I felt her eyes on me almost constantly.

'She's definitely cute, though – maybe I should go introduce myself; she might be shy…' Olly mused.

'Just concentrate on what you're doing.'

'Yeah, yeah, I got this. I'll go talk to her later. So, is this going to be like a permanent thing?'

'What?'

'You and your bro working on separate jobs?'

'Well, if this commission goes well and I can get more work like it, then hopefully, as a company, we can offer landscaping as well as maintenance.'

'So Lester will still run the maintenance team and what, you'll have, like, a landscaping team of your own?'

'That's the plan.'

'Can I be in your squad?'

I laughed. 'Maybe. I think Lester needs you back next week; I've only got you on loan.'

'But this place is massive, you'll never get it all done by yourself.'

'Thanks for the vote of confidence, Olly.'

'But it's true; it's gonna take you, like, forever.' Straightening up he gazed off towards the lake in the distance.

'Lucky for me the client isn't in any particular hurry – I'll get there.'

'Yeah, I guess. But it's cool working here; repairing the balustrades, relaying slabs – this terrace looks a million times better and we're not even finished yet... I feel like I'm actually learning something here, y'know...?'

'Good, I'm glad.' Sitting back on my haunches I glanced up at Olly; he looked uncharacteristically glum. 'Look, maybe you can come back and work with me once the cold weather sets in. Things will ease up maintenance-wise, Lester won't need you so much, and there'll still be plenty to do here.'

'Sweet,' he said, flashing me a grin and crouching back down over his work.

In a rare moment of quiet I savoured the melodic tune a robin was emitting from within a cherry tree and identified what I thought might be a skylark singing in the distance.

'Maybe I'll offer her a cuppa tea next time I see her, whaddya think?'

'Leave her alone, Olly.'

'What? It wouldn't hurt...'

'It might – I wouldn't wish your tea on my worst enemy.'

21

Chapter Six

Ugh. I was behind with my work; I still had a manuscript to finish correcting by the end of the week, but I was restless and couldn't concentrate. It wasn't so much the amount of noise they were making, because I could easily sit on the other side of the house where even the rhythmic whirr and thump of the cement mixer couldn't be heard. It was their very existence here; knowing that they'd invaded my private space; *that* was the issue.

If I was honest, they intrigued me. Not the younger one so much – the gangly teenager who talked too much – but the big one. I still found the monstrous scale of him morbidly fascinating. He looked marginally less fierce now that the swelling and bruising on his face had subsided, and his movements were oddly unhurried, deliberate and assured – engrossingly so.

I noted the precise way the muscles in his arms, legs and back, bunched and stretched as he worked; the ease with which he lifted enormous slabs of stone; and the accuracy with which he troweled mortar into the narrow gaps between the flagstones, with a practised scoop and flick of his wrist. Patches of sweat slowly spread through his faded T-shirt as the sun rose, bright and burning, in the sky above.

I had virtually no experience of men at all. Gregory had always encouraged me to stay within the safe boundaries of the property – supposedly out of concern for my welfare – and I was happy to go along with that most of the time. Instead of going out, everything I needed came to me. But most of the visitors to this house were women – a proliferation of housekeepers, cooks, cleaners and tutors had been here over the years, but very few men. A faceless assortment of uniformed couriers came and went, but they had instructions to leave all deliveries in an outbuilding, so I hardly ever saw them, regardless of whether a signature was required or not.

Every three months Finnegan arrived to clean the outside of the windows, repair anything that might need fixing, and touch up the paintwork. But for all his spryness he was at least seventy years old; a stringy fellow with skin like creased leather.

Once a team of Polish guys came to repair the roof. They winked and waved at me from the scaffolding, but barely spoke any English. They were boring to watch and before long I simply forgot they were there. With no real friends and no television, my main experience of men came from books, horror movies and, more recently, the World Wide Web. I'd *never* come across a giant like Mr Hunt before.

I was staring again.

The doorbell rang and I jumped, startled by the rare sound. It couldn't be *him* because he was still on the terrace below; it must be his loquacious assistant. I hesitated, tempted not to answer at all, but then what would be my excuse for such antisocial behaviour? He knew I was here. It rang again and I hurried through the house, down the back stairs and along the hall to the front door.

23

'Alright? Sorry to bother you, I saw you through the window; figured I'd come and say hello.' He had sunburn across his nose, a smile like a wide-mouthed frog and something, which looked like porridge but was presumably wet concrete, smeared in his floppy fringe. 'I'm Olly, by the way. We're fixing up your patio back there,' he said, jerking his thumb over his shoulder. 'It's perfect weather for it, nice and dry...' His smile faltered slightly when I didn't react. 'Anyway, I'm off to put the kettle on and I wondered if you fancied a cuppa...?'

This time his eyes narrowed slightly at my lack of response so I shook my head.

'No? OK, no worries.' He stepped backwards away from the door and I closed it, firmly, before he had a chance to say anything else.

Mentally congratulating myself on a situation well-handled, I headed back upstairs and returned my attention to my manuscript with fresh determination.

Soon after six the two men piled into their van and disappeared down the drive, leaving me entirely, blissfully alone. It was warm on the terrace. The smart, newly-pointed paving had been washed down but was already drying in continent-shaped patches. Slipping off my shoes I walked barefoot, letting the smooth warmth radiate up through my soles. I squatted where the giant had been crouched, running my fingertip along the firm damp channels between the stones, where the mortar he had so adeptly introduced was now setting hard. There was no staining, no gap still to be filled, no bits he'd missed as far as I could tell; he took pride in his work and it showed. In one corner where a tree cast shade, I found a wet hand-print, where he had braced himself for balance while reaching for a brush. The print was already fading but I placed my own hand in the centre, where it was dwarfed by his palm, and where each of his long fingers outstripped my own.

In what was once the old tack room, in the stables on the north side of the house, lay the landscaper's tools – a large shovel crusted at the edges with rust and dried concrete; a still-wet but empty bucket, ringed with tide lines; a soft broom; a stiff brush; and a flat, pointed, metal hand-trowel. This last item had a smooth, worn, wooden handle. It was too big for my hand but as I wrapped my fingers around it I imagined it moulding neatly to Hunt's ample palm.

Across the back of a chair was the padded jacket he had arrived in almost two and a half weeks ago when it was cold and pouring with rain. Lifting it up to my face I inhaled. It had a soft fleecy lining and still held his scent – a subtle, not-unpleasant, soapy smell – though I'd not seen him wear it since. He wouldn't need his jacket on an evening as mild as this, but had he missed it on Tuesday night during that heavy thunderstorm? Was he out then, or tucked up warm and dry at home? What did a man like that do in his spare time? Drink? Fight? Fuck lots of women? That was the correct verb wasn't it? With a shiver I returned the jacket to the back of the chair and stepped back out into the evening sunshine. Why did I even want to know?

Chapter Seven

I'd spent the best part of a fortnight getting snagged, scratched and stung while I single-handedly dug out great swathes of nettles, thistles and brambles from the area up near the house. But I was in my element. To reinstate the structure of the neatly-edged beds I'd run a series of string lines and clipped the miles of box hedging back into shape, and between the parterres I'd strimmed and mown the formal lawns so that they now resembled shaggy green carpets rather than meadows. Together with the freshly-restored terrace, the immediate vicinity of Wildham Hall was now taking shape and looking fantastic – if I did say so myself.

Of course the beds were devoid of flowers at the moment because I wanted to wait for autumn. If I planted in the height of summer, the poor buggers would struggle to get enough water to stay alive, let alone get their roots established. And the lawns would require further weeding, feeding and scarifying before they were anywhere near croquet-playing standard. Even so, I was pleased with the progress I'd made and enjoying my work.

Now I was venturing further into the more rural parts of the grounds and clearing out the undergrowth in the cooler shade of the trees.

But I had company. It seemed the mysterious lady of the house was no longer content with watching me from the house and had taken to hiding behind bushes. It would be amusing if I wasn't so concerned about her getting injured. Olly had been right; she was young. From a distance I'd thought she might be a child – her petite size, coupled with the girly dresses she wore, gave that impression, not to mention the ongoing game of hide and seek. But she was not a child.

Three days ago, on my way back to the van to fetch a bigger pair of loppers, I'd stumbled across her. She was leaning against the trunk of an oak tree, her head tipped back, her eyes closed against the sun, and a serene expression of contentment on her face. I'd only had time to look from her face down to her hand, unconsciously searching for a wedding ring, before she saw me and darted away. But in that brief glance I'd clocked the writing scrawled down her arm and across her left hand in black ball-point pen, the colourful plastic wristwatch she wore, and the blue varnish on her bitten-down fingernails. There was no ring.

I hadn't had a chance to decipher any of the words on her skin, but perhaps she suffered from absent-mindedness. Despite her peculiar behaviour I'd decided she was somewhere in her early twenties – too young for me, but a woman nevertheless.

As I laboured I listened to the birds singing in the trees. Now and again I paused to toss a worm to the robin who was also keeping an eye on me, albeit brazenly and with a chirpy song. I gathered the assorted weeds and brambles in a wheelbarrow which I periodically emptied onto the compost heap, while the woodier prunings I piled in a clearing out of view of the house; it would make for a terrific bonfire once autumn arrived.

It was satisfying work – tiring and repetitive, but no less enjoyable for all that – and it left my mind free to wander aimlessly across the countryside and beyond. I thought about the new woman in James's life (I'd never seen him so enamoured) and I pondered Maire's news. At the pub on Tuesday night she'd announced that she was pregnant. In six months' time Lester would become a dad, and I would become an uncle for the first time. I was still trying to get my head around the idea. I suppose I'd always assumed that Cally and I would become parents one day – though the fact that neither of us had ever mentioned the possibility, in six years together as a couple, perhaps indicated otherwise.

She'd finally called me a few days ago on her birthday to let me know she was OK. She still hadn't provided an adequate explanation for her sudden departure but, to my surprise, it no longer bothered me. Yes, I missed having someone to go home to, someone to cook and care for, but other than that I didn't miss Cally as intensely as I'd expected to. It was enough to know that she was happy and safe wherever she was – maybe we were never meant to last.

But I would still like the opportunity to be a dad one day. Perhaps James was right when he said I needed to get out and start meeting women again…? It was OK for him; he'd found someone special. The mere thought of dating filled me with dread. If I couldn't make a relationship work with someone as patient and understanding as Cally, what chance did I have with any woman? What girl in her right mind would look twice at an oaf like me?

Chapter Eight

A sinister nightmare woke me with a start. It was the same one I always had; the same shadowy figures and faces; the same sense of searching for something I could never find; the same intense sense of hopeless desolation. While I waited for the usual panic to subside and my heart-rate to return to normal, I lay in bed staring at processions of black poodles marching around the pink walls.

The nursery had always been my bedroom. Gregory occupied the master, Cornelia haunted the adjoining room, and the spare bedrooms were cold, cluttered and draughty. This room benefited from being situated above the kitchen, so it was cosy warm. It also had an easterly aspect and large windows; which afforded a clear view over the walled garden and the woodland beyond, and allowed the sun to wake me each morning. But it hadn't been re-decorated since the fifties – it had been stuck in a time warp so long that it was almost fashionable again – and the wallpaper was undeniably childish.

Now that my bad dreams had retreated back into my subconscious, I pushed my numerous and varied stuffed toys aside and reached for the largest – a brown bear with a pink bow and a knowing smirk whom I'd named Beauty. Gregory had brought her back from one of his many trips abroad, Germany I think. He'd gradually gifted me my entire collection over the years; I had stuffed teddies from nearly every corner of the world, though half of them where actually made in China or Taiwan. They covered my wardrobe, chest of drawers, dressing table, shelves, and swamped my four-poster bed. But Beauty harboured a secret.

Turning her over I unzipped the central seam of her back, opened the concealed compartment within, and withdrew my secret hoard. A pink lipstick; a pair of sixties-style sunglasses; three plastic disposable lighters in fluorescent colours; a tortoiseshell comb; a pen featuring a naked lady down the side; an Eiffel Tower keyring; half a smoked joint and two foil-wrapped Durex. There were three condoms originally, but when sheer curiosity got the better of me I'd opened one; unravelled and inspected the limp, slimy, balloon-like contents, and then, disappointed, thrown it away.

But these assorted treasures were not things I'd bought or been given. Each and every item had been carefully pilfered from the handbag or coat pocket of people who'd visited the house over the years. I only ever stole one item from each person, and even then I tried to only take things they wouldn't miss, but I felt they were clues to lives I would never truly understand.

The maths and English teacher, Miss Prichard, had half a dozen different lipsticks rolling around in the bottom of her purse, ranging from Candy Creme through to Raspberry Shimmer. My chosen hostage was called Rosewood, and the most muted of the lot, though far richer than my natural colour. It was thick and greasy on my lips as I pouted at myself in the mirror like a dead-eyed woman from a magazine. How many people had she kissed with this particular shade?

The joint I'd pinched from Finnegan's secret stash. I'd smoked half of it simply to find out what all the fuss was about. It made my throat tickle, my head swim and my eyes water, but otherwise it had little effect. I probably wasn't cut out to be a pothead – my life simply wasn't stressful or exciting enough to require narcotic relief. What I was saving the other half for was anyone's guess – I had no intention of smoking it.

To my collection I added my latest and most prized acquisition: a men's wristwatch. I was breaking my own rules because Hunt was bound to miss it – but he shouldn't have left it just lying there by the sink in the stables; I couldn't resist taking it for myself. The dial was shiny and complicated with several other smaller dials on the face; telling the date as well as the time. But it was the sturdy brown strap which really appealed; it was soft and malleable and there was a clear impression in the leather to show where he always fastened it. Slipping it onto my arm like a heavy bracelet, I marvelled at the sheer magnitude of his burly wrist compared to my slender one. What must it be like to be a man that size? To carry all that physical strength, power and influence around , inside your body?

The front gates rang out with a clang as they closed and I shoved my booty safely back inside Beauty, leapt off the bed and raced along the corridor to the west side of the house in my nightdress. Gregory had given Mr Hunt his own key fob to activate the gates so that he could come and go as he pleased. As the mornings grew lighter he seemed to arrive earlier each day. I reached the window in time to see him park his van, emerge, yawn widely, scratch his jaw and stretch his enormous arms above his head. I hoped he might be working close to the house today, where I could keep an eye on him without resorting to hiding in the bushes, but when he returned from the stables with a mug of something steaming hot and a selection of tools, he strode off into the long grass and disappeared beneath the trees.

My hands and feet were getting stiff with cold in the draughty window, so I threw on Cornelia's fluffy pink robe and a matching pair of slippers and left the bath running with hot water while I made toast with marmalade in the kitchen. Before eating my breakfast, I returned to the now-full bath and settled my body beneath the bubbles; scattering the cloud-like suds with crumbs and licking my sticky fingers with satisfaction.

At nine o'clock Mrs Daly arrived as usual; banging doors, clattering crockery and then powering up the vacuum cleaner and shoving it about. All Mrs Daly's movements were angry-sounding; as if she was constantly bitter and resentful of her life. Or maybe mine. During her first week here I'd made the mistake of asking for a cup of tea – I didn't drink it because it was obvious by the scum on the surface that she'd spat in it, and I never asked her for anything again. Whatever her problem, she made a point of pretending I didn't exist and I afforded her the same courtesy in return.

But I was still finding the landscaper difficult to ignore. I still didn't trust him and wanted to know what he was up to. Admittedly the work he'd done so far was a great improvement – the terrace, the formal beds and the lawns were starting to resemble the garden from my memory. But even so, with Gregory away I had a responsibility to keep him under surveillance. And it was my home; I shouldn't have to hide. I was pretty sure Mr Hunt knew I was watching him anyway. So today I would be bold about it; I would take a book and sit in the grounds to read it – that was a perfectly normal thing to do. I could catch up on my work later.

Having spent far too long prevaricating over which dress to wear and which book to take with me, I finally set off along a narrow track that had been trampled through the long grass on the south side of the house. The hot sun had long since burned away the morning dew, and the grass, which reached up to tickle my elbows in places, was lush and beginning to swell with seed. I'd worn a big hat to protect my face from the sun, and I was absentmindedly watching my feet as I picked my way through the grounds, so it was a shock when I stumbled across the landscaper, unnaturally large and powerful, and a mere few feet away.

He was digging out roots where a dense thicket of brambles had invaded a crumbly section of path, but thankfully he had his back to me and hadn't seen me yet. I stood, holding my breath, mid-step, my blood pounding in my ears as I stared at him. Using his bodyweight he stamped a spade into the stony earth with a booted foot, levered tearing roots to the surface and then bent to snatch them out of the ground with his rough, bare hands, repeating the process over and over again. He wore trousers covered in lots of pockets, a holster at his waist carrying a sharp implement, and a baseball cap with a peak to shade his eyes. But it was the nakedness of his expansive back which really captured my attention – a vast wall of shifting muscle, browned by the sun and glistening with sweat. I was close enough that I could smell him – the same warm, soapy scent but sharper, tangy with sweat, so that I could almost taste it.

He paused in his work, leaving the spade embedded upright in the ground and wiping his forehead on his right bicep as he turned. I witnessed the flash of surprise on his face before I averted my gaze, heat rushing to my cheeks. I hadn't meant to get so close. Why hadn't I kept a better eye out for him? Now I couldn't double back without looking foolish.

Disregarding him completely, I boldly waded into the long grass, awkwardly parting it with my hands and feet until I came to the large old stump of an elm tree. It had a rotten hole in the middle, which served as a birdbath when it rained, but the outside of the stump was solid enough to provide me with a seat. Perching on the edge I opened my book and made a show of scanning the lines with my eyes, all the time monitoring him in my peripheral vision. After a moment he took a long swig of water from a large plastic bottle, took up his spade and returned to his labouring without a word.

As the butterflies in my stomach began to settle, I sneaked furtive glances at him through the gap between the brim of my hat and the top of my book; noting the flash of paler skin beneath his arms, and above the waistband of his trousers as he crouched, and the way the fabric tightened around his meaty bum and thighs as he did so. He was hairier than any man I'd ever seen in the flesh; it sprouted from his armpits, and his nipples nestled in a curly fuzz across his chest. The thought of how his body might feel to touch made me jittery.

He made no attempt to talk to me, for which I was grateful, and only acknowledged my presence by smiling at me occasionally. For a beast of a man he had an unexpectedly attractive smile; his heavily furrowed brow lifting, his eyes softening and his mouth curving up lopsidedly into one cheek. I didn't return the gesture; I automatically returned my eyes to my book and turned a page without having read a word. But I began to consider smiling at him; testing the idea in my mind and fretting over the possible implications.

Because, weirdly enough, I was enjoying myself – sitting there in the sunshine, listening to the birds singing while a man dug up brambles. I was proud of myself for holding my ground; not letting a stranger intimidate me and push me out of my own territory. And the silence between him and me was not as strained or awkward as it could have been; for once it was oddly comfortable, and soon I began to relax; my breathing calming and my body slouching. I even read a few pages of the book in my hand – it was my favourite, after all.

At midday Mr Hunt set aside his spade, dusted his hands on the back of his trousers and retrieved an aluminium foil-covered package from the dense shade beneath a rhododendron bush. I tensed with anticipation as he carefully unwrapped it and then took two slow strides in my direction. He blocked out the sun as he loomed over me, but once I was sure he was stopping there and not coming any nearer, I slipped off the stump and carefully peered at what lay within his outstretched hand.

My bottom had gone numb and now tingled with pins and needles as I eyed the stack of neatly-cut, triangular sandwiches. Glancing up at him I found him staring back at me from beneath his cap, unnervingly close and potentially as unpredictable as a savage animal. But there was no denying I was peckish. Plucking a sandwich from the stash in his hand, I rapidly backed away, keeping my eyes on him.

Without a word he hunkered down on the ground in the shade of an oak tree and collapsed against the gnarled and pitted trunk. Opening his mouth wide he took great crescent-shaped bites of food, his head falling back, his cheeks bulging as he chewed, and his eyes closing on a silent sigh. The way he ate made my mouth dry and my insides ache in a disconcerting way. I didn't know what to do with myself. The great brute looked for all the world as if he belonged there; as if he owned the place, and I glared at him in consternation. But he didn't open his eyes and I was too unsettled to hang about.

Abruptly turning I stomped back along the path, up to the house and through the back door, bypassing Mrs Daly on the landing, and not stopping until I'd reached the safety of the nursery. Once there I sat down, breathing hard, sweat tickling my hairline. Why did he annoy me so much? Why did I let him get to me? I wanted to open a window and let air in, but the leaded panes had always been sealed shut; presumably to prevent small children from accidentally plunging to their deaths.

Dropping my book I stared at the sandwich still clasped in my other hand – I could see cheese and lettuce poking out of one side. Once the ringing in my ears had subsided, I tentatively lifted it to my mouth and took a bite. It was warm and slightly soggy, but tasted delicious and I couldn't stop smiling as I ate.

Chapter Nine

It was strange the way she watched and followed me about, as if gardening was a spectator sport, but I'd grown accustomed to the prickling sensation at the back of my neck alerting me to her presence. At first it had crossed my mind that she might be disadvantaged in some way; perhaps a little slow or mentally deficient, but her pale grey eyes were bright with intelligence and her movements perfectly controlled. Maybe she was autistic? Arnold Chambers at the corner shop had Aspergers – he was a nice chap with a superb memory and a gift for mental arithmetic, but he found it difficult talking to customers. Either way, this girl had been keeping me company for weeks now and had still not said a word – I didn't know her name, her age, or anything else about her.

She also had an unconventional way of dressing. I was aware that past styles had come back into fashion – had become 'retro' or 'vintage' – but I got the impression that this girl's dress-sense slightly missed the mark. Her dresses where loose and floaty and trimmed with lace, ending midway down her calves, and her tiny leather shoes – low-heeled and embellished with buckles – were entirely unsuitable for roaming about in the undergrowth. Sometimes she wore a shawl around her shoulders or a big floppy hat with a scarf tied around it, and she always carried a book – an ancient-looking, leather-bound copy of Daphne du Maurier's 'Rebecca'. Sometimes she looked like she was from another time. I didn't believe in ghosts, but even if I did, the trodden grass and small footprints she left behind in the earth attested to her physical existence.

Today was a picture-perfect summer day; the sun a searing blow torch in a cerulean blue sky, scattered with puffs of white cloud which drifted steadily like steam from a cartoon train. The gentle breeze stirred the leaves in the trees, tickled the long grass and caressed my clammy skin, tempering the late afternoon heat. The lilac bushes I was currently attacking had sprouted suckers and advanced across the open grassland like an invading army, establishing into a stubborn thicket of unwieldy, unyielding, shoots and roots. It was a while since we'd had any substantial rain, and the ground on this section of slope was like rock – I'd resorted to attacking it with great swinging blows of a mattock.

Meanwhile my watcher was lying peacefully nearby like the Lady of Shallot, marooned in the sea of long grass, almost hidden from sight. But as I paused to catch my breath and glanced over I spotted one pink knee where the hem of her dress had ridden up. Had she fallen asleep? Was she wearing sun screen? Picking up my spade I dug away at the earth I'd loosened, but that patch of rosy skin played on my mind – I didn't want her to get burned.

Leaving my spade in the ground, I straightened up and stretched with an audible groan, but she didn't stir. Grabbing my water bottle I took a long drink, the plastic contracting noisily in my hand, but still she didn't stir. Pointlessly I glanced at my empty wrist. Somehow I'd managed to misplace the watch my mother had given me – it was too big and grown-up for me at the time, but I'd matured into it over the years and now it was one of the few possessions I had with any real sentimental value. I was still hoping it would turn up somewhere and wasn't lost for good. Reaching for the mobile in my back pocket I checked the time. It was almost midday and the sun was at its highest. Clearing my throat I took a few steps towards sleeping beauty, stopping once she was in full view.

Nestled in the grassy hollow she was curled on her side like a child, her book discarded, her elbow bent and her head resting in her tiny palm. Her left arm had been scrubbed clean of ink in recent days and her nail-polish had changed from blue to a quirky green. On the inside of her thigh, four inches above her knee was a pale brown birthmark about the size of a ten-pence piece. It was symmetrically shaped, like an ink blot or a butterfly, and I felt guilty for having seen such an intimate mark. She looked innocent and vulnerable; her lips parted, her fine red hair mussed up, and her torso rising and falling with each slow breath.

It occurred to me that it must be lonely living here, with Sinclair away so much of the time, perhaps that was why she sought my company. But why me? Why not go visit other people; other places? And why had she made no attempt to make conversation? Was she just shy? Could she be deaf? She had caught the sun on her cheek, her forearm and her lower legs, and although I didn't want to wake her, I knew that I should.

Instinctively I sank down into a crouch, to make myself smaller and less intimidating, and pushed my cap further back on my head, before clearing my throat for a second time. This time she woke with a start, her eyes widening and locking onto me as she scrambled up into a seated position. Her hat lay flattened on the grass where she had rolled onto it.

'I'm sorry to wake you,' I said, my voice jarringly loud against the soft background buzz of insects. 'I was concerned that you might be getting sunburnt.'

Her sharp eyes stared at me, slate-grey and wary. I gestured towards her arm and she risked a downwards glance at her reddened skin before returning her gaze to mine. Absently she rubbed at her arm with her other hand while I reached into my back pocket, pulled out a bottle of factor thirty, and offered it to her. She hesitated before accepting it, and even then made no attempt to thank me or actually open it.

'I'm Liam by the way...'

She made no reply but her eyes dropped to my mouth as I spoke, making me self-conscious. Was she lip-reading? I thought she'd woken up because she'd heard me...

'You live here?' I said, gesturing back towards the house for emphasis.

Finally she nodded; it was the slightest of responses, but it was progress and I couldn't help but smile. She blinked back at me, as if confused, and I decided not to push my luck by asking her more questions.

'You have a lovely home,' I said, standing up and retreating back to the crater-like hole I'd dug. By the time I'd picked up my spade and turned back to her, she was gone; fled back to the house, leaving only the bottle of sun-cream, abandoned and unopened, lying in the grass.

She was a weird one. I wasn't surprised by her vanishing act, but I was oddly disappointed that she had gone.

Chapter Ten

I woke late on Friday. I never usually slept past seven o'clock, but I'd been up half the night trying to get a dry market analysis report checked in time for the submission deadline. As a career, proofreading suited me; I'd always had a good eye for detail and the work didn't require me to leave the house, but it was difficult checking for someone else's typos and spelling errors when you were tired enough to create new mistakes of your own. In the end I'd resorted to re-reading the whole report backwards in order to catch them all.

The other half of the night I'd spent chasing off my bad dreams; the same old mysterious strangers, alien places and threatening voices; all the details blurred and just out of reach. How could the same dreamt-up scenario – one that I didn't even understand – be so frightening? Maybe that was what made it so potent – the not knowing? Either way, I had no desire to dwell on it.

At first I thought it was the sound of Mrs Daly vacuuming that had woken me, but the persistent whine was coming from outside and gradually turned into alarm bells ringing in my head. What was that man up to now?

There was no visible sign of him through the windows. My breath caught suddenly in my throat. Throwing on yesterday's dress and only pausing on the landing long enough to glimpse my reflection and claw my fingers through my hair, I hurried from the house.

This was what happened when I let my guard drop and took my eye off the ball. Just because he hadn't caused any damage so far – just because he offered me sandwiches and sun-cream and didn't try to interrogate me like everybody else I'd ever met – didn't mean I should trust him. He could be carrying out all kinds of destruction out there.

Once I'd spotted him I started running full pelt across the terrace, realising too late that I'd forgotten to bring my book or put shoes on. But there was no time to stop; the great brute was wearing bright orange ear-defenders and wielding a chainsaw – immediately making me think of *The Texas Chainsaw Massacre*. Heavens to Betsy, was he cutting down trees?

My heart banged like a drum in my chest as I ran, flailing, towards him; adrenalin coursing through my veins and grass whipping at my legs and toes. He was stood before a sprawling, medium-sized tree, set apart from the others in what was once a sweeping lawn. The tree might not look like much right now, but it was old and produced pretty flowers every year – I would not let him butcher it. Without slowing I dived into the space between Liam Hunt and the tree, flattening myself back against the trunk, my arms splayed wide.

'Whoa, shit, careful!' He swung the offending power tool away from me and switched it off. 'I almost took your head off, what are you doing?' The colour had drained from his face and he pressed a hand to his chest and closed his eyes behind a plastic pair of safety specs, as he blew out a heavy breath.

As the sudden silence pulsed in my ears I began to question the prudence of my actions – I was now trapped in close proximity to an angry man with a weapon.

'I'm not going to cut the whole tree down, if that's what you're worried about,' he said gently, opening his eyes and lowering the ear-defenders to around his neck. Reaching up he fondly patted a low branch of the tree as if petting a dog. 'This magnolia's a beauty; must be at least fifty years old; and I bet it produces masses of flowers in early spring, am I right?'

I nodded uneasily, unable to stop trembling. The large, jagged-toothed chainsaw still dangled from his other hand, as if it weighed nothing.

'See this branch here?' he said, redirecting my attention. 'See how it's growing in the wrong direction and crossing these other two branches here and here…?'

I nodded, intrigued, despite myself.

'If it's left to rub against them like that it will create wounds, which might get infected, and if that happens you could end up losing the whole tree. So, you see, I was only going to remove one or two branches that are causing harm and leave the rest alone.'

That made sense. I believed him. My face flamed hot with embarrassment as I lowered my arms to my sides and willed myself to stop shaking. Cautiously he smiled, his warm hazel eyes intent on mine and making me look away. For something to do I plucked a leathery green leaf from the magnolia, consciously committing the name to memory, and stroking the cool, smooth surface across my cheek. Maybe I should try to give this guy the benefit of the doubt. Life wasn't really a horror movie, no matter

45

how thrilling that might be, and this man, regardless of how dangerous he looked, seemed to care about plants.

Standing well back I observed Liam as he surgically removed a few wayward branches without so much as nicking any of the others. Patiently he explained how he undercut each limb before removal to prevent tearing, and the importance of leaving an angled cut that would guide rainwater away from the trunk. His knowledge, skill and precision surprised me, and as he gradually worked his way across the grounds, expertly tending to each specimen tree and even climbing up into them, I found myself fascinated by arboriculture, where previously I'd had no interest at all.

As midday neared I returned to the house, slipped on my shoes, brushed my hair, and noticed, with dismay, that I was wearing my dress inside out. Idiot. Having made myself more presentable, I made my way back to the murky depths of the lime avenue, armed with a platter of cold meats and a flask full of iced tea. Liam's eyebrows lifted in surprise as I set my offerings down near where he stood, but I wanted to thank him for his efforts in my garden, his patient generosity, and for everything he didn't ask of me in return.

'Thank you, this is delicious,' he said with grease on his chin and a half-eaten chicken leg in hand. The simple pleasure on his face made me smile – really smile – for the first time in a long time. He did a double take when he caught my expression before grinning in return. But this sort of interaction was unfamiliar territory, so I focused on pouring tea into a plastic cup and setting it down in the grass where he would be able to reach it without having to make any physical contact with me.

I maintained a wary eye on him as we ate, ready to spring away the moment he made a wrong move. But he never did. Not only that, but he didn't even attempt conversation of any kind, as if he knew I wouldn't welcome it. We ate our lunch listening to the birds singing and the insects buzzing in the undergrowth, while the dappled sunlight and shadows shifted and danced across the path beneath the trees. And then we parted ways without a single word between us, and I marvelled once again at his otherworldliness. Here was someone I could share a long silence with, without feeling awkward or alone, and that was rare indeed.

Chapter Eleven

We were in the walled garden when Gregory Sinclair appeared out of the blue. The air was cooler than it had been for a while; the sky hazy with cloud that diffused the intense heat and light of the July sun. I was taking the opportunity to clear the vegetable beds and weed the fruit-cages while the high-sided, sun-trap of a garden was not churning out the stifling heat of an oven.

I had discovered a hoard of summer-fruiting raspberries and the lady of the house was picking and eating them with nimble fingers, her skin and lips staining with the juice, her eyes alight with glee. It was hard to take my eyes off her. She was a conundrum with the sharp gaze of a wise old woman and the seeming naivety of a young girl. And she had a guilelessness about her – her every emotion, good and bad, played out across her face without restraint or censorship. It was disconcerting at first, but made her refreshingly easy to read. Which was helpful since she'd still not uttered a word and I still didn't even know her name.

Despite her silence, or maybe because of it, I found myself voluntarily talking far more than I normally would. And not out of an urge to fill the silence – things didn't feel awkward between us – but because she hung on my every word. I waxed lyrical about nature; about the trees and plants, the changing seasons, everything right down to the leaf-cutter bees who made holes in the rose leaves; all the stuff my friends would have found dull, but which she seemed keen to hear.

Today I'd introduced her to a variety of different herbs as I came across them; mint, rosemary, thyme, chives, fennel... There was something sensual in the way she touched everything – lifting them to her nose to smell them; caressing them with her cheek and brushing them across her lips – as if exploring them with all five senses. Maybe hers were all the more acute due to her solitude and silence, or maybe she was simply tactile by nature.

When she abruptly bolted out of the fruit cage and disappeared behind the ramshackle tool shed, I stared after her bewildered at first. It wasn't until several seconds later that I picked up the sound of footsteps heading my way.

'Ah, Liam, here you are.'

'Mr Sinclair, you're back,' I said, carefully disentangling myself from a vicious gooseberry bush, straightening up to my full height and wiping my hands on my jeans.

'Gregory, please,' he said, slipping his own hands safely into his suit pockets and gazing around at the tangled foliage strewn about. A thistle had snagged the edge of one neatly-hemmed trouser leg, but he hadn't noticed yet. 'Just a fleeting visit I'm afraid, I fly out to Japan on Tuesday morning, but I wanted to touch base.'

'Right. I'm still clearing this area, as you can see...'

'Yes. The area around the house is looking much better,' he said without looking at me. 'When do you think you'll cut the rest of the grass – it's still very long.'

'I was aiming to cut it at the end of the summer – the ride-on mower you have in the stables won't start, so I'll have to fix it before I can use it.'

He nodded. 'And the lake?'

Sinclair was the sort of client who preferred to focus on all the things you hadn't done yet, rather than thank you for those you had. He was probably like that with all his staff; perhaps he liked to feel masterly and in control.

'I should be able to start dredging next week.'

'Good, good,' his words were distant as he continued to avoiding my eye. 'You haven't seen anyone else in the grounds have you?'

I hesitated. 'No, like who?' The blatant lie, and the instinctive ease with which I told it, surprised me – I rarely told fibs, and when I did I was unconvincing at best. But the girl and I had sort of become friends; I felt strangely protective of her, and if she was hiding from Sinclair I figured there must be a good reason. Luckily he made no attempt to scrutinise my expression and seemed to take me at my word.

'Oh, no-one. It's nothing, forget it. We'll talk again when you've finished all the clearance work.' As he turned to leave, the rogue thistle pulled at his leg and he kicked it away with irritation before marching off, his back ramrod-straight and his shoes ringing out on the brick path.

Once his footsteps had faded into the distance, my silent friend climbed out from behind the tool shed looking sheepish.

'I'm never going to find out your name, am I?' I said ruefully.

She raised her delicate little shoulders in an exaggerated shrug and I smiled at her, resigned. As I clambered back into the fruit cage she left the walled garden by the gate opposite the one in which Gregory had departed from, and I spent the rest of the day alone, speculating once again on the life of others.

Chapter Twelve

Gregory had buggered off again – hallelujah – he'd been in a strange mood all weekend. On Friday evening he insisted we sit and eat a formal dinner together in the dining room, like Lord and Lady of the manor – an excess of silver tableware and four tediously long courses interspersed with at least three different wines. He got a caterer to come in and cook our dinner on the weekends when he was home. Yvette was a retired French chef who lived nearby with her long-term partner, Jade, and cooked everything to Gregory's exacting standards without complaint. The Eiffel Tower keyring was hers before I pinched it. She was usually kept too busy in the kitchen to acknowledge me, but was considerate enough to make and freeze extra portions of the dishes she made, so that I would have something nutritious to eat during the week. It certainly made a nice change from microwave pizzas and spaghetti hoops on toast. I'd never learned how to cook.

Why Gregory had requested such an elaborate meal for that particular evening, I couldn't be sure – the date held no particular significance as far as I was aware, and he mentioned no cause for celebration. I suspect he hoped I would get tipsy and foolish, but I was careful to only take a few sips from each wine glass, while he progressively pickled himself.

Gregory quizzed me repeatedly on my work, the manuscripts still requiring my attention and the books I was reading; eager to know every detail of how I spent my time. Twice he remarked that I seemed to have caught the sun on my skin – but he was either too drunk or too cowardly to pursue the matter with any conviction.

As I tried to escape to bed afterwards, he hugged me; grabbing me too tight and jamming my face against his shoulder. Once upon a time I'd longed for Gregory to hold me, but back then he was reluctant and behaved as if it were a chore. I went to all sorts of desperate lengths to get his attention: sliding down the bannisters of the main staircase, deliberately overfilling the bath, and even cutting all my hair off – but it only made him keener to stay away.

Now that I was older, he seemed to want the closeness that he'd denied me in the past, but it was too late. The feel of his clammy hands on my back, his hot breath against my ear and the sharp sting of his aftershave in my nostrils only made my stomach turn. I thought he might be weeping as I pushed away from him, but any sympathy I might have for him was diluted by having to wash my hair three times to purge it of cigar smoke. The rest of the weekend we spent carefully avoiding each other.

This morning I'd waited for Gregory to depart for the airport before taking the back stairs up to the second floor and rifling through the heavy wooden chests and leather suitcases filled with clothes. It was stiflingly hot and stuffy up in the old servants' quarters, tucked under the eaves. The rooms had long been stripped and relegated to storage space; a jumble of spare furniture draped in plastic sheeting and the air thick with dust, cobwebs, and that distinct but indescribable mothball odour. I had the house to myself on Tuesdays and Thursdays (Mrs Daly's days off) so I was free to rummage about without being nagged about making a mess. Gathering armfuls of garments, I carried them back down to the nursery and proceeded to try them on.

Several of the items may once have belonged to Cornelia, but many of the others seemed to date back generations. They'd presumably been retained for children to play with and parade around in, or for fancy dress parties, but to my knowledge Wildham Hall had not hosted a single party of any sort. At least not since I'd lived there. I tried on a variety of pinafores, blouses, skirts, belts and scarves, one after the other and sometimes in combination, analysing ruffles, hemlines and demure sections of lace, and repeatedly scrutinising myself in a floor-length mirror. Recently I'd been browsing online music videos to gain an idea of what was fashionable and what was not – and this stuff was definitely not. But I had an eye for detail, a sewing machine and a streak of stubborn determination a mile wide. And anything else I needed could be sourced second-hand on eBay.

Of course I didn't dwell on my reasons for suddenly wanting to update my wardrobe – I told myself it was long overdue and nothing whatsoever to do with the gentle giant I'd made friends with in the garden. As I hastily unpicked, pinned, and re-sewed the hem of a dress, I stole glances at him in the distance through the window. It looked like he'd started dredging the silt and muck from the bottom of the stream this morning and was working his way towards the lake, though he was too far away for me to be sure.

Was I right to consider Liam Hunt a friend? I had no experience to go on, but everything I'd read on the subject of friendships made me quietly optimistic. He didn't treat me like a freak and that alone was a great sign.

Every carer, housekeeper or tutor I'd ever had resented my silence. Many would start out seemingly understanding, patient and kind, only to inevitably turn angry. They found my failure to speak peculiar, frustrating and offensive, and often took it as some kind of personal insult. But so far Liam appeared to be different; he refrained from questioning or snapping at me, and he never grabbed at me either. Despite his size and the amount of time we spent together, he was careful not to touch me at all – a simple courtesy that most people, in my limited experience, didn't bother with.

And I enjoyed the way he talked to me as he worked; explaining his actions and teaching me things without expecting anything in return. I liked the way he was clever with his big, rough hands; the way he ate messily and without restraint; and the way he smiled at me with a golden warmth in his eyes. In short, I liked spending time in his company and surely that was what friendship was all about, wasn't it?

My alterations complete, I slipped the dress on over my head, snugly buckled a belt around my waist, and stood back to eye myself in the mirror, marvelling at the waft of air circulating around my bare knees. It would have to do. In the bathroom I spent time scrubbing at my forearm with soap and hot water in a futile attempt to erase my communications with Gregory, and made a mental note to stop using my own skin to write on.

In the kitchen I removed the leftovers from the fridge and packed them into a wicker hamper along with a chilled carton of orange juice. Did Liam like orange juice? I guess I'd find out. Pleased with my preparations, I slipped on a pair of sandals at the back door and made my way down to the lake.

The man was wearing welly boots attached to weird rubbery trousers, which extended right up to his chest and were held up by braces – making him look like an ogre from an illustrated fairytale. His arms were coated in mud past his elbows and he was sweating profusely, but Liam smiled when he saw me.

'If it gets any hotter I'm going to have to strip off these ruddy waders and do this job in my undies.'

I stopped a few paces short and blinked at him as I tried to process this unexpected possibility in my mind.

'I'm joking,' he said with a grin. Clambering up the bank he unhooked the braces from his shoulders and peeled the 'waders' down to his waist. I was both relieved and faintly disappointed to see he was wearing another pair of trousers underneath. 'What've you got there, lunch?' He indicated the hamper with a jut of his chin, while his eyes skimmed my new outfit; my chest, my waist, my hips and my exposed bare legs. It was a fleeting glance, but it weighed more; as if his gaze alone warmed my skin. The curious sensation was not unpleasant and I was glad to have made an effort.

Liam used a couple of lengths of twine to tie back the trailing branches of a willow tree, like swagged curtains either side of a stage. By doing so he created a shady green arbour on the bank of the stream. 'After you, mi'lady,' he said with a mock bow. He waited for me to make myself comfortable before dropping down beside me, just out of reach.

While I set out the food, he talked me through his progress, emphasising that the water would run clear again once the churned up silt had settled. He'd left great mounds of excavated mud and roots at intervals along the bank, so that any wildlife he'd disturbed would have a chance to return to the water before he cleared the debris away for good. It was only once I'd opened the orange juice that I realised I hadn't brought any cups.

'We can just swig from the carton,' he suggested with a shrug.

My face must have betrayed my misgivings as I looked at him.

'But I understand if you don't fancy sharing – I can have water instead...'

In my haste to shove the carton at him, juice spilled from the top, but after only a moment's hesitation he accepted it. I stared as he took a drink; his soft-looking mouth yielding around the opening and his Adam's apple shifting beneath a fine sprinkling of golden stubble with each swallow. He handed it back to me and I kept my eyes on his as I took a sip myself, the juice tangy and refreshing on my tongue. My thoughts were racing and my lips tingled afterwards as I licked them. Sharing saliva with a man I barely knew was oddly intimate – in my over-active imagination I had just kissed him.

Chapter Thirteen

I only realised I'd been set up when I returned from the camp-site facilities to find a female interloper bent over pitching a two-man tent, not five metres away from mine.

'Ah, Liam, there you are,' Maire said, slinging her arm casually around my smirking brother's waist. 'This is my friend Bridget – she's joining us for the weekend.' The interloper straightened up, and turned to me with a smile, dusting her hands on her jeans. 'Bridget, this is Lester's little brother, Liam.'

'Little?' Bridget said, clearly amused and looking me up and down as we shook hands. 'If you say so…'

She herself was tall for a woman – maybe five foot nine or ten – with long, chestnut hair pulled back in a ponytail and womanly curves in all the right places. Her open smile and her firm handshake were warm and appealing, and though I was irritated by my sister-in-law's ambush-style attempt to set me up, I wasn't about to take it out on Bridget.

'I understand you're a gardener too, is that right?' she asked.

'Landscaping more than maintenance, but yes… how about you; what do you do?' Taking a handful of loose pegs from the ground I squatted to secure the guy ropes on her tent. I'd never been one for introductory small talk – especially not with women.

'I work at the British Library in London, have you been?'

'I'm afraid not, no – what's it like?'

Thankfully Bridget was content to waffle on about her job with minimal encouragement from me. It started to rain and under Maire's direction we unloaded the collapsible table, deck chairs, camping stove and other equipment from the back of Lester's van, while he erected a waterproof tarpaulin over the communal space between our three tents.

It was a long-standing family tradition that my brother and I went camping on the first weekend in August – regardless of the weather – we'd done it every year since we were small. Once he got married, Maire started tagging along with us. It might have bothered me, but Lester and Maire had been together since high school so I was used to her being around, and they were good at not making me feel like a spare wheel. Maire and I had repeatedly tried to get Cally to join us, but she never fancied it – she'd never been much of an outdoor person.

In our youth, Lester and I would venture into the wilds of the Scottish highlands, the windswept coasts of Ireland and Wales, and the peaks and valleys of the lake district, making camp wherever we ended up. But recently, a concise travelling duration had become the priority when picking a destination, in order to make the most of our limited free time. This year we'd booked pitches on a working farm in Suffolk – albeit a picturesque one – and the onus would be on me to make polite chitchat with a stranger all weekend.

While Bridget was busy lacing up her walking boots I shot Maire a disgruntled look, but she smiled to herself and pretended not to notice. Now that she was four months pregnant and the worst of her morning sickness was over, nothing got her down. For me, this trip was not going to be the relaxing break I'd hoped for.

*

By midday on Sunday I was ready to admit defeat; cut the long weekend short and head home. It didn't help that the weather had been against us, though it wasn't really the wind and rain that was getting to me. We'd managed a decent hike or two, and Bridget was lovely; attractive and friendly, and genuinely seemed interested when I described Wildham Hall. She backed off once she realised that I wasn't big on conversation and, for the most part, left me alone with my thoughts. But, as it turns out, that was my real problem – my thoughts.

I couldn't get *her* out of my head – the girl from Wildham Hall; my silent stalker; my sylph-like student; my shadow – and it was driving me to distraction. Was it crazy to miss someone when you didn't even know their name?

Every little detail about her had me fascinated. The way she ate, for example: the other day she'd opened a packet of cheese and a bag of crisps, broken the cheese into chunks and then taken the time to garnish each individual crisp with a precariously-balanced piece of cheese. Once her food was arranged to her satisfaction she steadily consumed each bite-sized morsel, delicately one by one with her fingertips. Something inside of me yearned to be on the receiving end of her precise attention. I'd never wanted to be a piece of cheese before…

And her ongoing, comprehensive silence was intensely intriguing. Was she simply reluctant to speak or actually unable to? And if it was the latter, was that due to a physical problem or psychological trauma? Her tongue looked healthy enough when she was licking orange juice from her lips, and there were no outward signs of scarring at her throat – on the contrary the skin there looked as smooth as white marble, the delicate throb of her pulse visible beneath the surface.

But not all her skin was flawless; her left arm showed faded evidence of more writing. I assumed that was how she communicated with Sinclair when he was at home – when she wasn't hiding from him, of course. It was pointless making assumptions based on a jumble of scribblings which may, or may not, represent one side of a conversation, but words like 'no' and 'please don't' seemed to leap out at me and made me worry about relations between them.

In the last few days her outfits had changed – her clothes were shorter at the leg, lower at the neck line and more-closely fitting – not indecently so, but enough that she no longer resembled a rag doll or a child. I couldn't help thinking that these changes might be for my benefit – a concept both flattering and worrying in equal measure. I still had no idea if she was my client's wife or daughter, but either way, and regardless of whether they got on or not, she was off-limits for me. I did not get involved with clients.

Besides, she was not the sort of woman I wanted to get mixed up with – she was far too unpredictable, mysterious and complicated. I needed someone who was normal, easy-going and straight-forward; someone I could rely on; someone more like Bridget, maybe...

'I might head off early,' I said.

'What, why?' Lester looked genuinely disappointed. 'We're booked in for a session at the shooting range tomorrow...'

'I know.'

'You won't have to kill any real animals – it's just target practise – it'll be fun.'

'It's not my thing.'

'That's kind of ironic – with your name being Hunt,' Bridget said.

'Yeah, I guess,' I shrugged.

Lester put a hand on my shoulder and steered me away from the women. 'What's going on?' he said in a low voice.

'Nothing, I'm just tired.'

'I thought you and Bridget were getting on – you look great together – don't you like her?'

'No, she's a lovely girl, it's not that.'

Lester sighed. 'You can't stay hung up on Cally forever – I know she hurt you, but—'

'No, it's not that either, I don't know, I—'

'Look, you didn't hear this from me, but Maire mentioned that Marguerite knows where Cally is. Maybe you should go down to London and see her? Then maybe you can put that relationship behind you and move on.'

It was no surprise to me that Marguerite had Cally's address; she'd probably had it all along. Was unfinished business with my ex really holding me back? It was definitely easier to let Lester think that than try to explain how I was being haunted by a strange female client. 'OK, maybe I'll do that.'

Chapter Fourteen

He was back! He'd mentioned he was going to be away for a few days but I hadn't expected it to feel like a year. I watched from a bedroom window as he made his way down to the lake, a blue T-shirt stretched tight across his shoulders and his waders dangling limply over one arm like a deflated sea-creature. It was only 7 a.m. – still early – too early to go and see him. But the sun had been up for over an hour; as had the birds; as had I...

'Morning,' he said, his face lifting into a big smile and making my stomach lurch with excitement and fear. I had a ferocious and entirely foreign urge to hug him, but instead I grinned back at him like a fool. 'The water's looking much clearer, don't you think?'

Stepping over I stood beside him at the water's edge, and as the sleeve of my cardigan brushed his arm he shifted away.

'I've still got to tackle the clump of reeds at that end by the boathouse, but then I reckon it will be good enough to swim in.'

This was a surprise. Why would anyone want to swim in it? Peering through the water at the murky bottom I shivered. Admittedly I didn't know how to swim – but the idea of sinking barefoot into all that cold mud didn't appeal at all, and I'd never known Gregory or anyone else to swim here. Reaching past Liam, I idly ran my hand up the tall upright stems of the bulrushes, letting the long, brown velvet heads skim through my fingers. Again my sleeve brushed his arm and again he shifted away from me, a subtle sign of respect that I would have been grateful for in anyone else, but which left me crushed. I wanted to touch him; I wanted him to touch me. More than that; I wanted him to *want* to touch me, as disturbing as that concept may be.

'I brought you something,' he said, withdrawing a small notebook and a Biro from his pocket. 'You might think it's silly, and you don't have to use it, but… just in case you ever want to tell me something… anything…'

It was amazing that he had waited this long to try to get me to communicate, and even now he was doing it in a gentle, unpushy way. And yet, I couldn't help feeling disappointed. There was a certain safety and security in my anonymity – once he got to know me he might not like me anymore. With reluctance I accepted the pen and paper, still warm with his body heat, and stared at the blank white page. Where should I start? What should I say? Thank you for being so kind to me? I like being around you? Touch me…? No, it was no good, he would run a mile.

'You don't have to write anything right now.'

With an apologetic smile I tucked the pad and pen into my pocket and he set about pulling on his waders. It seemed improper to watch him dressing, so I wandered over to the nearest tree – the large old cypress with distinctive spreading limbs, which provided a striking focal point when viewed from the house. In the past I'd climbed up and sat in it, but over time the lowest branches had been removed and now, as I reached up on tiptoe, bracing a foot against the trunk, I found I could no longer scale it without making an ass of myself.

'Want some help?' He was standing close behind me as I turned to look at him, and my heartbeat picked up with anticipation. 'If I help you up there do you promise not to fall and break your neck?'

Smiling, I nodded.

I don't know what I'd been expecting; maybe I'd imagined he'd crouch down and give me a leg up; a boost, but instead he cupped my waist in his enormous hands, lifted me straight up into the air as if I weighed nothing, and gently set me down on a branch six foot off the ground. My hands automatically shot out and gripped his shoulders as all the blood rushed to my abdomen and left me light-headed, but he kept a firm hold of me, gazing up at me with concern.

'You OK? You're not going to fall, are you?'

I blinked a few times, breathless with the exhilarating physical sensation his touch provoked inside me. It was unlike anything I'd ever experienced. Was this desire? Coming to my senses I snatched my fingers back from where I'd been clinging to his body and grabbed the branch either side of me instead. Once he was sure I'd regained my balance, he slowly withdrew his hands and their warmth lingered like a pleasant ache long after he had walked away.

After that I became obsessed with thinking up new excuses to make physical contact; the heady rush of heat I got from his touch was addictive. As he worked I tried to predict which tool he might require next, simply so that his long coarse fingers might skim mine as I passed it to him. When we ate lunch together, or walked side by side, I tried to position myself close enough that his arm would brush mine. And every time we came across a suitable tree I would climb it, with his obliging assistance of course, that and his large and powerful hands. It made me smile every time. Who was this person I'd become?

Chapter Fifteen

A messy oil change and a brand new carburettor later, the lawn mower finally growled into life. It was built like a small tractor and made a farmer of me as I drove up and down creating stripes across the land. The steady monotony gave me time to reflect on recent events. In a disturbing case of history repeating itself, my best mate's girlfriend had left him – abruptly walked out on him, like my ex had four months previously – as if the urge to run away was catching. But the more I thought about it, the more convinced I became that the situation was completely different. James and Kat were suited to each other in a way, I now realised Cally and I *never* were. Their relationship was obviously complicated but I had enough faith in them to believe they would work it out. Whether I'd ever figure out my own love life was another matter.

The ride-on machine didn't have an attachment for collecting the cuttings, and it was hot, back-straining work raking them up by hand. But as the underlying slope of the main lawn began to take shape, forming sweeping curves and revealing the elegant trunks of trees, I couldn't help being pleased. The unfurling green carpet led the eye effortlessly down through the landscape, providing a perfect canvas for the spectacular view, framed by trees and sky. On the east side of the estate, a good half-mile away from the house, the long grass was dominated by wild flowers – a proliferation of ox-eye daisies, purple knapweed and yellow loosestrife, buzzing with insects. On impulse I left the area of flowering meadow almost intact, deciding instead to mow a track around the periphery and one sinuous path meandering through the middle, from which the space could be enjoyed from within.

But by lunch time the temperature had reached thirty degrees; I was soaked with sweat and itchy with cut grass, and the cool, clear water of the lake called to me. Keeping my trousers on – so as not to offend the lady of the house, who was reading her book in the shade of a nearby tree – I emptied my pockets, peeled off my shirt, and threw myself in.

The water was deliciously refreshing and almost sweet as I swam a few lengths with a lazy front crawl and then stopped in the middle to simply float on my back with my eyes shut. After a while, a sound drew my attention to the water's edge, where my silent companion was gingerly tiptoeing into the lake in her white cotton dress; her limbs rigid with tension. Was it the shock of the cold or was she genuinely afraid? Turning over I trod water and watched as she inched forwards, the water rising up her calves, over her knees and soaking into the hem of her dress. Abruptly I turned away, cursing under my breath, when I realised her clothes were becoming transparent.

But a splashing sound had me turning back to where she must have slipped and submerged herself before she was ready – the water now reaching her chin. The abject terror on her face had me swimming towards her.

'You OK? You *can* swim, can't you?'

Shaking her head she folded her arms defensively across her chest, her eyes wide and locked on mine. I stopped a few feet away from her.

'Right, well you should be OK as long as you don't come any further – the bottom drops away quite sharply, as I guess you've discovered.'

She didn't respond to this, but kept staring at me as if attempting telepathy.

'Unless... I mean... I could try to teach you to swim, if you like?'

She smiled, and for a split second I felt fantastic until the reality of the situation hit me and I recognised my spur-of-the-moment offer for the bad idea it really was. Unfortunately she looked too excited by the prospect for me to take it back.

For the next half hour or so I gently supported her in my up-turned hands; issuing instructions and encouragement while she kicked her hands and feet. It was torture. Keeping her from drowning was the easy part. The sheer effort of not noticing the soft feminine contours of her body, her raspberry-like nipples or her seductive scent, was rivalled only by the immense concentration involved in not letting her detect my hard-on.

At last she returned to the water's edge like a bedraggled mythological nymph, exhausted but exultant, while I swam the deepest, coldest parts of the lake in order to regain my composure. It had been many, many years since I'd been so physically affected by a woman. In fact I couldn't recall ever having been so turned on before.

By the time I joined her on land, she was wrapped safely inside a shawl and brandishing a long stick in her hand.

'What've you got there?'

Crouching down to where water had lapped onto the shore, she scratched something into the soft mud, before standing back to reveal two words.

'Melody Sinclair?'

She pressed a palm to her chest, her expression tight with anxiety.

'That's your name? Melody?' The cruel irony of it was shocking and explained her reluctance to share it with me. And yet she had. She could have lied – made something up or shortened it to something else, but instead she had gifted me with the truth.

Melody was scrutinising my face; silently gauging my reaction and waiting for a response. So I said the only honest thing I could:

'That's a beautiful name.'

71

Chapter Sixteen

At first the shock of the water made me gasp and grit my teeth; my clothes dragged as they grew heavy, and mud oozed between my toes, sucking at my feet and filling my mind with notions of swamp monsters and decay. But it had all been worth it. Not only was I learning to swim, something as alien and exciting to me as flying, but it gave me the perfect excuse to be close to him.

Even now, as I returned to the house, damp and itchy in my shawl, I could still sense the heat radiating from his body; the imprint of his strong hands on my belly; the splay of his long fingers as he held me up in his calloused palms with a look of intense concentration – as if he were presenting something precious to the Queen.

I tried to focus on his instructions and advice by taking deep breaths, putting my face in the water, relaxing my body and kicking my toes… but a secret voice in my head spent the entire duration begging him to move his hands – either higher up to cup my breasts, or lower down to where I ached between my legs. But of course, frustratingly, he kept his hands on my stomach the whole time.

Liam Hunt didn't resemble any of the male pop stars or models I'd been curious about in my teens, but I could no longer deny it – he turned me on. All the songs about lust and desire I'd heard; all the sex I'd read about in books and on the internet; all the hype and fuss I'd once considered irrelevant to me, disregarded and skimmed over, now seemed vitally significant. I wished I'd paid more attention. For instance, how was I supposed to know if he wanted me the same way I did him, or if he was simply being friendly?

He'd said my name was beautiful – which was the kindest thing anyone had ever said to me – but he hadn't tried to hold my hand or kiss me or anything. For a moment in the lake I'd felt something in his trousers prod my hip, and hoped he might be aroused too, but I couldn't be sure, and with all the mud I'd churned up splashing about, the water was too murky for me to see.

Wasn't the man supposed to make the first move? What would he do if I tried to kiss him? Oh crap, what if he was married?

The thought brought me up short and I stopped abruptly on my way through the laundry room, dripping water on the stone floor. He didn't wear a ring, but that didn't necessarily mean anything. He was certainly old enough to be married... and have kids... several kids in fact. Over the past few weeks he'd mentioned his brother Lester, his pregnant sister-in-law, various friends (someone called James in particular) and several guys he played rugby with... surely by now he would have mentioned a partner or children if he had them...?

'Just look at the state of you.'

The unexpected voice made me jump as I passed the kitchen and turned to find Mrs Daly stood there with her arms crossed and a mocking expression on her face. It was Tuesday, she didn't work on Tuesdays – what was she doing here?

'Having fun out there were you?'

Unease unfurled in the pit of my stomach.

'Oh yes, I saw you. He knows you're frolicking about half-naked with the gardener, does he?'

I scowled at her, pulling my shawl tighter around me. How dare she speak to me like that.

'No, I'll bet he doesn't. How's about I mention it to him when he's next home, see what he says...?'

It was moments like these, in which any normal person would simply open their mouth and verbally defend themselves, in which I felt my mutism most acutely. It was bullies like her who made me reluctant to venture out into the world – and here she was threatening me in my own home.

'What's the matter, cat got your tongue?' she crowed.

Pushing past her into the kitchen I grabbed the white board where Gregory left her instructions and wrote: *What do you want?* in marker pen.

'Now there's a good question,' she said, smirking.

Slapping the pen down on the counter and trembling with fury, I stared at her with my jaw clenched while she made a show of deliberating.

'Well now, let's see, for a start you can clean your own bedroom and bathroom from now on – seems to me you have plenty of time on your hands and I have enough to be getting on with in the rest of the house... and now that you ask, a bit of financial appreciation wouldn't go amiss – you know – in recognition of all my hard work...'

I don't have any money, I scrawled.

'Is that so? Explains a fair few things that does – your dress sense for one,' she added, eyeing me disdainfully.

74

'But, now, I'm sure you could find some cash, if you put your mind to it... or shall I inform Mr Sinclair of your floozy ways and see how quickly your man disappears, never to return?'

Bitch. Pursing my lips I blinked my acquiescence.

'What was that? I can't hear you?'

Chucking the pen across the room, I stormed out, my feet slapping the floor. Her cackling laughter followed me all the way up the back stairs.

In the bathroom I locked the door, plugged the bath and turned the taps on full blast before catching sight of myself in the mirror. Was there ever a more pathetic sight? In a fit of rage I swept my toiletries into the sink where they clattered, bounced, and smashed against the enamel, the din reverberating off the tiles. Then I ripped all my damp clothes off, flinging them in too. But I stubbed my toes on the clawed-foot of the bath and with the shot of pain I collapsed to the floor. Powerless, naked and alone, I huddled in the corner listening to the cascade of rushing water, with angry tears spilling down my face.

Chapter Seventeen

From Liverpool Street Station I caught the Metropolitan line four stops back to Kings Cross. The morning rush hour was over and I managed to get a seat opposite a woman with talon-like fingernails, wearing an indecently short gold skirt and stiletto heels. Despite her dark shades I could tell she was fast asleep; her head lolling back against the window and her lipsticked mouth gaping slackly. I idly wondered what her story was; whether she'd been out all night partying or whether she was a sex worker. I tried not to judge people by their appearances or for their life choices, but I hoped for her sake that it was the former and not the latter.

The train jolted on the track and she woke with a start, glancing around self-consciously. As she raised a hand to her hair, a tattoo – a faded string of hearts – was revealed along her arm, and I offered her a sympathetic smile, but she didn't seem to notice. The train stopped, she disembarked, and was quickly swallowed up by the city.

My unannounced visit to my ex-girlfriend had gone well, all things considered. She didn't own, or even rent, the swanky penthouse apartment she was currently living in – few people could afford that kind of abode in central London. Marguerite worked for a house-sitting company, and Cally was simply contracted to stay there, as some kind of caretaker, until the rightful owner returned.

It was strange seeing Cally again, but not as uncomfortable as I'd imagined. She too had looked tired and she'd lost too much weight, but despite that she seemed happier; more confident, almost glowing with a vitality I'd never noticed in her before. It confirmed my suspicion that we'd never been right for each other; friends – yes – but lovers...? I'd never induced her to glow like that, and she'd never aroused me the way someone else had recently – someone I barely knew.

So we made polite conversation, my ex and I, over a cup of tea, and as I was leaving I met the man she'd become involved with – her neighbour; a man who had clearly fallen for her hard. He was openly hostile and belligerent towards me, but I figured that anyone who could draw Cally out of her shell and cause her to shine the way she did could not be all bad. At her request I was prepared to give him the benefit of the doubt for now, and reserve judgement until I knew him better.

From Kings Cross tube station I made my way over to the British Library where someone in the Registration Office checked my ID, issued me with a reader's pass and quietly directed me to a Reading Room. At the security desk I flashed my new pass, switched my mobile to silent, retrieved a notebook and pencil from my pocket and gazed around the room.

For once I didn't feel too big for the space I found myself in. It was a vast angular room with a central atrium, several storeys high, which drew in diffused natural light for an arrangement of balconies and mezzanine floors, which in turn were supported by lines of boxy white columns. Rows upon rows of smart writing desks spread out in regimented succession across the floor – each one with its own leather-upholstered chair, reading lamp and power socket – primed for the serious matter of studying in earnest.

Most of the seats were occupied, and I found the respectful hush of the place perversely stimulating; giving me an urge to clear my throat much like churches and art galleries did. Don't get me wrong, I appreciated libraries; I'd read my fair share of books, and such places were invaluable resources to both local communities and civilisation as a whole. But a profound, prolonged quiet in a building filled with people seemed unnatural, unsettling, as if the air itself was tense with potential sound. Then again, given the choice, I always preferred to be outside surrounded by nothing but trees, birds and sky.

'Liam, you made it,' a low voice said behind me. I turned to find Bridget smiling at me, hands on hips.

'You got me intrigued.'

'Good,' she whispered, '… follow me.'

The last time I'd seen Bridget she'd been clad in high-vis waterproofs on a windswept hillside, rain dripping off her nose. I recognised the same warm smile, but she now sported a glossy haircut, a pencil skirt, high heels and an officious-looking lanyard around her neck. As she led me across the room I couldn't help but notice the assured swing of her hips, and I wasn't the only one; heads turned and eyeballs swivelled as she navigated the space; Bridget was a sexy woman.

Stopping at a desk where she had already deposited a sheaf of papers, she gestured for me to take a seat. Her knee brushed mine as she pulled up a chair beside me and started talking in a hushed voice.

'I did a background search on Wildham Hall and, to be honest, not a great deal turned up. The house itself isn't particularly old or large, or even especially grand compared to other country estates in the area, and it has always stayed in the Sinclair family, so there are no records of sale or auction details to go on.' Bridget looked at me, her eyes bright with enthusiasm; clearly in her element.

'I can hear a 'but' coming…' I whispered.

She smiled. '*But*, in 1878 Aubrey Benjamin Sinclair commissioned the famous French landscape architect, Édouard Marcel, to create a rose garden in the grounds of Wildham Hall, and that was big news at the time.'

The copies of articles she showed me were from the Herts Guardian and the Bedfordshire Times, both dating from the 1870s. In a few brief sentences, the appointment of Monsieur Marcel was announced in a typically understated, British manner. But there was no disguising the sense of civic pride written between the lines, and I myself was impressed reading the news, over a century later.

'So why was he famous?'

'He was a leading horticulturalist as well as a landscape architect, and during his career he designed many private parks for nobility, right across Europe; from France to Lithuania. But the really exciting news is that in the 1870s he was in regular correspondence with a British plant hunter called Montgomery Broome, who kept all his letters…'

'And you have them?'

'Yep – the British Library has the complete collection archived.' Leaning across the desk she retrieved a smart-looking folder. 'These two letters refer to the rose garden at Wildham Hall, by name...' Opening the file she carefully turned the crinkly, faded, hand-written pages within before I had a chance to read them, '... and on this page Marcel loosely sketched out the design itself!'

'Wow,' I muttered, studying the geometric pattern inked into the paper. The central layout of the design was instantly recognisable; a clear footprint for the sunken rose garden that was now drowning in weeds.

Bridget left me alone to read the documents from beginning to end; jotting down all the various rose varieties that Marcel mentioned, and carefully photographing the sketch plan on my phone for printing out later. In the second letter the Frenchman also made reference to a grotto that he had been asked to advise on at Wildham Hall – presumably the same locked-up, 'dangerous' structure Gregory Sinclair had pointed out to me. But Marcel was cryptic and vague on the details. Maybe it was just a vocabulary issue, though his written English was excellent, but I got the distinct impression that Marcel had misgivings about the grotto; reservations which he was reluctant to put into words.

'How's it going?' Bridget murmured, leaning over my shoulder from behind.

'Great, thanks, I think I'm just about finished, but it's been really useful.'

'Wonderful, do you have time to grab lunch before you go...?'

I insisted on paying for our drinks and sandwiches to thank Bridget for all the trouble she'd gone to on my behalf. She argued that searching the archives was her job and her passion, but I wanted her to know I appreciated it anyway. We sat across a table in the busy café, and while we ate she seemed content to do most of the talking again; feeding me anecdotes about the various things she had discovered in the archives since working there. As she chatted and laughed and flicked her hair with her fingers, there was no denying her appeal; she was friendly, smart, down-to-earth, and talkative, without being brash or loud. Bridget was the sort of person I could care about; date; settle down with, and this was the perfect opportunity to ask her out. But somehow, I still couldn't summon up the words. As we stood up to leave, I thanked her again for the information she'd found and she waved it off with a smile.

'Liam, forgive me if this is too forward, but I was wondering if you'd like to go for a drink sometime...?' She held my eye with confidence as I tried out various awkward excuses in my mind, but they all sounded weak and cowardly.

'I'd like that. How about Saturday evening?'

By the time we parted I had a firm date lined up with a desirable woman. So why didn't I feel more excited?

The one word answer sprang up in my thoughts making me feel guilty before I could stop it; the three syllables lingering on my tongue: 'Melody'. A wet vision of her swam into my mind's eye, accompanying the sound of her name, and I swallowed in response as if tasting something forbidden and delicious, and cursed under my breath.

Between the Library and the tube station I checked my mobile, dismayed and concerned to see I had no less than fifteen missed calls from Olly. Taking a deep breath, I called him back.

'Dude, thank fuck! Where've you been? I've been calling and calling...'

'What's the matter, Olly?'

'It's Lester – he's had an accident and Maire's doing her nut – can you come to the hospital...?'

Chapter Eighteen

With Cornelia's diamond tiara perched on my head, I sat beneath the willow tree in the rain, and poked at an ugly blister on my foot. Last week I'd spent a stuffy forty-eight hours holed up in the nursery. Liam had mentioned he'd be away for a day in London, and I wanted to avoid another run in with Mrs Daly; I was so furious, I was afraid of what I might do to her. Liam had said his visit would be brief; that he was hoping to learn something about the history of the garden, whatever that meant. But that was five days ago and he still hadn't come back.

A duck paddled out of the rushes, gliding across the pitted surface of the lake at an unconcerned pace. I watched as it neared, before chucking a cold sausage roll in its direction, narrowly missing its head. It paddled away again, with an apathetic quack, while my miserable offering sank without trace.

Until now I'd been happy with my uniquely solitary lifestyle. I was used to it. As a child I simply made up imaginary friends to keep me company, and they were infinitely preferable to the real people I occasionally came into contact with. Gregory had always refused to have a television set in the house. I'd discovered a stack of movie DVDs from his student days in a box in the attic, which I surreptitiously viewed on my computer. But those violent glimpses of society aside, I didn't really understand what I was missing. By the time he'd hooked me up with limited access to the internet, I'd grown fond of my quiet way of life, my own space and my privacy.

As I got older I ventured into town every now and then – mainly out of mild curiosity. But it usually turned out to be a frustrating and highly disappointing experience, and I was always glad to get home again. If I craved escape I simply cycled around the grounds on my bike – before the paths became too overgrown to do so.

No, as far as I could see there was a certain amount of weakness involved in interacting with lots of other people – constant compromises, criticism and, ultimately, betrayal. I preferred to be strong, independent and free to please only myself most of the time.

And then along came Liam. Damn him.

Where the hell was he? Was it the weather keeping him away? There had been heavy rain and even a thunderstorm since he'd been gone, but I'd seen him work in the rain before. Was he deliberately avoiding me?

At the weekend I'd gone out on my trusty green bicycle; racing up and down the deserted streets of Wildham at night, cloaked in darkness and enjoying the wind in my hair and the sense of freedom it evoked. I was safe on my bike in the early hours of the morning – there was no-one around and I pedalled too fast for anyone to catch me. I'd hoped I might spot Liam's van and thereby discover where he lived, but apparently there were hundreds of vans in Wildham and I didn't manage to find one bearing his name.

In my mind I replayed our first swimming lesson over and over again, searching for clues to his disappearance. Had I made a mistake; a faux pas; a social blunder? Or had I simply made such a fool of myself that he was reluctant to face me? What if it was worse than that; what if he was sick or injured or dead? I couldn't contemplate that last one – it induced a painful sensation behind my ribs.

Had Mrs Daly said something to him? But no, that didn't make sense – it was *me* she was trying to blackmail, and if she warned Liam off she'd not get a penny. She was away on a fortnight's holiday at the moment, which at least gave me time to work out how to deal with her.

What little I earned by proofreading went straight into an online account. I usually spent my wage on books and music, and I'd recently blown a load on second-hand clothing. There wasn't much left; certainly not enough to satisfy that greedy, manipulative cow. Each week I used Gregory's credit card details to order groceries, toiletries, and general household items from an online supermarket, but he kept a close eye on his statements and regularly perused the itemised delivery list to monitor my spending. I didn't have the actual card to enable me to withdraw funds from a cash-point, and anyway, Gregory would simply cancel the card if I abused it by purchasing anything non-essential. So where was I going to get a load of cash from?

Of course, Gregory had a safe hidden in his wardrobe, which was probably full of money. I'd never seen inside it, or managed to get it unlocked, but it was a while since I'd tried, so maybe it was worth another look. I should be doing that right now, instead of moping around the grounds in Liam's ginormous wellies and Cornelia's finest crown – it wasn't making me feel any better.

I just wanted my rugged landscaper to return. I didn't care if I'd already made a fool of myself. If he appeared right now I wouldn't hold back; I'd throw my arms around him and never let him go. I'd jot down anything he wanted me to; reply to any question; write whole paragraphs, letters, entire essays if he wanted me to – anything to encourage him to stay.

I'd always been content to be alone, but that was no longer true; not now that I'd met Liam Hunt. Now I was lonely.

Chapter Nineteen

As I was parking the van, the huge front door was flung open from inside. Melody stood there on the threshold, dwarfed by the architecture and barefoot in a short, blue summer dress, a long string of pearls, and with what looked like a peacock feather stuck in her hair. But the huge smile on her face slipped dramatically as she registered that I was not alone.

'Morning!' Olly yelled cheerfully through the open passenger window as I switched off the ignition.

Melody's grim expression adequately conveyed her annoyance, even before she slammed the door shut with an almighty bang.

'She's as friendly as ever,' Olly said, hopping out and loudly whistling a tune as he began unloading tools from the back. I sighed.

The last few days had been exhausting. On Wednesday, Lester had lost his balance at the top of a ladder and almost cut his own leg off with an electric hedge trimmer. Thankfully he hadn't fallen very far and he'd missed his femoral artery, thereby narrowly avoiding bleeding to death. The hospital had made a good job of stitching him up, but it was a deep laceration, he'd suffered nerve and ligament damage, and it would be at least two months before he stood any chance of playing rugby again.

I'd spent the remainder of that week supervising my brother's garden maintenance crew in the pouring rain, while he lay on his sofa at home, and drove poor Maire up the wall with his complaining.

Now, against all medical advice, he was back at work; hobbling about on crutches and complaining. But as a thank you, and in recognition of my efforts, I'd been bestowed with Olly's questionable company and assistance for a few days. The rain had dried up, the sun was shining, and I was looking forward to catching up on a few of the two-man jobs that needed doing at Wildham Hall. And I had to admit, to myself if no-one else, I'd been looking forward to seeing Melody again.

She was an enigma – the woman piqued my interest like nothing and no-one else on earth, and was never far from my thoughts. I had a suspicion I'd even started dreaming about her in my sleep. The last time I'd seen her she'd finally told me her name and I was hoping to learn more about her. That was until today. If the thunderous look on her face this morning was anything to go by, I'd blown it, big time.

Together, Olly and I embarked on the arduous task of repairing the many miles of hoggin path that snaked their way around the estate; weeding them, reinstating the edges where they had disintegrated, filling pot holes with hardcore, and resurfacing the bald patches with a fresh mix of gravel, sand and clay. Olly did most of the donkey work; shovelling and depositing barrowfuls of material into position, while I did most of the heavy pounding – using a thick plank of wood and a sledgehammer to compact and bind the repairs. It provided a good physical workout and the sun beat down on our backs as we settled into a steady working rhythm.

'Hey, didn't you go on a date at the weekend?' Olly piped up, pausing, shovel in hand.

I rolled my eyes. 'Where did you hear that?'

'I overheard Maire telling Lester.'

'Oh. Great.'

'So? Who is she and how did it go?'

'It's not really any of your business, Olly.'

'Aw come on, don't be like that. Her name's Bridget, right? And she's a friend of Maire's…?'

'You obviously have big ears as well as a big mouth.'

'So, is she hot? What's she like?' It would seem that not even my most glowering scowl was going to deter Olly today.

'You're too nosey for your own good,' I muttered, still labouring in the hope that he would drop it. I had indeed met Bridget in town for a few drinks on Saturday night – we had a perfectly pleasant evening and even exchanged a brief kiss goodnight before her bus pulled up – but I wasn't about to discuss it with Olly.

'Does she look anything like Renée Zellweger?'

I sighed and paused, wiping the sweat from my brow, leaning on the handle of the sledgehammer and breathing hard. 'Who?'

'Y'know, from *Bridget Jones's Diary*…'

'Oh, I see. Maybe, a bit…'

'Yeah, I knew it – she's hot.'

I shook my head, bemused by Olly's logic as I repositioned the gravel board, widened my stance, and wrapped my hands around the sledgehammer again.

'So, are you seeing her again? You're going on another date, right…?'

'Get back to work, Olly.'

As the week wore on, I learned to tune out Olly's prying questions and we made good headway around the estate. But the stretch of path along the stream and down by the lake had been so badly damaged by flooding that it required complete relaying. To make the job easier I rented a vibrating roller from the local hire shop, and let Olly take turns steering the heavy machinery across the newly laid surface. Our progress was clear to see, which helped make it all worthwhile, but while Olly jabbered on about everything from drinking games to *The Smurfs*, Melody stayed away.

And I missed her.

By Friday afternoon every inch of the snaking paths leading around the grounds had been restored. I left Olly to sweep the last completed section and load the van with tools, while I returned those that we'd borrowed to their rightful place in the stables. On my way back I passed a back door to the house which was propped wide open, as if in invitation. I hesitated. Was it an invitation or was someone simply airing the house? I hadn't seen the cleaner in days, or Gregory Sinclair, or Melody come to that; she'd made a neat job of avoiding me all week.

The door was on the north side of the house and opened into a shadowy flagstone-floored interior. I knocked and called out hello, but there was no response from within. Ducking my head and stepping inside, I wiped my dusty boots on the mat and rapped my knuckles on the door again; harder and louder this time. As my eyes adjusted to the gloom I could make out several large sinks and a couple of industrial-sized laundry machines, but a male voice drew my attention through another open door, on the far side of the room.

Was that Sinclair? Had he come home for the weekend? Perhaps I could talk to him about my findings from the library. The second doorway led onto a large, open space with a partially glazed roof and several other doors leading off it. But I hesitated again before stepping out of the shadows and into the light-filled hallway. Maybe this wasn't a good idea. Perhaps I should go back around to the front door and ring the bell.

As I was about to turn away Melody appeared at the far end of the hall, making my chest tighten and my blood pulse loudly in my ears. She resembled a fairy, wearing a pink floaty dress which had wing-like sleeves, but which only just covered her bottom, and a matching pink scarf tied around her hair. I observed in stunned silence as she flounced across the room closely pursued by Sinclair.

'Don't walk away from me while I'm speaking to you!' He grabbed her upper arm, halting her mid-step and swinging her round to face him. 'Why are you dressed like this, if not to welcome me home? You must have known it would provoke a reaction...'

Melody had her back to me, so I couldn't see her expression, but her shoulders were rigid with tension. It was discomfiting trespassing upon such a private scene, but I couldn't leave, or even move, without drawing attention and potentially landing both Melody and myself in trouble. So I lurked motionless in the shadows, praying I wouldn't be discovered.

'I know you must be lonely,' said Sinclair, his voice softening as he peered into her face. 'I am too. If you'll

91

only let me in; let me get close to you...' Melody squirmed out of his grasp and for a moment, as she backed away from him, his eyes seemed to crawl all over her body with lascivious intent, making me nauseated. The next moment Melody was gone; she'd disappeared through a doorway, leaving Sinclair behind. He made no attempt at chasing her, but sighed heavily and shook his head, pausing only to adjust the front of his trousers with one hand before turning on his heel and walking back the way he'd come.

A disproportional sense of despair descended like a black fog in my mind as I quietly retreated back outside. No decent man would look at his daughter, his sister or even his niece, like that – Gregory and Melody must be husband and wife.

In a daze I returned to the van, climbed into the driver's seat beside Olly and started the engine while he enthused about his plans for the weekend. Carefully reversing around Sinclair's gleaming Mercedes, and avoiding the worst potholes, I coaxed the van into the dark tunnel of driveway, and out of sight of the Gothic hall. But as I drove away, the gnawing pain and discomfort in my chest confirmed what I'd long suspected and ignored: I was falling for her – Melody – a married woman and my client's wife. God help me, I was in trouble.

Chapter Twenty

It was still dark when Gregory got up and made preparations to leave for the airport. I waited in a window seat, wrapped up in Cornelia's silk dressing gown, admiring the sun as it rose above the horizon. The robe was apricot with a delicate oriental motif, and for a transient moment I perfectly matched the optimistic glow of the sky at daybreak.

Once he'd gone I strolled into his bedroom, removed a section of wood panelling from inside the wardrobe, and inspected the safe. Mrs Daly would be back from her holiday in two days and I was running out of time to find a means of buying her silence. The steel strongbox was a newer version to the one I remembered, but still basic by modern standards with a standard keypad and an LED display requiring a six-digit code. I tried all the obvious dates first – our birthdays; Gregory's, Cornelia's and my own; the date of their wedding and that of her untimely death, but all to no avail. With a buzz of fresh inspiration I tried the month and year that Wildham Hall was completed, but again with no luck. A quick search of the rest of his sparse bedroom yielded no new ideas. Time to move on.

The study was part library, with one whole wall, from floor to ceiling, taken up by old books; all of which I'd read or at least leafed through. The rest of the room served as an office, so I rifled through the desk for clues. Sitting cross-legged in Gregory's swivel chair, I was regarded from above by a large stag's head mounted on the wall. Ignoring the unfortunate animal's bleak stare, I spun slowly round and round while scanning endless customs invoices and dreary sales reports on my lap.

Gregory worked in the import/export business – high-end, one-off decorative ornaments and antiques; procuring them for peanuts abroad and then selling them at highly inflated prices in specialist showrooms. Evidently interior designers, home stylists and celebrities were prepared to pay top dollar for the pieces he found. Of course it was Cornelia who'd started the business; she had the instinctive eye and had trained his. Gregory once confided that the two of them used to do the travelling and buying together, and that Cornelia referred to it as 'treasure hunting'. She liked to discover new diamonds in the rough, rescue them and elevate them to glamour status by re-homing them in the residences of the rich and famous. I couldn't see the appeal at all.

Eventually I grew dizzy and bored. Having checked every draw and file and found no new dates or numbers to try, I climbed back upstairs to Cornelia's bedroom, leaving a trail of toast crumbs behind me.

Her latent existence was apparent in nearly every room of the house, and not only in the flowery wallpapers and furnishings. She hadn't been able to resist keeping for herself some of the 'treasures' she found, rather than selling them on. Everything from Japanese Cloisonné vases to blown-glass Christmas baubles – she had quite a collection and it was still growing, because Gregory kept bringing things back for her, even though she could no longer appreciate them. Her coats hung by the back door;

her favourite perfumed soap adorned the lip of every bathroom sink; and her reading glasses sat on a side table in the drawing room – as if she'd recently popped out, rather than died fifteen years previously.

But it was her bedroom which Gregory maintained as a real shrine to her. It was through these things that I'd garnered everything I knew of Cornelia Sinclair; I had no clear memories of my own, and Gregory's grief was so great that he rarely spoke about her. Sometimes he would wander in here in the middle of the night to sleep on her bed or touch her shoes, or whatever else it was he did, in order to feel close to the love of his life. I was fairly sure he conducted relationships with various other women while he was abroad; living, breathing ladies who bought him ties and cuff-links and aftershave, and knew nothing about me at all. But no matter how long he stayed away, he was always, eventually, inevitably, drawn back to this room and the emotional hold Cornelia had over him. It couldn't be a healthy way to live, especially for a man not yet forty, but that was Gregory.

Carefully I leafed through the pile of books beside her bed – five in total; two lame romance novels (I'd read them out of curiosity), a buyer's guide to inlaid Indian furniture, a true crime book about missing children, and a hard-back collection of photographs of fifties Hollywood actors. In each book a page was neatly folded to mark her place, but there were no passages underlined and no notes written in the margins – no dates or numbers worth trying on the safe.

Gregory had long since removed any letters, papers or diaries from the room, assuming they'd ever existed.

Whether he had kept or disposed of such items I had no idea – maybe they were in the safe? But with none of Cornelia's personal correspondence to look through, I was running out of options. Running an eye over her clothes, accessories, toiletries, make-up and jewellery, I re-familiarised myself with it all without moving anything. Cleaners were banned from this room and Gregory liked everything to be kept as she left it, right down to the used handkerchief on the dressing table.

There had only been a few exceptions over the years. On my eighteenth birthday Gregory had gifted me a few pieces of Cornelia's jewellery; a diamond tiara with matching necklace, bracelet and earrings. It was a complete set, in mint condition, and worth a fortune to be sure, but for the most part they lived in a box in my dresser. I'd never been invited to any public occasion where I might wear them, and the earrings were no use to me whatsoever since my ear lobes were not pierced. Would Mrs Daly accept diamond earrings as payment to keep her silence?

Hearing the van approaching I peered apprehensively out the window, and sagged with relief at the sight of the empty passenger seat. Liam had abandoned me for almost two weeks; first he'd stayed away and then he'd brought that stupid boy along with him. I'd monitored their progress from the safety of the house as they worked their way around the grounds, but not once had Liam attempted to make contact with me; not even to say hello. But then what had I expected? With all the friends and family he had, he didn't need my company the way I'd come to depend on his. To him I was of little consequence. Maybe I should just try to forget about him altogether.

Quietly unlatching the front door, I sat down on the top step while he lifted a deadly-looking selection of loppers and saws out of the back of his van and deposited them in a rusty wheel barrow. But upon seeing me, he abandoned his tools and approached, his boots crunching on the gravel, his eyes locked on mine. At the foot of the steps he stopped.

'Morning, Melody,' he said softly.

I tried to smile, but my heart wasn't in it.

After a few beats of silence he dragged his gaze away from mine and looked down at the palms of his hands. 'Do you mind if I sit down?'

I hesitated, surprised by his request, but then I shuffled over to one side and he climbed up and seated himself beside me. His T-shirt-covered bicep was warm where it brushed my shoulder. We sat in silence for a while, listening to the birds singing in the trees and I had an urge to cry; I couldn't bear the thought of losing this; of losing him.

'I've missed you,' he said.

It was an innocuous sentence; three ordinary words, but at that moment they meant the world. An ugly sob burst from my mouth and I threw my arms around his neck, hiding my face against his chest. It was an awkward embrace; my body twisted at the waist, my arms stretched upwards and my legs squashed against his thigh, but as he wrapped his huge arms around me and held me close, I'd never felt better.

'I'm sorry I was away for a while,' he said, his voice emanating from his body and rumbling through mine. 'My brother injured his leg and I had to help out with that side of the business until he was back on his feet...'

Once I was sure my tears had stopped, I pulled away from him and wiped my eyes and nose on my sleeve. There was a damp patch left behind on Liam's chest which made me smile. He glanced down, following my eye line, and then smiled too with a shrug. Reaching inside my dressing gown pocket I pulled out a blue ballpoint pen and wrote on my palm: *Ask me something*. He read the words in silence before returning his warm hazel eyes to mine.

'I don't know where to begin. I don't want to be rude, or nosey.' I shook my head and urged him on with my eyes. 'OK, but, for example, it's rude to ask a lady her age...'

I quickly scribbled: *21, you?*

'Thirty-two,' he said warily. I smiled but he still looked uneasy. 'And... you're Sinclair's wife?'

Is that what he'd thought all this time? I stared at him a moment before shaking my head, pushing up my sleeve and writing along my arm: *Gregory is my father*.

I studied his face as he read my words, but he didn't seem reassured – quite the opposite in fact – as he returned his gaze to mine he looked alarmed. 'Your biological father?'

I nodded, but his expression didn't change. *What?* I mouthed.

'Nothing... it's nothing, I'm surprised that's all... he doesn't look old enough...'

He turned away from me, looking off into the distance and I wondered what he was thinking. Was that it? Just two questions? Was that all he wanted to know about me? I'd prepared myself for the Spanish inquisition and should be relieved to get off so lightly, but I was disappointed by his apparent lack of interest.

I scrawled: *What are you working on today?* And nudged him with my elbow to draw his attention.

The tension faded from his face and he smiled. 'I thought I'd make a start on the rose garden. Did you know it was originally designed by the famous French landscape architect, Édouard Marcel, in 1878?'

I raised my eyebrows and smiled, instantly warmed by his enthusiasm.

'It was much bigger when it was first created – much grander than it is now – I think it must have been scaled back at a later date to reduce the level of maintenance required; maybe during one of the wars. Anyway, I've found a plan of it; look…' From his pocket he withdrew a folded piece of A4 and handed it to me.

The photocopied plan showed a neatly laid out formal garden – a complex but symmetrical pattern of intersecting lines, triangles and circles.

'First I need to clear all the weeds out, prune back the surviving roses, topiary and box hedging, and mow all the lawned areas around it. But then we can have a look; see if we can find any evidence of the lost parts, what do you think?'

I beamed back at him, having written one word on the edge of the photocopy: *Awesome*.

He laughed in response, hooking one arm around me and gently squeezing my shoulder as he rested his head on top of mine. I loved being included by him, close to him, and it was unexpectedly gratifying making him laugh. For once someone was laughing with me, rather than at me, and it made me tingle all over with pleasure.

'I should get on.' Releasing me and rising to his feet, he re-pocketed the plan, offered me a big strong hand, rough with callouses, and helped me up. 'Come and find me when you're ready – I can give you a lesson in pruning roses if you like.'

As he wheeled his barrow full of tools round to the side of the house and disappeared from view, I hugged my gown tighter around myself; not because I was particularly cold or self-conscious, but because I missed him already.

Chapter Twenty-one

Hanging out with Melody again, was a joy. She was a peculiar sight to behold in what looked like a belted Victorian petticoat, a pair of plimsolls, an eighties sun-visor and a smart, tailored set of leather gloves, but she was a quick learner and naturally green-fingered – instinctively distinguishing between the plants and the weeds, and pruning the roses with neat, confident snips of the secateurs. I found her company intensely comforting, and not simply because of her restful silence.

Admittedly I didn't miss Olly's constant stream of chatter, but Melody and I had been working together for two days now and we communicated frequently. In order to make conversation, she'd threaded a spiral-bound notebook and a pen, onto a length of pink ribbon which she wore slung across her body like a handbag. Every now and then we would pause for breath and she would make a written observation, or pen a query for me, or respond to one of mine.

Amongst other things I'd learned that she'd always lived at Wildham Hall, had been home-schooled there and had never had access to a TV. But she enjoyed books, violent movies and music videos, and had a job working from home as a proofreader. She wrote that she was grateful for any excuse to get out in the garden because staring at printed words for long periods made her eyes sore. Her handwriting was beautiful – neat and curly, with an almost calligraphic feel to it – but her use of words, her 'voice' was not nearly as delicate as I'd imagined it to be. She was blunt, honest and to-the-point, and not just because she had to write everything down. She clearly knew her own mind, and now that we'd made friends she was no longer afraid to express it – which was refreshing and often funny.

Extricating herself from a rose bush, Melody flung her secateurs down on the grass, peeled off her gloves and studied her fingers with a frown.

'You OK?'

She quickly wrote something and I set aside the loppers I was carrying and moved closer to read where she'd written: *This one's a prickly bugger.* A small smudge of blood was left behind on the paper, as if proving it.

'Yeah it's a rugosa – they can be particularly vicious,' I said, taking her hand in mine and scrutinising her punctured fingertips. 'You don't have to do any of this, you know – I'm the one getting paid to do it.'

Snatching her hand back she scribbled something else onto the pad where it rested on her jutting hip and then angled it towards me with a grim expression. It read: *You're not getting rid of me that easily.*

I smiled. 'I'm not trying to get rid of you, I just don't want you to hurt yourself.'

We made eye contact and for a moment I was lost in the grey depths of her irises. What was she thinking? What was this thing between us? Was it my imagination or was this evolving into something deeper and more potent than friendship? Whatever it was it made me nervous, but she looked away and changed the subject by writing: *Who's your hero?*

I took a subtle breath of relief. 'That would have to be my dad. He's retired now, but he's a plumber by trade; hard-working, honest, fair. He pretty much raised Lester and me single-handedly, and he's always been a great role model, not just for us but for other boys in town too. He used to coach rugby at the school.' I hoped she wouldn't ask about my mother. 'What about you; who's your hero?'

Ellen Ripley.

I stared at her. 'As in the film *Aliens*?'

She nodded.

'The fictional character...?'

She nodded and I tried hard not to laugh while she jotted down an explanation: *What! She's a strong woman – brave, smart and selfless – and she doesn't have to act like an egotistical macho man to save the day.*

'Hmm, I don't know, she's pretty butch...'

She falls for Hicks and tries to be a mother to Newt – she's still a woman – but a strong one.

Melody looked infuriated, which made me want to wind her up more, but I refrained. 'You're right – I've never thought about it like that before. Good hero,' I admitted, and she smiled, satisfied.

As she began to pull her gloves back on it occurred to me that Melody was probably motherless like me, and perhaps hadn't had many 'real' female role models in her life. The realisation was sobering.

'Just so you know – not all men are egotistical.'

She looked up at me in surprise and then, before I had a chance to move, she rose up on her tiptoes and pressed her lips to my cheek. It was a slow, lingering kiss that caught me off guard, filled my nostrils with her scent, chased the blood to my groin and left me light-headed. And when she drew back and looked at me there was no trace of innocence in her expression – she was deliberately flirting with me.

I stepped back away from her, rattled by the look in her eyes and unsure what to do or say. My natural instinct was to scoop her up in my arms and kiss her, properly, on the mouth; I'd wanted to for days, weeks, even. But I couldn't.

Technically I was dating someone else – I'd taken Bridget out for dinner at the weekend – and anyway, I was still haunted by the scene I'd witnessed between Melody and her father, my boss. Admittedly I'd missed the beginning of their conversation, but whichever way I replayed it in my mind, something wasn't right about the way he'd looked at her. Now that I had some understanding of the life Melody had lived – isolated from the outside world and starved of human contact – my suspicions about her father were growing. I feared that he might be abusing her, and until I was convinced otherwise, I would not take advantage, no matter how much I wanted her.

Turning, I stooped down to pick up the almost empty bottle of water we'd been sharing. 'I'm just going to go and refill this so that we don't get dehydrated,' I said, backing away.

Slowly she nodded in acknowledgement, but I could tell by the look on her face that she was puzzled by my behaviour. Without meaning to I was almost certainly giving her all kinds of mixed signals. Hell, I'd never felt more conflicted in my life. Cursing under my breath I told myself to get a grip as I walked away.

Chapter Twenty-two

I was ready and waiting for Mrs Daly the moment she put her key in the lock of the back door. Perched on top of the tumble dryer I had a height advantage, a clear view of the room, and two separate escape routes available to me if necessary. After all, wasn't that Sun Tzu's advice in 'The Art of War' – hold the high ground and wait for your enemy to come to you?

Armed and prepared I was ready to fight to keep my relationship with Liam under wraps. Though, admittedly, I was unsure exactly what that relationship was. Yesterday I'd kissed his cheek by way of a thank you, but once I was there, touching him with my mouth like that, it became difficult to pull away. A friendly peck on the cheek almost became something else, something more, and I know he felt it too, even though he walked away. Regardless, I was ready to do battle; to protect what we had; do whatever it took to keep seeing him.

Mrs Daly jumped when she saw me but recovered quickly, her lips pressing into a hard line of disapproval as she wiped her shoes on the mat and set down her bag.

'Got something for me, have you?'

With a jerk of my chin I gestured to the note I'd left on the counter, and waited while Mrs Daly deliberately took her time retrieving her reading glasses from her handbag and putting them on.

'I can't get hold of any cash...' she said, reading my words aloud, '... but take these, I'm sure you can get a good price for them.' Flipping open the folded handkerchief beside the note, she cast a beady eye over the neatly laid out pair of earrings. They glinted as they caught the light. 'Real diamonds are they?'

I nodded.

'What's to stop me getting accused of stealing them?'

I held another, pre-prepared sheet of paper out to her, and she took it grudgingly. 'These have been in my possession a long time – Gregory won't miss them,' she read out. 'Thought this through, haven't you,' she muttered under her breath.

With claw-like fingers she hastily folded the hankie into a tight package around the precious stones before stowing it deep inside her handbag. 'This is a good start…' she said, preparing to leave the room, '… but it'll take more than some old jewellery to buy my silence indefinitely.'

Her predictability made me smile as I thrust my final note in her direction. She hesitated, eyeing me with unconcealed loathing as she debated walking away, but eventually curiosity got the better of her. Snatching it from my fingers she read my final statement in silence:

Breathe a word about me to Gregory or anyone else and I will point out the silverware that has gone missing from the dining room – you will be fired and almost certainly arrested.

Her face paled and she scrunched the paper up in her fists with irritation. 'Fuck you,' she muttered, dropping my last note on the floor and marching out the door without further comment.

Her inability to meet my eye told me everything I needed to know. I'd got her. At the end of the day Gregory would always take my word over hers and we both knew it. She could have the earrings – they were no use to me anyway – and keep the candlesticks and whatever else she'd stolen in the past. I'd even let her keep her job for now – better the devil you know – but her power over me was gone for good.

Smiling to myself with satisfaction I hopped down off the tumble dryer, disposed of the handwritten notes, grabbed a cold carton of orange juice from the kitchen and skipped out the back door into the sunshine.

Chapter Twenty-three

Sinclair's Merc was sitting on the drive when I pulled up on Monday morning. As I was unloading my tools, he stepped out of the house to meet me, looking as dapper as ever in a complete, three-piece, pinstriped suit, despite the mounting heat.

My inappropriate feelings for Melody had thrown me for a loop and I'd spent all weekend trying not to think about her. I'd taken Bridget out again – this time to an Indian curry house – and I must have made a good impression because she'd invited me back to her place for a 'nightcap' afterwards. And yet, despite being horny as hell, I'd turned her down with a feeble excuse about feeling tired. The truth was I couldn't bring myself to sleep with her, not when my head was full of someone else. Bridget took the brush-off well, considering. But Melody's lecherous father was the last person I wanted to see right now.

'Morning, Liam. How are things progressing?'

'Really well, I think. I was hoping to speak to you actually; I found out something interesting about the rose garden…'

'Oh yes?'

As I relayed my library findings, we walked side by side to where Melody and I had cleared and restored the four circular beds centred around an old sundial. Once I'd shown him where the original design had extended out to, and described the formal arrangement of columns and rope swags we could reinstate, I paused to see what his reaction would be.

'That all sounds very interesting, and I appreciate all the trouble you've been to, researching the original design etcetera, but... they're rather old fashioned aren't they, rose gardens...?'

This comment was not what I'd expected or hoped for, and for a moment I was at a loss for what to say. 'Well, yes... I suppose so, but they're in keeping with the period of the house and the rest of the gardens. I know it looks a bit untidy right now, but once I've re-planted these beds and the roses are in full bloom I really think it will look stunning...'

Sinclair cleared his throat. 'I don't want the rose garden extended. In fact it might be an idea to scrap it completely. My friend, the sheikh, was showing me his garden of exotic succulents last week. They're very low-maintenance and really provide a spectacular display of colour, texture and form...' I fought to maintain a politely neutral expression on my face as I waited for him to continue. 'If we ripped these old shrubs out we could have something far more interesting and contemporary, don't you think? I mean, it's a prime location up here near the house and it's quite a sun trap...'

My heart sank as he talked of creating a desert garden of cacti, yuccas and palm trees arranged around a fake dry river bed, mulched with crushed sea-shells. 'Do you think you could design something like that?'

'Um, yes ... I'm sure I could come up with something, and... although an exotic garden would be a great addition to the grounds... I do wonder if this is the right spot for it. I'm not sure if it would complement the existing Victorian architecture or the traditional layout of the terrace. Maybe a desert garden would be better located on the far side of the walled garden, where it would still benefit from sunshine and—'

'But no-one would see it over there! No, I'd like to be able to view it from the drawing room when I'm entertaining – something to comment on and admire...'

'Oh, right...' I hadn't been aware that Sinclair did any entertaining, but then I was never there at weekends.

'I don't see any reason to stick rigidly to the sentimental idea of a rose garden when we have the opportunity to do something remarkable with the space instead.'

'No, I understand,' but even to my own ears I didn't sound convincing.

As Sinclair and I toured other parts of the grounds that morning, he made several other suggestions (instructions), which I didn't agree with – replacing a brick path in the walled garden with smooth concrete, for example, rather than repairing the frost damage; and removing a cluster of ancient rhododendrons instead of simply cutting them back. But these poor decisions didn't bother me nearly as much as his dismissal of the Marcel rose garden. Melody had been as keen to see it take shape as I was, and based on my suggestions she'd been googling different species and varieties of roses all week. My only hope was that she might be able to talk her father out of his new scheme, where I had failed completely.

It was mid-afternoon by the time I saw Melody. She only emerged from the house once Sinclair had left for the airport, on his way to the Middle East. I was busy dragging blanket weed out of the lake with a long-handled rake when she came running towards me through the trees in a flurry of yellow cotton. I smiled and threw down my tools when I saw her.

'How can you run about in this heat?'

She didn't slow as she neared, and I caught her as she launched herself at me in an enthusiastic wide-armed hug. Apparently she'd missed me as much as I had her. I returned the embrace and then set her down as my body inevitably began to react to her softness and her delicate, appealing scent.

'Gone again, has he?'

She nodded.

'How long for this time?'

She held up three fingers.

'Three weeks?'

She nodded again, grinning happily up at me and, before I realised it, I was putting my hand to her face and stroking her hair back from where it was sticking to her cheek. As she leaned into my fingers, her longing gaze locked with mine, I swiftly reminded myself that she was simply lonely and in need of a friend.

We sat on the footbridge over the stream as I told her about Sinclair's exotic new plans for the garden and witnessed her expression fall.

'Maybe if you tell him you want to keep the roses, he'll change his mind?' I suggested. She wrote something down and showed it to me: *Then he'll know we've talked.*

'Is that really so bad?'

She nodded.

'But we're just friends, right? I mean, he can't mind you having friends…'

She frowned slightly before writing again: *He wouldn't understand.*

I sighed in frustration. 'OK. In that case, maybe we can transplant the existing rose bushes somewhere else; plant them in the other beds. They don't always survive being moved, but if we do it later in the season they'll stand less chance of drying out…'

Melody looked upset and stared off into the distance as I spoke, and I had a feeling it wasn't because of the roses. I didn't need to see it written down in black and white to suspect she wanted to be more than friends. If I was honest I wanted that too, but her circumstances were so complicated. I'd never felt this strongly attracted to anyone before. It was consuming me and truthfully, it was scary.

Rising to my feet I picked up the rake and returned my attention to the surface of the lake. My insides ached as she wandered away from me, dejected, in the direction of the house.

Chapter Twenty-four

Upon hearing the hum of Liam's van pulling up on the drive, I slipped out the back door unseen and made my way down to the lake, armed with a bath towel. The night had been long, sultry and sleepless; my limbs were weary with restlessness, and my skin felt sticky with yesterday's sweat, and yet today it was only going to get hotter. I was still angry; mad at Gregory for wanting to do away with the rose garden that we'd worked so hard to restore, and furious with Liam for only wanting to be friends.

He was all I could think about. The more time I spent with him, the more desperately I wanted him to kiss, hold and touch every part of my body. It was as if he was channelling the power of the sun and causing a restless burning deep inside me, which yearned for release. And yet, infuriatingly, he always held back.

I may not have an in-depth understanding of men, but the internet led me to believe that they all wanted sex. Through conversations with Liam I'd confirmed that he was unmarried and lived alone, and from the appreciative way I sometimes caught him looking at me, I'd ruled out homosexuality, so what was stopping him from making a move? Was he simply afraid of losing his job? Yesterday I'd literally thrown myself into his arms, but instead of taking the opportunity to ravish me, he'd let me walk away.

At the side of the lake I ruthlessly stripped down to my underwear and waded into the crystal clear water on my tiptoes, taking my time, inch by inch and huffing out breaths as I adjusted to the sting of the cold. Despite the rising heat throughout most of August, Liam had not been swimming and hadn't offered me another lesson since that first one. I wanted to impress him with my bravery and lure him into holding me again, and a swimming lesson was the perfect excuse.

When the water finally reached my chest I practised pushing my arms out the way he'd shown me, ignoring my shivering and trying to adjust to the chill. Lifting first one leg and then standing on the other, I tested my balance and let the water buoy me up. Then, recalling Liam's gentle words of advice, and feeling reassured, I attempted to lift both feet off the muddy floor and kick my legs out behind me, while still paddling my hands. Immediately I began to sink and stumbled to my feet, unnerved without Liam's hands to support me. But I was determined to get it right, and after several more attempts and a mouthful of water, I managed to lift my bottom and propel myself forwards with my head above the water.

Elated, I splashed my way around the edge of the lake, parallel to the shore, enjoying the feel of the now temperate water as it eddied around my body. Was Liam on his way? Could he see me yet? Would he be impressed with my progress? With new-found confidence I pushed myself out a little further from the shore, where the water was cooler and darker.

But it occurred to me that I must look as ungainly as a baby elephant splashing about; the noise almost violent in the quiet of the grounds, blocking out the birdsong and making me feel self-conscious. I wanted to look graceful and elegant. In an effort to achieve this I minimised and slowed my movements but sank almost instantly, water stinging my eyes and filling my nose as my feet flailed about searching for a floor that was no longer there. As I began to panic I writhed about gasping for air, spluttering and swallowing more water. Realising that the lake bed was too far below me to reach with my outstretched toes, I lifted my legs high again, my pulse thundering through my body and pulsing in my ears as I broke the water surface, and gratefully sucked in air. But then a cramping pain shot up through my right calf and I inhaled more water as I gasped in shock, reflexively grabbing at my leg and dropping back below the surface.

I'm drowning; I'm going to die, right here in my underwear in this stupid lake and no-one will ever know what happened to me! I'll never learn to dance the tango, or publish a novel, or figure out what my bad dreams mean. I'm going to die a bloody virgin and I can't even scream!

Kicking out with all my limbs I was straining my head upwards, desperate for air, when something warm and solid hooked around my waist and dragged me back and upwards through the water. I broke the surface with an almighty choking wheeze. By the time I'd worked out what was happening, I was lying on the grass, convulsing and coughing up great lungfuls of water while Liam leaned over me, dripping, his face white and eyes wide with worry.

'What the hell were you doing? How could you be so stupid?' he shouted, his anger distracting me from my discomfort and my near-death experience. I gaped at him, my body shaking uncontrollably as humiliation began to crawl through me. 'You know you can't swim, you could have drowned!' His voice softened slightly as his eyes searched my face.

He had every right to shout at me; I'd been foolish, I could see that now, but the obvious anxiety etched on his face was surprising. He cared; this lovely big man really cared if I lived or died; the realisation flooded me with warmth.

'Are you OK?' His voice had finally reduced to an emotional rasp as his anger waned. I nodded and his eyes closed as relief washed over his features. His passionate concern, coupled with his bare-chested proximity, roused my feelings for him ten-fold and before he had a chance to open his eyes I sat up and pressed my mouth, inexpertly, to his.

For a split second he stilled in surprise, before his lips softened against mine, his hand cupping the back of my head and inducing a rushing sensation inside my body. His mouth was moist and warm as it moved against mine, his breath hot as his lips parted slightly. I let my own mouth open in response, and was rewarded with a low vibration of sound as he half groaned, half sighed with pleasure. It was the most erotic thing I'd ever heard, and it spread through me like molten lava, heating me from within.

Encouraged, I tentatively licked the inside of his upper lip, light-headed with my own daring, and he used the tip of his tongue to stroke mine. The sensation was almost overwhelming and I found myself wrapping my arms around him, thrusting my fingers into his hair and pressing my chest to his, in an unconscious attempt to hold him there indefinitely.

He groaned again, this time louder and deeper as I brazenly explored his mouth with my tongue, drunk on the taste of him and anxious to commit every millimetre to memory. My body ached with a hunger I'd never experienced and in every place my skin made contact with his, it seemed likely to burst into flames.

But then he cupped my face in his big hands and pulled back away from me, breathing hard, his eyes burning darkly beneath his furrowed brow.

'This isn't right,' he said.

What?! I stared at him in disbelief. Nothing had ever felt more right to me in my whole entire life; surely he felt the same; his eyes told me he did. I tried to kiss him again but he held me back with no effort; my strength no match for his.

'We can't do this.'

Frustration lashed through me and before I knew it I'd slapped him hard across the face.

Chapter Twenty-five

God she was beautiful.

For an agonising moment, when she disappeared under the water, I was terrified I might lose her forever, and now here she was, bedraggled, beguiling, and attacking me with unrelenting spirit. Her right hook had caught me off guard even more than her kiss had; the force of it enough to turn my head, heat my skin and almost make me come, right there and then, like a pubescent schoolboy.

The kiss we'd shared was stirring enough – I'd fantasised about how good she might taste and the reality was even sweeter; her obvious inexperience and eagerness was downright endearing. But it was the sudden sting of pain that followed it which almost had me losing all control. Such passion from someone so seemingly small and innocent was intensely arousing. Her eyes burned with fiery reproach more clearly than words ever could, and I found myself wanting her to hit me again.

As if reading my mind, she back-handed me across the other cheek, my hard-on jerking in direct response, and I returned my mouth to hers, kissing her hungrily while she scrambled enthusiastically up onto my lap in a tangle of bare legs and arms. This mysterious girl provoked and confounded me at every turn. Right now I wanted nothing more than to bury myself inside her, right here in the grounds of her stately home, but reality crept back in.

What the hell was I doing?

Summoning the last of my willpower I pried her off me and staggered to my feet. Dragging air into my lungs I made an effort to calm down while she sat half-naked on the grass, gazing up at me, open mouthed and panting. She was breathtakingly sexy. I wanted to taste every inch of her body; to kiss that perfect little birthmark on her thigh and explore all her other secret places with my tongue. In desperation I grabbed her clothes from where they lay folded and handed them to her.

'Put these on, please.' She hesitated, a perplexed expression written across her face, but then, to my great relief she began to dress.

Turning away from her I pulled my own shirt back on, hiding the prominent jut of my erection, which was still refusing to subside. God I was confused.

Once Melody was covered up, she retrieved her notepad and pen and it was with apprehension that I read: *Do you want me or don't you?*

Her blunt question was a reasonable one under the circumstances and made me ashamed of my own cowardice in comparison. Heavily I sat down on the grass beside her, just beyond her reach.

'It's not that simple,' I began, pushing aside my jumbled emotions and trying to construct a sensible answer. 'We hardly know each other...'

She cocked a sceptical eyebrow at me.

'I mean, how many men your own age do you really know? Are there any?'

She looked down at her hands, confirming my suspicions.

'Have you had a boyfriend before?'

This time Melody looked away across the lake, her features tightening with irritation.

'I'm not trying to make you feel uncomfortable. It's just... I get the impression you're rather isolated living here and I don't want to take advantage of you. There are so many guys out there closer to your age... I may not be right for you...' I wasn't explaining myself well and she deserved to know the whole truth. 'And anyway I'm... I'm kind of seeing someone...'

She flinched at this and my heart contracted painfully in my chest as a tear escaped from the corner of her eye.

'Please don't be upset...' I reached out to her, despite my resolution to maintain a safe distance, but she shrugged away from me, swiping hastily at her tears as she rose to her feet.

'I'd still like to be friends... I'll happily teach you to swim if that's what you want...'

I stared after her as she walked away from me, yet again. I desperately wanted to run and catch her; hold her and show her how badly I wanted her, but I knew, with my head if not my heart, that I should let her go. It was for the best.

Chapter Twenty-six

Dammit why was I crying? So he was seeing someone else and I'd made a complete fool of myself – so what – I'd get over it. I swiped at my cheeks as I stomped dejectedly back to the house, my clothes clinging uncomfortably to my damp underwear. Maybe it was delayed shock from almost drowning; for a moment there I'd thought my life was over, and my lungs and throat were still raw. In fact I had a headache now too, but then again, none of that had prevented me from enjoying my first proper kiss.

Wow. I'd tried to envisage it plenty of times in the past, but I'd never imagined anything as spectacular as the wonderful, all-over melting sensation of kissing Liam Hunt. I enjoyed it so much that I was furious when he wanted to stop – angry enough to hit him. Twice.

But I wasn't crying over him. He was just a stupid man; some idiot guy who didn't seem to understand what his own body was telling him – what his body was telling me. It was in his eyes, in the way he kissed me, and in the bulge of his trousers – I was sure of it – and yet he kept pushing me away. Who was this other woman? She couldn't mean that much to him if he was only 'kind of' seeing her. And what did it matter that I'd never had a boyfriend? How was I supposed to gain any experience if he wouldn't let me? Stupid man. I wasn't upset like he said, I was thoroughly pissed off and frustrated.

The sun hurt my eyes making me squint as I crossed the terrace, and despite the furnace-like heat bouncing off the stonework I began to shiver. It was a relief to reach the shade at the back of the house, but I wrapped my arms around myself feeling nauseated and dizzy. What was wrong with me? Was it shock, or had all the lake water I'd swallowed made me ill? In the kitchen I made myself a cup of tea, stirring in plenty of sugar, grateful that Mrs Daly wasn't around to express her disapproval.

Slowly and carefully I made my way along the hall, but by the time I reached the bottom of the main stairs I was hot and cold and clammy with perspiration, and my hands were shaking so hard that I had to set my slopped tea down on a side table. A wave of nausea swept over me and I doubled over, clinging to the newel post for support. What was happening to me? This wasn't right... I need to get upstairs and lie down...

Before I could take another step a ringing started in my ears, darkness clouded into my peripheral vision, and the chintzy hall carpet rushed up to meet me.

*

'Are you likely to live, do you think?'

At the sound of the voice, I tried to open my eyes. My whole body ached, my head throbbed and my tongue was so thick and dry in my mouth that it was a struggle to swallow, and when I did, my throat burned with pain. It took me a while to make sense of my surroundings. There was a fox staring down at me, and for a confused moment I thought it was Mr Fox from the garden and that he was talking to me. But then I took in the bristly carpet beneath me and the mountain of stairs advancing up to a high and distant ceiling; it wasn't a talking animal after all, it was a stuffed hunting trophy in the hallway. A sour-looking woman stood over me, with her hands on her hips.

'Ah, you're still alive then,' Mrs Daly said with undisguised disappointment as I blinked up at her from the floor. I tried to move but my head felt disconnected from my body and I couldn't seem to summon up enough energy to shift my twisted torso into a more comfortable position.

She pressed a papery palm to my forehead and tutted. 'I thought maybe you fell down the stairs and broke your neck, but seems like you're sick with something. I could call you a doctor I suppose... or I could just leave you here and crack on with the cleaning, what do you think...?'

Bugger and blast it. Not only could I not speak, as usual, but now I was too ill to move, and at the complete mercy of a woman who hated me. If she was here that meant it was Wednesday morning and I'd been lying here for hours. Gregory wouldn't be back for another fortnight and no-one else would know to come looking for me; not even Liam. With a building sense of panic I tried to move again. This time I managed to roll over onto my back and raise my head but the pain and the strain of staying conscious was too much. Mrs Daly tutted again and I witnessed one last sneer of contempt as I helplessly slipped away.

Chapter Twenty-seven

As I worked my way along the winding driveway to Wildham Hall, one tree at a time, pruning the overhanging canopy, I missed Melody. A lot. It was a task that needed doing; a lot of the crowns were congested; the boughs criss-crossing, interlacing and blocking out much-needed light. I was removing those branches that were causing problems, but also cutting back and reducing the canopies for aesthetic effect. It was absorbing work, involving prior consideration, skill and concentration, and if I was honest with myself it was no coincidence that I'd chosen a job about as far away from the lake as I could get. After what had happened on Tuesday I'd deliberately set about creating space between us – only I hadn't expected to be quite so successful.

Having started up a relationship with Bridget, it was her I should be thinking about, not Melody. I'd convinced myself I couldn't have Melody; because she was young and inexperienced and possibly even the victim of abuse. But the more time that passed, the less sure I was about the exchange I'd seen between Melody and her father. What if I'd got it wrong? If she was being sexually harassed or abused, would she really be so keen to get physical with me? She was twenty-one – not a child – and clearly knew her own mind. Perhaps I should give her the benefit of the doubt; respect her wishes and trust her to know what she wanted.

Maybe all my doubts about Melody were simply excuses to mask my own fear of getting hurt. Because if anyone on the planet now held the power to wound me, it was Melody Sinclair.

I hadn't seen her for two days and I missed her with every breath – her quiet company, funny facial expressions and blunt written remarks; I even missed her quirky dress sense.

The cleaner had come and gone as usual, and yesterday a middle-aged woman in a Fiat Punto had briefly visited the house, but I'd seen no sign of Melody at all and I was starting to worry.

I hated that she might be deliberately avoiding me, though she had every right to, of course; I'd behaved abominably. What kind of man got turned on by a woman who slapped him in anger? What sort of monster did that make me? I was ashamed of myself and still considered her better off without me, but not seeing her at all was proving unbearable.

I had fallen for her hard.

Having reached the end of the driveway and finished pruning the tree nearest the front door, I chopped up the last few branches and barrowed the logs round the side of the house, where I added them to the over-stuffed wood store in the stables. As I was returning to the drive, the dour-faced cleaner emerged from the back door of the house, handbag on shoulder, ready to leave for the weekend. I nodded and smiled to her, she didn't bother smiling back, but as I continued on my way she spoke, stopping me in my tracks.

'Scarlet fever.'

I turned. 'I beg your pardon?'

'She's sick with scarlet fever. My grandson's just had it. Uncommon in adults apparently, but the doctor's been and says she'll probably recover eventually. Only I'm not paid to be a nurse and I haven't time to be coming back here to check on her at weekends...'

'Sorry, what? Melody's sick?'

'That's what I said, isn't it?'

'So who's looking after her?'

'Well not me, that's for sure. I've already done more than I'm contractually obliged. You go on up and see her if you want, but don't expect to be rewarded with scintillating conversation.' Leaving the door open she began to walk away and I stared after her, stunned.

'Wait! How do I find her – which room is she in?'

Rolling her eyes in irritation she turned back. 'Top of the main staircase, end of the corridor, last door on the right.' Without further hesitation she stalked off.

It was peculiar entering the grand old house without a proper invitation, like I was trespassing, but the thought of Melody lying there sick and suffering all alone prevented me from hesitating long. Kicking off my boots I padded my way through the laundry room, through the atrium-like space, past a vast kitchen and round a corner into a long hall. A macabre collection of stuffed animal heads were mounted at intervals along the walls; a deer, a badger, some kind of antelope, a fox... it was like a set straight out of a horror film, their eyes seemingly following me as I went. Several high-ceilinged, formal-looking panelled rooms led off the hallway but I bypassed them, heading straight for a wide, elaborately-carved staircase and mounting them quickly.

The house was undeniably impressive but felt more like a museum or a stage set than a home, with each piece of furniture positioned for effect, and every surface cluttered with ornaments. At the end of the upstairs corridor was a closed door labelled 'nursery', which couldn't be right, but I knocked and waited for a response anyway. When nothing happened, I turned the handle and opened the door to a large, dimly-lit bedroom.

The curtains were drawn against the sun, but as my eyes adjusted to the muted light I could make out various pieces of furniture heaped with mounds of stuffed toys set against sugary pink patterned walls. But it was the occupant of the vast four-poster bed in the centre of the room who really claimed my attention.

She looked like an angel lying there with her hair fanned out around her head and a white sheet twisted around her tiny frame. Her eyes were shut, her breathing was shallow and her skin glistened with sweat, but her alluring scent was everywhere, drawing me closer to her almost against my will.

As I whispered her name she frowned in her sleep but otherwise did not stir. Reaching out I brushed the hair from her forehead, confirming for myself the fever that burned inside her. A rash of fine red spots was visible above the neckline of her nightdress, but a sense of propriety prevented me from checking to see how far downwards the rash might extend.

On the bedside table, beside a prescription pill bottle, was an empty drinking glass which I took into the en-suite bathroom to refill. I also found a flannel hanging beside the sink, so I rinsed it with cold water, wrung it out, and took it back to the bedroom.

When I perched carefully on the edge of the mattress, she opened her eyes. They were darkly dilated, glassy and unfocused as she stared at me in confusion.

'Hey, it's just me, everything's OK.'

She tried to push me away at first, but I gently cradled her head and shoulders in one arm as I put the water to her lips and she drank greedily from the glass before collapsing back onto the pillow. I leaned over to lay the flannel across her forehead and for a moment her eyes rolled back, she shivered and her lips moved as if she were silently muttering something, but no sound came out. Her eyes closed again on a long sigh as she drifted back into a fitful sleep.

Having carefully studied the dosage instructions on the bottle of penicillin, I fetched more water and tried to open a window to introduce fresh air into the stuffy room, but the diamond-pattern leaded windows were sealed shut. After several minutes spent Googling scarlet fever on my phone, I came to the conclusion that all I could do was stay with her, keep her hydrated and make sure she took the antibiotics regularly. But I hated seeing her this way – all limp and vulnerable – and the idea that she might have been suffering for days only increased my sense of guilt. Melody was so special to me, and she was so alone; I should never have pushed her away.

Chapter Twenty-eight

My room was on fire. Flames were licking at the curtains and igniting the bed sheets and my flesh was burning. I was running and running but every time I reached the top of the stairs I was back in the nursery again; the poodles on the walls taunting me with their upturned noses and smug smiles. I couldn't get away or breathe or scream for help, and I was thirsty, so very, very thirsty.

And then I was at the lake and it was completely clogged with mud and leaves, and Liam was there but I dove head-first straight into the filthy water and I drank and drank, my throat aching with relief despite the bitter taste. Liam was trying to pull me out – rescue me – but the water was so cool and refreshing on my skin that I didn't want to leave, so I struggled and pushed him away. And now I was drowning again, icy cold, my teeth chattering so hard that they shattered, shook loose and fell out, piece by piece. I tried to catch them in my hands but they were lost in the murkiness surrounding me as it grew denser and darker and turned black.

And then *they* were there; the shadowy figures from my nightmares; the same voices; the same repeated warnings: 'Keep quiet' and 'Not one word' and 'Do not make a sound…' If I'd ever known the reasons behind those threatening words, I'd long since forgotten, but the persistent sense of dread that accompanied them returned full force with every bad dream. The message was clear: my own voice could destroy me.

I was back in my room again and the fire had receded, leaving smouldering fabric remains, charred furniture and a stringent lemony scent. My soft toys were all blackened with soot but whichever way I turned their glass eyes were staring at me in fierce accusation. I tried to get away from them but the bed was too slippery to get any purchase on. And then Liam was there again – right there in my bedroom, with his heavy furrowed brow, colossal body and kind eyes, and I realised I must be dreaming, but I didn't care because it was wonderful to see him. He was saying something in a strange foreign language and I simply lay there, listening to the gentle rumble of his voice, letting it resonate through my body like distant thunder on a sultry summer's day.

*

I woke to the sound of snoring, convinced it wasn't my own. Holding my breath I listened, but the noise had gone. Opening my tired eyes, I was reassured to find that I was in my own bed and that everything looked normal, except for a glass of water by the bed I didn't remember putting there. Had someone been in my room? Slowly sitting up I lifted the glass to my lips and greedily drank the contents in one go. As I was setting the glass down again a snore broke the silence, making all my hair stand on end. With an intense sense of dread I turned around.

There was a man asleep beside me. He was fully clothed in jeans and a T-shirt and lying on his side, on top of the sheet that was over me, but it was still a shock. My instinct was to leap backwards out of bed, but then I took in the solid curve of his shoulders, the bumpy line of his nose and the familiar dirty-blonde hair and realised it was Liam. He looked so different with his facial muscles relaxed in sleep, his lips parted and his jaw shadowed with stubble.

Was I dreaming? I felt absolutely exhausted but a warm tingle of excitement spread through me at the unexpected appearance of this man on my bed. Reaching out I touched his tanned, hairy forearm. It was warm, solid and substantial, thrilling me to my core. He was really here! Spreading out my fingers I gently stroked his arm from his wrist all the way up past his elbow to the cuff at his bulging bicep. He'd stopped snoring but was still in a deep slumber.

Lifting my fingertips to his face I lightly traced his eyebrows, the coarse stubble along his jaw line, and then the soft pink swell of his lips, his breath hot and moist on my skin. Why was he here? What day was it? The last thing I could remember was walking away from him, not feeling well and making myself a cup of tea...

Shuffling closer to him I lay my head down on the pillow and gently placed my hand on his chest. The slow rhythmic pulse of his heart beat up through my palm accompanied by the steady rise and fall of his breathing; so soothing it lulled me back to sleep.

*

The next time I stirred he was conscious and smiling at me, his warm brown eyes causing me to wake with a start. He held my hand in both of his, nestled against his chest, but otherwise we weren't touching.

'Morning,' he said softly, making me smile. 'Are you OK? Do you feel alright?'

I nodded my head, though in truth I felt like I'd been run over by a ten-ton lorry. He started to get up, but I didn't want him to go and used what little strength I could muster to cling to the front of his shirt.

'I'm just going to get your notebook so you can talk to me – I'll be right back, I promise.'

Gingerly I sat myself up, pulling the sheet up over my nightdress, conscious of my own body odour and the lank, greasy texture of my hair. When Liam returned he perched on the bed beside me while I scribbled down my first question: *What day is it?*

'Sunday,' he said.

I stared at him in disbelief. My last clear memories were from Tuesday; where had the rest of the week gone?

'You came down with scarlet fever sometime during the week – the cleaner told me.'

Now that he mentioned it I had a vague recollection of Mrs Daly standing over me with a cup in her hand and a look of contempt... and then helping me up the stairs... crap, how humiliating.

'She called a doctor in to see you, but she said she couldn't stay and I didn't want you to be on your own...'

The idea of Liam the burly landscaper tending my bedside and nursing me back to health was both surreal and extraordinary – was there no limit to this man's kindness? Were other guys this caring and considerate? Not in my experience.

'You had a high temperature and a rash, but I think that's fading now – not that I've looked – but you seem much better... are you in any pain?'

I shook my head.

'Can I get you anything; you haven't eaten in days...?'

I was hungry. I'd been distracted by his presence, but now, as if on cue, my stomach rumbled and he smiled.

'How about some toast? I bought a few supplies and there's plenty of bread...?'

While he was gone I dragged myself into the bathroom to relieve my bladder. A hideous sight greeted me in the mirror as I washed my hands and splashed my face. It was tempting to take a shower, but I was afraid Liam would disappear if I took too long, so I settled for simply brushing my teeth before crawling back into bed.

Liam settled beside me with his back to the headboard as I munched my toast and passed him another sentence: *Thank you for looking after me.*

'My pleasure,' he shrugged, passing the pad back to me.

I'm sorry for hitting you.

His cheeks flushed as he read my words. 'Forget it,' he muttered, avoiding my eye.

Taking the note back I added another line: *Just friends is fine if that's what you want.*

As he read it I tried to bury my regret beneath a genuine sense of gratitude, after all he had saved my life, probably more than once, and was without doubt the greatest friend I'd ever had.

But he lifted his head and looked straight at me, his big brown eyes seeming to see right inside me. 'You don't leave here much do you? Not to go to the shops or into town…?'

I slowly shook my head, knowing what was coming next.

'Why?'

It was a fair question, but heat automatically rose to my face at the directness of it and the toast scraped my throat as I swallowed. I wrote: *People think I'm weird. And anyway I have everything I need right here.*

'You don't feel you're missing out on anything?'

I shook my head again, underlining my last seven words for extra emphasis.

'So you wouldn't want to go out to a restaurant for dinner… with me?'

I gaped at him, momentarily floored by this idea. *What about the woman you're seeing?*

'That's nothing. We've been on a few dates, that's all. She's been working abroad recently so I haven't seen her or had a chance to officially break things off. But I'm going to – it's already over – I'd just prefer to tell her in person.' He cautiously took my hand in his. 'You were right the other day – I… I *do* want you. I'm just not sure it's a good idea. Maybe if we got to know each other better… took things slowly? I'd like to take you out for dinner, once you're well again of course, what do you think…?'

It wasn't the most romantic of suggestions – I'd read better ones in books – but it was real and honest and more than a person like me could have hoped for. And yet my instinctive delight was evenly matched by a deeply-rooted reluctance to hang out in a publicly populated place. In my (admittedly limited) experience, most people were loud and rude and would stare, laugh and jeer at me, and then this lovely man would think me a freak and never speak to me again. Why was he asking this of me? Why couldn't we simply eat here, in private? The backs of my eyes prickled with tears.

'You don't have to give me an answer now,' he said, opening his arms and drawing me into a hug. Climbing into his lap like a child, I buried my face in his neck and revelled in his comforting scent as he held me close. 'Just think about it OK…?'

Chapter Twenty-nine

At the bar I bought drinks and carried them out to the beer garden on a tray. The round consisted of several pints of larger, a few glasses of wine, and a vodka-lemonade for James's girlfriend, Kat. Maire and I were on orange juice as usual. As I retook my seat at the picnic table opposite where Kat was perched on James's knee she blushed and smiled her thanks. Earlier I'd caught the two of them having sex in the rugby club changing rooms, though James was oblivious. I didn't begrudge them their post-match celebration – on the contrary I was glad James had finally found a woman to make him happy, and a smart, sensitive woman at that, but deep down I was envious of the relationship they shared.

Cally and I had never been overly passionate with each other, not even in the early days when we first started dating. Missionary position in bed with the lights off, that was us, and perfectly satisfactory it was too. Public displays of affection and sex in communal places had never been on the cards, and it had never occurred to me to question any of that until now.

Since meeting Melody my sexual imagination had kicked into overdrive. She'd hooked me with those stormy grey eyes of hers – all innocence one minute and openly devouring the next. The way she carried herself was utterly disarming – whether half-naked or dressed in crazy clothes, she was entirely comfortable in her own skin and artlessly appealing. And nobody had ever wanted me the way she seemed to – how could I not be turned on?

Of course Bridget seemed to like me too, and she might be an absolute animal in the bedroom for all I knew – I hadn't taken the opportunity to find out – hadn't wanted to. Now she was abroad and too preoccupied with work to contact me, there was no urgency to end things. But as soon as she was back, I would. As much as I liked Bridget, I didn't miss her. Whereas I missed Melody whenever I wasn't with her, particularly when alone at night in my bed.

Despite the anxiety her illness had caused me, I'd enjoyed looking after her all weekend. Those nights I'd stayed awake watching her sleep, wrapped in her scent and listening to her breathing, lingered in my mind; taunting my imagination with possibilities. I dreamed of waking up beside her every morning. I wanted her to be mine.

As I glanced around the table at my friends and fellow team mates, I tried to picture Melody there with me. I doubted she'd ever been to a rugby match, or even a pub for that matter. But my mates would like her, I was certain, regardless of her mutism or the style of her clothes. She was innately loveable.

And yet, public places filled Melody with dread – it was clear in her face. What if she point blank refused to ever leave the estate? What then? Once my landscaping contract ended, how would I see her? Would Sinclair give me permission to visit her, or would I have to sneak onto the premises whenever he was away? The idea was ludicrous, but the thought of never seeing her was worse.

'Alright, Liam?' Maire said, breaking off from her conversation with Kat and distracting me from my fears. 'You're a million miles away.'

'Yeah, sorry,' I shook my head in an attempt to clear it and picked up my juice. 'Just work, y'know.'

'Yeah, yeah, like I believe that,' she said with a knowing wink. I avoided replying by having a drink, and as she returned her attention to Kat I made an effort to tune into Lester and James's conversation about the latest Bond film, and forget about Melody Sinclair altogether.

Chapter Thirty

The White Bear was only a half-hour walk away; I'd
looked it up. Liam had mentioned it was where they went
after their rugby matches and practise sessions, so I knew
that's where he'd be this evening. With his friends.

All week he'd been busy relaying the gravel driveway;
starting at the gates and steadily working his way back
towards the house one section at a time – first scraping
away the old, mossy, weed-infested surface, then
restoring, compacting, and rolling the sub-layer before
finally re-surfacing with fresh, clean, finely-raked gravel.
It was not the sort of work I could easily help with, so
aside from bringing him an occasional cup of tea we'd
barely spent any time together.

I'd been recuperating for most of the week; sleeping a
lot, gradually re-building my strength and catching up on
a mountain of proofreading while I considered Liam's
proposition. He hadn't repeated his offer to take me out
for dinner, but it hovered, unanswered, in the space
between us. I liked Liam and I *did* want to get to know
him better, but the plethora of dating sites, blogs, articles,
tips and rules I'd found online only made me nervous, not
to mention the conflicting advice on etiquette.

So here I was on a Sunday evening, lurking behind the
trees in a pub garden. It had been a while since I'd left the
grounds of Wildham Hall, and tonight was a test for me of
sorts – a chance to get a feel for being out in public, in
daylight, without the safety of my bicycle; an opportunity

to try out the idea of dating in my head before committing to anything.

I'd worn my green velvet dress with the sensible neckline and the buttoned capped sleeves to give myself an air of grown-up sophistication and confidence. But a lifetime of Gregory's warnings about how cruel people could be still echoed in my mind. At the last minute I'd slipped on my comfortable pink ballet shoes and grabbed a large pair of sixties sunglasses to hide behind.

My dress turned out to be too warm in the sunshine, and it was tricky to walk normally while trying to avoid all the cracks in the pavement at the same time, but I'd managed to maintain a brisk pace with my head down and fists clenched, and no-one I passed had said anything to me.

Of course the idea of waltzing into a building full of strangers was inconceivable; I had no idea what to expect inside, so my intention was simply to observe from the tree line in the hope of catching sight of Liam as he left the pub. Consequently I was prepared for a long, boring wait, but to my surprise I spotted Liam immediately because he and his friends were sitting outside in the glimmering sunshine.

There were far more women in his social group than I'd anticipated. Most of the men were well-built and stocky, as you might expect for rugby players, though Liam was still the tallest. They sat, crammed shoulder to shoulder, around picnic benches with some of the girls sat on the laps of their guys to save on space. Together they formed a cheerful but rowdy and intimidating bunch, of which Liam was by far the quietest and most sober.

But it was the women who really intrigued me; so stylish, modern and refined, with their sleek hairstyles, tight denim, branded cotton and over-abundance of handbags, sunglasses and mobile phones. From where I stood I could be viewing an entirely different species to my own.

A pretty woman with hair almost as red as my own had been sociably working her way around the group, and now squeezed herself into a narrow space right next to Liam, making my fingers curl and my stomach tighten. Was this the other woman he'd been dating, or was she still away?

This woman was attractive, with a happy-go-lucky way about her and immediately began chatting as if it was nothing; as if she were free to say anything and everything to him; talk to him forever. I was too far away to hear what was being said, but my mind ran riot with possibilities. Was she regaling him with tales of her adventures in far flung places? Impressing him with her business acumen and superior intelligence? Dazzling him with witty jokes and feminine charm?

In all fairness Liam didn't look especially dazzled – he looked tired. He had a large bruise developing across one cheekbone and sat there as nonchalantly as he usually did. But that did not temper the hot jealousy that pulsed through my veins as I witnessed every flick of her hair, flutter of her eyelashes and pout of her lips. Was she flirting with him?

I'd never felt possessive of a man before and it was an oddly fierce sensation, far stronger than I could have imagined. Suddenly it didn't matter how many men there were in the world, or how suitable for me they might be, I only wanted this one. With all the time we'd spent together and the closeness we shared, Liam was now vitally important to me – my link to the outside world, a real friend, my own personal hero. Seeing him talking to another woman brought the reality home. If he wanted me to go on a lousy date with him, I'd do it; I'd do just about anything to keep him in my life.

But I still couldn't make myself go over there.

As it grew dark it became harder to discern all the interaction between Liam and his friends, even after I'd pushed my sunglasses up into my hair. But as various members of the group dispersed for the night, I was relieved to see the redhead leave with another man entirely.

Eventually, at about ten thirty, as I was starting to shiver with cold, Liam got up and said his goodbyes to the remaining few drinkers, turning down the offer of a lift in favour of walking home alone. As he shrugged into his jacket and set off towards the front of the pub, an impulsive rush of adrenalin spiked in my blood. Stumbling out from under the trees with stiff muscles, I ran across the grass chasing after his long strides. As I caught up with him at the side of the building, he paused and turned, presumably alerted by my frenzied breathing. But before he had a chance to register what was happening, I was throwing myself into the comfort of his big body, as if I was home.

'What the…? Melody…?'

Damn he smelled good; reassuringly warm and familiar and strong and safe. He lifted me right up off my

143

feet in a hug so that he could see my face, his eyes sparkling in the light of a nearby street-lamp, bright with surprise.

'You're here…'

I smiled at him while he searched my face with an open look of wonder.

'How long have you been here? You should have come and said hello, I could have introduced you…'

I pursed my lips at the thought.

'Next time. I can't believe you're here!' Two men walked past us making me tense up self-consciously, but Liam held my gaze with clear, warm reassurance until they'd gone and I was able to breathe again. 'I'm so proud of you,' he muttered, pecking me on the lips.

With exhilaration zinging through my veins and a savage sense of possessiveness still alive in my mind, a peck was not nearly enough. Ruthlessly grabbing his face in my hands I kissed him hard, assaulting his soft lips with mine and plunging my tongue inside. He tasted of tangy, sweet orange juice and groaned as he kissed me back. His hands shifted down to my behind to better support me, and I instinctively wrapped my legs around his hips, reluctant to ever let him go.

Even while I was focused on the delicious feel of his mouth on mine, I was aware of his arousal growing between my legs, a corresponding heat spreading through me; a yearning ache for more.

'Oh God,' he muttered, moving his mouth along my jaw as I tried to press my body closer to his. His hot breath at my neck made me shiver with pleasure as I tangled my fingers in his hair. 'What are you doing to me?'

Unable to answer I took his earlobe between my teeth and bit down on the tender flesh. He seemed to throb against me in response and softly moaned, giving voice to my own hunger. When he returned his gaze to mine, it was dark with desire, and I held it as I ran my tongue along the inside of his lower lip, addicted to the taste of him. Closing his eyes he tipped his head back out of reach and took a deep breath.

'Jesus. Slow down, baby; you're killing me.'

Once again Liam was squeezing the brakes, but my immediate frustration was assuaged by the endearment he'd used. The way he spoke to me, as if I was precious to him, made me want to burst with happiness. With a last drawn-out kiss I let him lower me to the ground.

'Does this mean you'll let me take you out to dinner?'

I nodded and his face stretched into a huge grin.

'Next weekend? I'll look after you and you won't regret it I promise…'

I shrugged and he took my hand and kissed it.

'It's late, let me walk you home, OK?'

It was a clear evening, the stars a scatter of glitter against an indigo sky. Liam draped his jacket around my shoulders and we walked in silence. I wished I'd brought my notepad with me, but the lack of communication didn't feel awkward. He held my hand all the way back to Wildham Hall, his thumb lightly skimming across my knuckles, and the sensation was so pleasurable and distracting that even when I trod on cracks in the pavement by mistake it didn't bother me.

We passed a group of five teenage girls, who probably should have been tucked up at home in their beds instead of loitering on a street corner. I was careful to avoid looking at them, but they sniggered and giggled, and without even identifying what had been said, I knew in my gut that their amusement was at my expense.

Thankfully Liam seemed oblivious to the girls and their pointed looks, but a wave of embarrassment and frustration still swept over me, making my skin prickle with unease. Gregory had always said I wouldn't like life beyond Wildham Hall; that people would laugh at me; and I hated it when Gregory was right.

As the iron gates to my home slowly swung open Liam glanced up the long driveway, which, thanks to his hard work, no longer looked as dark and foreboding as before.

'Shall I walk you to the door?'

I shook my head and kissed him on the cheek.

'You don't get scared, living here on your own night after night?'

I shook my head again. Once upon a time I'd been frightened, but I'd long since grown used to the solitude, and the estate was the only home I'd ever known. I was safe within its walls. I wasn't sure how much of this Liam could read in my expression, but he chose not to argue, told me to keep his jacket, leaned down and kissed me softly goodbye.

'I'll see you tomorrow?'

I nodded and he smiled.

'Sweet dreams, Melody,' he whispered after me, making me shiver. Once I'd rounded the bend, out of sight, I broke into a sprint; racing back to the safety of the mansion with a heady mix of exhilaration and fear chasing at my heels.

Chapter Thirty-one

My dinner date looked as though she was off to work in an office when I collected her from Wildham Hall on Saturday evening. Autumn had arrived in the form of a north-easterly wind, stripping the leaves from the trees before they'd barely had a chance to turn. In deference to the weather Melody wore a belted overcoat and a sturdy pair of heels, but, curiously, she also wore a pair of spectacles perched on her nose.

I'd never seen her wear glasses before and wondered whether they we prescription or merely for effect, but I refrained from asking. Instead I offered to drive us to the restaurant, so that she wouldn't get cold, but this idea was met with repeated shakes of her head. She was determined to walk and I couldn't really argue as that would involve a furious amount of writing on her part.

Melody clung to my arm as we walked, listening while I described the carpentry repairs I'd been carrying out on the old timber-framed glasshouse. She had seen most of the restoration work for herself, but hearing about it seemed to calm her, so I was happy to oblige. She had an amusing habit of avoiding the cracks and drains on the pavement as we walked; a superstitious task which required her to watch her feet in concentration, but by the time we'd reached the French bistro, she seemed to have given it up in favour of gazing about.

The wind had dishevelled her fine hair, her cheeks were flushed and her hands were trembling, but as she slipped off her coat the look of shocked admiration on the waiter's face said it all. Melody wore a slinky, knee-length evening gown; the soft, dove-grey satin hanging seamlessly from her delicately-boned shoulders, skimming her modest curves and perfectly complementing her eyes. She took my breath away.

The waiter was young, good-looking and armed with a charm-filled smile, but Melody simply nodded her head graciously in silent thanks as he took her coat. I felt conspicuously lucky and proud to be with her as we were led to our table; Melody's understated bravery and beauty were constantly astounding.

'Would you like a glass of wine?' I said once we were seated.

Nodding tightly she pointed decisively to a mid-priced Rosé on the wine list between us, before gazing around at our surroundings. The restaurant was modern and unfussy, but popular, with every table occupied and a continuous hum of conversing voices. Melody scrutinised her cutlery before moving it aside and then picked up her napkin, taking the time to smell it and brush it across her cheek before unfolding it across her lap. It was fascinating watching her get comfortable and I found myself sniffing my own detergent-scented napkin in turn. By the time the waiter returned to take our drinks order I was able to give him our meal choices too, and he retreated with a curt bow.

'You OK?' I said, gently taking Melody's left hand across the table.

She nodded.

'We can leave at any time if you start to feel uncomfortable, just let me know…'

There weren't many restaurants in Wildham, but I'd still agonised over where to take her before making a final decision. I'd wanted to choose somewhere decent, but laid back and informal; somewhere that wouldn't freak her out or suggest any weighty expectations. I still hadn't had a chance to break things off with Bridget, and my intention for the evening was to keep things fairly relaxed between Melody and I.

But now that we were here and she was sitting across from me looking so beautiful, bathed in soft lighting and serenaded by Debussy, it suddenly seemed like the most romantic place on Earth.

The suave waiter reappeared with our drinks and Melody took several large gulps from her glass while he was still pouring my mineral water. Once he'd left us alone again she slipped off her spectacles and produced a discrete little leather-bound notebook from her handbag, in which she wrote with an even daintier pencil: *It smells of garlic in here.*

I smiled. 'That's probably the mussels – they're really good – have you ever tried them?'

She wrinkled her nose and shook her head.

'You should try them.'

That suggestion was met with a sceptical expression, but I let it go as Melody sipped her wine and then returned her attention to her notebook. *Why don't you drink?*

I'd been asked this question repeatedly over the years, most often by other rugby players, for whom heavy social drinking was part and parcel of the sport. I always offered the same vague answers; that I simply preferred not to; that it didn't agree with me; that I was an unattractive drunk. They weren't lies as such, but it wasn't the whole truth either, and most people assumed I must be a recovering alcoholic.

Melody's expression was earnest and alluring in the candlelight as she patiently waited for my response. 'It has a bad effect on me.'

It makes you sick?

'Something like that. I do miss it sometimes, though. How's your wine?'

The look in her eyes told me she knew I was hiding something, but that she wasn't going to press me for an answer. I took a sip of water and she gently weaved her slender fingers through mine in unspoken support.

'Excuse me,' said a large woman at the next table, leaning towards Melody. 'I'm terribly sorry to interrupt, but I love your dress... I just wondered where you got it...?'

Melody paled and physically shrank back in her seat as if the woman had spat at her, making me want to leap to her aid. I was sure the stranger's polite curiosity was genuine, but it had clearly caught Melody off guard. As the two women stared at each other, I jumped in with the first words that came to my head.

'I think it's Vintage, isn't that right, Mel?'

They both turned to me, and then Melody nodded at the stranger with something like relief.

'Ah, you lucky thing, what a find! I can never seem to find the right things in second-hand shops... either that or they're never my size. Have you ever been to Glad Rags on Goldhawk Road?'

Melody shook her head.

'Oh you must! They have beautiful dresses – mostly too small for me, but they'd be perfect for a petite little thing like you.'

Melody managed a smile as the woman's dining companion returned to his seat opposite her.

'Well, I'll let you get back to your dinner, nice talking to you,' she added, moving away and immediately informing her partner of the dessert she had chosen.

Melody turned her smile on me and its warmth reached all the way down to my feet. She had handled the encounter well, with minimal help from me. Why I'd shortened her name to 'Mel' was a mystery; it had slipped out on instinct, oddly comfortable and familiar; as if we'd been friends for years, but thankfully she didn't seem to mind. Squeezing her hand I returned her grin while she sipped her wine.

The food was delicious and I enjoyed watching Melody eat. We shared crusty bread and olives and she nimbly licked the butter and oil from her fingers in order to jot down comments about our surroundings. She seemed to find the décor hilarious; the exposed pipes, bare brick walls, distressed paintwork and dangly naked light bulbs. I tried to explain that it was a rustic, industrial look but she insisted the owners must have run out of money. Despite this she enthused about the cosy ambience of the place and the fresh flowers and candles. She wrote: *I'm glad it's busy – everyone is too engrossed in their own food and conversation to notice me.*

When the main course arrived she tested the blade of her knife on the pad of her thumb before tackling a classic steak frites with gusto. It was wonderful seeing her happy and relaxed, but she wasn't going unnoticed. Our waiter was far more attentive to her than he was to anyone else; constantly offering her more wine and enquiring about her enjoyment of the food with increasing frequency. It was clear by the way he was always trying to catch her eye that he was attracted to her, and only my substantial presence prevented him from openly flirting. It might have been annoying, except that Melody, the enigmatic beauty across the table, only had eyes for me.

While we were waiting for our dessert to arrive, Melody surprised me by slipping off her shoe and running a bare foot up my denim-clad leg. The lower halves of our bodies were well hidden by the tablecloth, but even so, the bold sensuality of the move was completely unexpected and intensely arousing. Melody wasn't drunk, she'd only had the one glass, but the wine had made her brave. As her toes inched their way up to my knee, she held my gaze across the table with a sphinx-like smile, her eyes burning with mischief. But as she embarked on the sensitive inside of my thigh I was forced to halt her progress; grabbing her small, perfectly-formed foot in my hand, for fear of losing all control.

She flexed and wriggled her toes with frustration, mere centimetres from my straining hard-on, but I held her firm, suppressing a groan. With my thumb I blindly explored the delicate arch of her instep, gently kneading the muscles beneath her soft skin, and was rewarded with a quiet gasp and a convulsive shiver of pleasure from where she sat. Drinking in the sight of her, I continuing my surreptitious massage while her shoulders sagged, her eyelids drooped and her lips parted. She was only saved from the indignity of actually falling asleep by our over-enthusiastic waiter delivering two crisply caramelised crème brûlées with flourish.

Chapter Thirty-two

Liam took my hand as we left the restaurant and I leaned into him, wrapping my other hand part way round his huge bicep. The wind had dropped at last, but it was chilly and I was drowsy with an excess of good food and wine, and with the stress of being out in public. And yet, against all expectations, I'd enjoyed myself. The French bistro was weird-looking but delightful, and nobody was rude to me at all.

Was it Liam's presence that prevented people from staring at me and making snide comments? The bruising on his face was fading, but he was still physically intimidating, even in navy jeans, a collared shirt and a smart jacket – my own personal bodyguard. Whatever the reason, the only people who had spoken to me tonight had been surprisingly kind, and I was now light-headed with relief.

'Are you warm enough? Would you like to go somewhere else for a drink, or would you rather go home?' Reluctant to release him I mouthed the word *home* and he smiled.

'Home it is.'

This time I let him walk me all the way up the winding drive to the front door.

'I won't be here on Monday – I promised James that I'd help him with some fencing, but I'll see you Tuesday?'

Retrieving my notebook and pencil, I bravely wrote down the question I'd been too afraid to ask until now: *Stay?*

His eyebrows rose as he read the word, and an internal conflict was clear in his eyes as they locked onto mine.

Just for tonight, I added.

'I can't do that, Mel... I'm sorry.'

I loved that he'd shortened my name to Mel. I'd never had a nickname before, not a nice one anyway, and it made me feel closer to him; almost special. And yet, he didn't want to spend the night with me. *Why not?* I wrote.

'It just doesn't feel right... you're here on your own and I'm so much older than you... it would feel like I was taking advantage.'

You stayed before.

'That was different, you were sick. Look, we've only had one date; we don't have to rush this; I want you to be sure about what you want...'

I am sure – I do *know what I want. I trust you.*

He smiled. 'I'm glad you trust me, but maybe you shouldn't; not yet; you hardly know me...'

He gently brushed a wayward strand of hair from my face and I batted his hand away with irritation, rejection and anger swelling up in my chest.

Sighing, he pushed his hands into his pockets. 'I'm crazy about you – you do know that, don't you?'

I turned away, blinking as tears pricked my eyes. I'd worn these silly glasses as an extra layer of armour to hide behind, but now they were just annoying.

'I've got something for you. I was going to give it to you in the restaurant, but I wasn't sure if you'd want it – I'm still not sure...'

I turned back to see a small, black mobile phone held out in his hand.

'I realise we can't exactly call each other, but I got you a sim card with unlimited texts... I thought a mobile might be easier to carry around then a pen and paper and this way, if you want to, you can contact me even when I'm not here.'

I'd never had a phone before – until now there was no-one in my life I wished to contact. The concept was startling, but the reasoning behind his gift, and the idea of being able to reach him at any time, was almost overwhelming.

'It's only a basic model, but I've programmed my number in and set up an email account... it should be easy to use... have you sent texts before? I can show you how it works...'

As he rambled on, my tears escaped and I covered my mouth with my hand in a lame attempt to hold them back.

'Hey, please don't cry,' he said, pulling me into a warm hug. 'You don't have to use it; it was a stupid idea; I didn't mean to upset you; I'm s—'

Reaching up I pulled his face down to mine and quashed his apology with a long, slow kiss. Once I was sure I'd silenced him, I pulled back and scribbled *show me* in my notebook.

'Are you sure?'

I rolled my eyes, shoved my pad and pencil into my handbag and prised the phone out of Liam's huge hand.

Below a generously-sized screen sat a neat keypad, and when I pressed the largest button, the display lit up brightly with the current date and time. I grinned up at him, pleased with myself, and he smiled back at me, relieved.

'Maybe I'll come in for a little bit – just to show you how it works...'

I wasted no time unlocking the front door and leading Liam into the cosy warmth of the kitchen, quietly thrilling at the novelty of having company. He sat down in a creaky chair at the table while I removed my glasses, coat and shoes, and held the kettle aloft in silent offering.

'A coffee would be great, thank you.'

Liam only stayed long enough to talk me through the simple processes of using my new phone. But we were texting each other inane little comments deep into the night.

*

In the morning Gregory returned from his three-week trip abroad, filling the house with restless noises, pointed questions and cigar smoke. Switching my phone to silent mode I hid it deep inside Beauty, right where her heart would be if she had one. I wished I could conceal myself as easily, but it was near impossible in a house where none of the internal doors locked. Gregory didn't believe in locked rooms.

I was hunched up on the window seat in the linen room, hiding behind the clean towels, sheets and tablecloths, trying to read a book, when Gregory first sought me out. He tried to smother me in an awkward hug, but my knees got in the way and I stubbornly refused to move them, so he sat down on the seat by my feet instead.

'Mrs Daly said you've been ill with scarlet fever – that she had to call the doctor for you, is that right?'

I nodded, gazing out the window and across the grounds, idly hoping that his stringent aftershave wouldn't infect all the clean linen.

'Why didn't you email me to let me know? I could have come back sooner… looked after you…'

I shrugged and, although my gaze was still trained on the view through the window, I could tell his eyes were crawling all over my bare legs and toes. It wasn't the same warm sensation as when Liam looked at me; on the contrary it made me vaguely nauseated.

'Are you feeling better now? Is there anything I can get you? Yvette's coming to cook for us, is there anything in particular you'd like to eat?' I shook my head and he vented his usual sigh of frustration. 'I'm sorry I have to work away so much. It doesn't mean I don't care…'

Technically it wasn't Gregory's fault that I resented his presence so much. Experiencing a pang of guilt I offered him a half-hearted smile which was all the encouragement he needed.

'Look, I've brought you something – sorry it's not wrapped.' He handed me a plastic carrier bag from which I withdrew a garish, bright-yellow stuffed toy. The thing was capsule-shaped with big goggly eyes, wearing a gormless smile and a pair of blue dungarees. A mobile phone it was not.

'It's called a Minion,' Gregory explained, all the kids are into them, isn't it cute?'

I'm not a kid. I tried to smile with gratitude, and it strained on my face, but he didn't seem to notice. He placed one soft hand on my foot and it took all my self-control not to kick out at him or shrink away from his manicured touch.

'I'm going to stay at home for a while, keep you company, I want to hear about all your news...' I turned back to the window to hide the irritation in my face. 'Maybe we could go out somewhere, I could take you to the opera, you wouldn't have to speak, what do you think...?'

I shook my head.

'I'd like us to be friends, Melody, you're a grown woman now...'

Something about this last line made me uneasy and I snatched my foot away from his grasp under the guise of adjusting my position. He seemed about to say something else but cleared his throat instead and stood up, smoothing the creases from his suit.

'We'll be eating in the dining room at seven-thirty this evening. Make sure you bring something to write with,' he added, leaving the room.

As the week progressed I tried to avoid Gregory as much as possible, and behave in the same way that I always had. But Liam had made me feel restless; impatient; alive; and Gregory seemed to sense the difference in me. He inspected the supermarket invoices more carefully than usual, scrutinised my browser history and even read the boring manuscripts I'd been editing. When he found nothing incriminating he tracked my movements from room to room, and hounded me with nosey questions dressed up as concern.

I'm ashamed to say his overt attention only brought out the devil in me, and I started thinking up subtle ways to encourage him to leave. At first I simply took advantage of the fact he was jet-lagged in order to mess with him. While he was asleep I crept through the house and turned all the clocks backwards or forwards by an hour to confuse him; his alarm clock included. I also swapped the jar of strong coffee in the kitchen with the decaffeinated one, so that he became increasingly sleepy after breakfast and keyed-up in the evenings.

But when he continued to hang around, I progressed onto more drastic and devious measures: such as pricking the surface of his contact lenses with a pin at night so that they irritated his eyeballs during the day, and lacing his evening drink with water tablets so that he was up half the night urinating. I am not a good person.

It was probably just as well that Liam ended up being absent for most of the week, and not just the Monday as he predicted. A drama involving his friends meant that Liam spent days at the local hospital waiting for news. Late at night we kept each other updated by exchanging a few furtive texts, but it wasn't the same – I missed his smile, his warmth, the rumble of his voice and the way he held my hand. Above all else I missed the magical spell of his kiss.

As autumn took hold in the grounds, rain set in and I was forced to stay indoors. Gregory was unable to go hunting and grew restless and irritable with lack of sleep. He chewed relentlessly at his cigars, no doubt frustrated by my secrets, but his questions stopped. Instead he took to pacing backwards and forwards, or sitting and jiggling one leg up and down, or simply staring at me in silence – which was by far the worst experience and would force me to leave the room.

By the time Liam arrived on Friday morning, the air of tension inside the house was unbearable. My heart leapt in my chest at the familiar growl of his van pulling up on the drive, and then plummeted into my stomach as Gregory strode purposefully through the house and out the front door to confront him.

Chapter Thirty-three

'You're back,' Sinclair stated, from the top of the steps.

'Yes, did you get my message? I had a family emergency, but I'm back now. How was your trip?'

'I assume you'll make up the time?'

'I'll do my best,' I said tightly. It had been a difficult few days. I'd witnessed a violent attack and a shooting and then spent the aftermath between the police station and the hospital, waiting for news on a friend. I'd missed Melody like crazy throughout and I was seriously lacking sleep. The last thing I needed right now was Sinclair's patronising tone.

From the back of the van I retrieved a spade, a fork, a large plastic trug, and crunched my way across the gravel and round the side of the house. It was peeing with rain but the parterre needed a final bit of weeding in preparation for planting. Sinclair followed me, despite the weather, his footsteps ringing out on the stone terrace.

'Where are you with the new exotic garden?' his tone suggested more of a demand than a genuine question as he cast a disparaging eye over the old rose beds, now stripped of their jewel-like scented blooms.

I sensed movement in a window above Sinclair's head and I knew that if I looked up, I would get a glimpse of Melody for the first time since our date nearly a week ago. We'd exchanged a few texts since then, nothing more, but I got the distinct impression that she and her father hadn't been getting on. The urge to turn my head and reassure myself that she was OK was almost overwhelming, but I didn't want to give myself away to Sinclair, so I fought the impulse with everything I had.

'I've prepared the ground, as you can see, but if I plant new tender species now they'll rot and die over the winter before they've had a chance to establish. I can plant that area in the spring once the soil warms up.'

'And these beds?' Sinclair gestured to the box-edged parterre, his shoulders hunched against the rain.

'I've got all the bulbs and biennials on order, they should arrive in the next couple of weeks.'

He nodded and I stabbed my fork into the ground to work at a dandelion root a couple of yards from his feet. 'I noticed that the glasshouse in the walled garden isn't finished yet...'

I sighed, sank my fork deep into the earth and straightened up, looking directly down into his bloodshot eyes. He shifted uneasily as I towered over him but refrained from actually taking a step backwards. 'No, it's not. But I've cleared it out, removed and replaced the rotten woodwork, and filled, sanded and re-painted the timber frame. It's all ready to take the new panes of glass when they arrive, but it'll be a two-man job getting them fitted safely and we'll need a dry day – it's not advisable installing glass in the rain – it makes it slippery and difficult.' *Like you*, I added silently.

'I see,' he said, feigning nonchalance and taking a sideways step away from me. 'As long as things are progressing as they should – I don't like unnecessary delays.'

'Neither do I, but gardening is subject to the weather and the seasons. It's not as if I've been sitting on my hands…'

'No?'

God he was rude. 'No. I relayed the entire drive while you were away – you might have noticed on your way in…'

'Look, Mr Hunt, I'm merely trying to establish which work you have completed and that which is still to do, and I'd prefer it if you didn't use that sarcastic tone with me – I do pay your wages after all.'

I pressed my lips together, aggravated by his ignorance and superior attitude. How had a man like him fathered someone as smart and generous as Melody? But he took my non-answer as an insult.

'If you're no longer satisfied with your position, Mr Hunt, I'm sure I can find someone who is – you are welcome to leave.' His fists were clenched tightly at his sides, and as his voice rose, I realised he was shaking with a pent-up rage, out of all proportion to our conversation. A less passive man than myself might have thumped him – given him the fight he was spoiling for – but he wasn't worth the trouble.

Instead I took a deep breath. Tempted as I was to walk away from this ridiculous little bloke in his soggy designer suit, I'd worked too hard on this project; I wanted to see it through, and anyway, I couldn't leave Melody.

'If it's all the same to you, I'd prefer to stay and honour the contract we agreed,' I said calmly.

Sinclair nodded curtly, lips white with tension, before marching stiffly back to the house.

I was relieved to have avoided being fired, but I still had my pride, and being dictated to by an idiot had seriously pissed me off. Abandoning my tools where they were I retreated to the stable block to make myself a cup of tea and count to ten.

Fifteen minutes later I was still in the old tack room, the rain hammering down on the slate roof above, when the door flew open to admit a rain-drenched Melody. Slamming the door shut behind her she leaned against it breathing hard. Her hair was dripping, her face was streaked with rain, or tears, or both, and her thin dress clung closely enough to reveal the outline of her underwear. She was a sight for sore eyes.

I got up to go to her, but she put up a hand to stop me, a determined look in her eye.

'Has he gone?'

She nodded.

'How long for this time?'

Shaking her head she shrugged her shoulders, droplets of water spotting the dusty floor. I took another step towards her, dying to scoop her up in my arms, but again she stopped me and this time held up her phone. Clearly she was mad at me and had something to say, so I waited patiently while her thumbs, a blur of speed, tapped out a message. She'd had a mobile for less than a week, stubbornly resisting the predictive text function, and yet her messages where impressively fast and typo free. My phone vibrated in my back pocket and she eye-balled me as I retrieved her text:

What are you doing? You mustn't argue with him - he'll sack you!

'I haven't done anything. He tried to start a fight and I deliberately didn't retaliate.'

Her eyes flashed and she fired off another accusatory text: You goaded him.

'No, I didn't.'

He wants to get rid of you.

As I looked at her I finally recognised her anger for the fear it really was – this beautiful creature was afraid of losing me. The realisation was humbling. 'He can try, but I'm not going anywhere,' I said, shoving my mobile back into my pocket and advancing on her despite her shaking head and furious expression.

She pushed her phone into my chest to stop me, and I willingly absorbed the discomfort as I gathered her in my arms and tilted her head back to look at her. Tears leaked from her eyes with frustration.

'Even if I don't work here anymore, I'll find a way to keep seeing you. I'll keep coming back for as long as you want me to, understand?'

Why? she mouthed.

'Because I like you.'

Moving up onto her tiptoes she kissed me, softly at first and then feverishly, with all the intoxication of her anxiety. As she pressed close, moulding her damp body to mine, desire engulfed me like flames – I'd missed her so much; my silent temptress; passionate, proud, innocent and alluring – a perfect mess of contradictions that I could no longer live without.

With a mischievous smile she jumped up higher in my arms, wrapping her legs around my waist and kissing me all over my face. I squeezed her bottom in my hands as I carried her over to the table and sat down with her straddling my lap. Relinquishing her phone she pushed her fingers into my hair, tugging painfully at the roots while I plundered her mouth with my tongue. God I wanted her. She might be a virgin, but right now she was horny as hell and loudly begging me for relief with her body and her dilated eyes.

On impulse I cupped a hand between her legs and she pushed against the base of my thumb, the cotton of her knickers hot and wet with her arousal in my palm. At first the expression on her face was somewhere between awe and stubborn determination, but as she began to rock her hips she found a rhythm and started panting; her lips parted, her cheeks flushed, her eyes glazed and fixed on mine. I'd never seen anything more erotic or more beautiful in my life. She seemed to hold her breath in the taut seconds before she came; her musky seductive scent filling my nostrils and the hammering of the rain intensifying, as if spurring her on. And then she peaked; exhaling in a great, juddering rush, her head falling back as her body convulsed over and over again with pleasure.

I almost came myself from the sheer intensity of watching her fall apart in my hand. While she was still catching her breath I eased her off my lap and gently set her down in a chair. Counting to ten in my head, I deliberately pictured spreadsheets full of boring figures, willing my erection to subside. Once I was sure I had control of myself, I crouched down before her and looked up into her face.

'Are you OK?'

A slow smile spread out across her mouth and she bit her lip as she nodded, her emotions as obvious and infectious as ever.

'You are so beautiful,' I said smiling back at her. 'Was that... have you ever...?' Why was it so hard to say the words out loud? Taking my mobile from my back pocket I tapped out a message while she waited with a bemused expression.

Have you ever come like that before?

I half expected her to laugh at me, but she looked serious as she read my question, considering her reply and keeping me dangling with anticipation. At length she looked straight at me, defiantly, and shook her head; and I knew it was the truth. Oh lord, I'd corrupted an angel, I was going straight to hell.

'God I'm sorry, Mel, did I hurt you?'

She shook her head adamantly and squeezed my hand, but it didn't assuage the sense of guilt that was now creeping inside me. Rising to my feet I rubbed my face with my hands, traces of her delicious scent taunting me, while she retrieved her own phone, tapped out a message and shoved it under my nose.

It was amazing — I want more. Please.

Her polite audacity made me laugh out loud and she grinned back at me unfazed. 'I'm glad you enjoyed it,' I said, pulling her into a hug, 'but I really should get back to work.'

169

Chapter Thirty-four

Holy moly. So that was an orgasm!

I'd read all about it of course; I'd swotted up on the theory behind the vagina, the clitoris and the G-spot, but touching myself there had always been about as underwhelming as a medical examination. Nothing like being touched by Liam.

For a moment there I'd been afraid I was going to wet myself – pee all over his hand like an excited puppy. But wow was it amazing. I actually saw stars! Splodges of coloured light anyway, and now my whole body felt relaxed as if all my bones had been separated and put back together again more loosely. And if Liam could do that to me with one hand, fully-clothed, I couldn't possibly imagine what the rest of his naked body would do to me...

I think he thought I was joking when I asked for more, but I really meant it – I even said please. I hope he meant it when he said he liked me and that he wouldn't leave, because I was in no way ready to let him go.

The heavy rain diminished to a persistent drizzle as Liam worked his way methodically around the terrace and then the walled garden; weeding beds and turning the earth as he went. I wanted to join in and help, but he was surprisingly insistent about my staying indoors. I sat in the upstairs bedrooms sulking – splitting my attention between proofreading the website text for a company which made pregnant bumps for the entertainment industry, and watching Liam digging with mesmeric masculine power and skill.

As the day wore on I started to worry. Was he regretting what had happened between us in the old tack room? Was my inexperience a turn off? I'd considered lying about it but he'd have seen straight through me. And why didn't he orgasm? He looked aroused and yet he'd kept his clothes on and held back again. Was he going off me?

From the nursery window I could see him carefully weeding around the rosemary bushes, pulling out handfuls of spaghetti-like mint roots. On impulse I picked up my phone and messaged him:

`Why won't you let me help? I want to be near you.`

He glanced up at me and smiled as he paused in his work, breathing hard. Wiping his forehead on his bicep and his hands on his thighs, he then reached into his back pocket to retrieve his mobile. I didn't have to wait long for his reply:

`I want to be near you too, more than you know, but I don't want you getting ill again.`

His words were touching, but it was not the answer I'd wanted, so I sent another:

`I won't - I'll wear a big coat.`

He laughed as he read it; I could make out the lovely warm rumble right through the glass, but he shook his head as he replied:

`Stay put, you're too distracting.`

Sod that. Discarding my manuscript I ran down the back stairs, past the kitchen and towards the back door; but he'd anticipated my impatience and I ran straight into a wall of hot, damp muscle as he intercepted me in the laundry room.

His distinctive earthy scent engulfed me as he bent down and kissed me firmly on my startled mouth.

'I mean it, Mel,' he growled. 'You're all I can think about and I have so much to do. If I stand any chance of holding onto this job, then you have to let me work.'

His confession gave me hope – he was all I could think about too – but I didn't want him to lose his job. It dawned on me that I was letting my newly discovered lust get the better of me. One orgasm and I was behaving like a fool.

'And anyway it's miserable out there,' he added more softly. 'How about I take you out on another date at the weekend? Anywhere you like…'

I shook my head.

'We could go for dinner again, or go see a movie…?'

Stepping back away from him I stared at the phone in my hands. Why was he so keen to make me leave this place? I was happy here and if he kept his job we could stay friends without my having to leave.

'Are you afraid of what people will think of you? Because you shouldn't be.'

I tapped out a reply: I couldn't care less what people think of me.

'Then why are you so reluctant to go out in public?'

172

Just because I'm comfortable with who I am doesn't mean I like being stared at and taunted.

He gaped at me in surprise. 'Mel, if people stare at you it's because you're beautiful and they're envious – either that or they want you for themselves. And I can't imagine anyone *taunting* you, why would they...?'

As much as I appreciated Liam's kind words, he obviously didn't understand what it was like being different; being an outsider; being me.

'Mel?' His features were drawn with concern.

I shook my head again, abandoned my phone on the side, stepped around him and stalked outside to the stables. Dragging out my trusty bicycle I hopped up onto the saddle and steered myself out into the rain. Liam stood observing me from the terrace, and I regretted the look of worry that was clear on his face, but I needed this. With a life like mine, full of frustrations, I needed to feel free; and this was the best way I knew how.

Leaving Liam behind to get back to work, I pedalled fast along the smooth pathways that he and Olly had so skilfully restored. The sinuous surface provided the perfect track on which to race around the grounds; free-wheeling down the slopes and skidding around the bends; the wind in my hair and the rain on my face. Maybe I was crazy, and maybe Liam was realising that and would never give me another orgasm. Maybe I would remain a virgin forever. Right now I didn't care, I only needed to ride.

Chapter Thirty-five

It had barely stopped raining for three weeks. Once or twice an abrupt downpour descended from the skies, batting the last leaves from the trees, drilling the surface of the lake and spattering the paths with mud. But for the most part it was a persistent misty drizzle; the kind that hung in the air, slunk between the trees and subtly seeped into your hair and clothes until you were soaked to the bone. All that moisture kept the night temperatures from dipping too low, and softened up the ground which made planting easier, but I saw far less of Mel.

I used the time to fill the flower beds with scented wallflowers and sackfuls of spring-flowering bulbs – narcissus, tulips and alliums – to provide a successional display of colour once the winter had passed. In the walled garden I re-stocked the herb beds with fresh marjoram and sage, cut back the summer-fruiting raspberry canes, planted garlic and onion sets and sowed several rows of a hardy variety of broad bean. Working long hours I kept myself busy and tried to think about other things.

Recently, and unexpectedly, I'd bumped into my ex-girlfriend. It wasn't clear from our brief exchange whether she was back in Wildham for good or not, but it was strange to realise it made no difference to me. Cally was caught up in her own life, and though I still cared about her, in truth, I'd moved on.

Lester was back in rugby training now that his leg had healed, and was grateful for the physical distraction. Though Maire was doing well and her scans showed a healthy baby, my brother was worried about the birth. Whenever he wasn't with his wife, he was checking his phone continuously. We all teased him about it, but I understood his concern; I knew how much Maire meant to him, now more than ever.

Once I'd run out of planting work, I ripped up the entire formal lawn below the terrace. I began by stripping out the lumpy, weed-infested grass; enriching the ground with fresh topsoil, sand and fertiliser; and rolling and raking the bare earth to a perfectly level finish. Laying and piecing together the fresh green lengths of turf was like completing a giant jigsaw puzzle, but the result would be an emerald carpet neat enough to play croquet on.

It was no coincidence that the projects I chose to focus on were all within reach of the house; I was drawn to Mel as if she held gravitational power over my mind and body. For the most part she simply worked inside where it was warm and dry; casting an occasional glance in my direction through the windows. But for an hour each day she emerged through the mist like an apparition to meet me for lunch in the stables. I looked forward to those moments every minute we were apart.

Through unspoken mutual agreement, we maintained a careful physical distance between us; covering safe topics of conversation like the grounds, the changing season, rugby and music. I discovered that she liked Paloma Faith and Natalia Kills – artists I knew little about, but made a mental note to look into. One day she brought an absurdly outmoded disc-man with her, and I donned her headphones while she played me 'Go' by Delilah.

There was something intensely intimate about listening to a song she'd chosen; maybe because she had no voice of her own. I found myself concentrating on the lyrics as if they might contain vital clues to Melody herself, and speculated about how her vocal chords might sound. They could be deep and husky for all I knew, though I suspected not. The song stayed with me long afterwards, the words looping around my head on repeat. Did she want me to go? I hoped not.

Gregory came and went again during that time, but thankfully did not make any attempt to speak to me. I couldn't stand the man and held him personally responsible for Mel's solitude, though in fairness, she had never implied he was to blame.

As the days passed and our friendship grew, I learned more and more about Mel; her likes, dislikes, tastes, quirks and foibles. But now there was an awkward tension between us that was never there before. The longer we refrained from making bodily contact, the more I yearned to touch her, hold her, kiss her; make her come again.

The ghost of her silent orgasm haunted me; crackling and reverberating in the space between us. I felt hideously guilty about groping her like that in a grubby outhouse as if she was nothing. She deserved so much more than that; so much better; she deserved to be properly romanced and gently made love to by someone closer to her own age and infinitely more worthy. But the way I'd carelessly rejected her afterwards made me feel even worse. She'd said she wanted more and I had thrown it back in her face

– suggesting another date, when leaving the estate clearly made her uncomfortable. No wonder she was now keeping her distance.

But what should I have done? Carried her straight off to bed and savagely taken what I wanted? I was stuck – I had no idea how to fix things, how to dissolve the tension between us and move forwards. And it was killing me. I wanted her so badly it hurt – I'd never been so horny in my life. I could no longer eat or sleep properly and it was even affecting my game. Last weekend I'd messed up a tackle allowing the other team to score a try. I'd been experiencing an uninvited flashback at the time – Mel's erect rosy nipples poking through wet cotton – like a ptsd sufferer at the complete mercy of his memory. From the sidelines, Lester, frustrated that he was still not fit enough to play matches, had loudly berated me with an array of colourful language. Thankfully the Warriors had still won the match, but it was no thanks to me.

And it seemed wrong to masturbate to thoughts of Melody; dishonest somehow. But if I didn't I had wet dreams and woke up sticky with my own seed like a hormonal adolescent. How could one innocent young woman have such a powerful, debilitating and downright embarrassing effect on me?

Today was a perfect autumn day; the rain had cleared, the sky was blue and the air was almost, but not quite, cool enough to see your breath. Sunlight shafted low and golden through the naked trees, illuminating piles of curling leaves like russet paper-chains as I made my way through the woods to the grotto garden.

Using the loppers I cut away vast armfuls of the creepers, which tumbled and cascaded down over the crumbling walls. The overgrowth didn't only obscure the locked door, but also Gothic-arched, glassless windows, set into the stonework on two sides. They had been boarded up in the past, presumably to exclude prying eyes, but the timber had rotted and was easy to remove. As I did so I peered in through these apertures, but the congested forest of self-sown tree saplings trapped within a dense tangle of brambles made it impossible to make out anything of the interior. I tried the oak door, but despite a little obvious rot at the bottom, it was solid and locked tight shut.

Sensing Mel's presence I turned to find her crouched under a nearby tree like a feral cat, cloaked in a shabby fur coat and observing me with a steady, feline gaze.

'I figured I'd take a look inside, have a go at restoring it, but I don't have the key,' I said.

Rising to her feet, which were bare, she walked towards me, the muddy hem of her coat dragging through the fallen leaves and making a shushing, whispering sound as she approached. Three feet from me she stopped; her pale, heart-shaped face sombre as she held out her hand. A large, rusty iron key sat in her palm; ornate, old-fashioned and evoking thoughts of fairytale secret gardens.

My fingers brushed her soft, smooth skin as I took the key from her, and the sensation burned its way up my arm. Had she anticipated I would come here, or did she always carry this key around?

Even with the door open it took me most of the day to hack away at the jungle of foliage that had taken hold inside. As the sun rose higher it grew unseasonably warm within the shelter of the chapel-like stone walls, forcing me to strip off my sweatshirt as I went.

Eventually the semi-primeval interior landscape of the garden was revealed – the four walled sides creating a mossy green room, open to the sky and the elements, but providing a humid micro-climate for the lush fernery within. A collection of irregularly-shaped stone boulders traversed the centre of the space like large pieces of furniture rising from a frothy green sea. They were stacked higher and more tightly compacted as they rose to a peak in the back corner of the space, where a natural spring bubbled out from between the stones, the water trickling and escaping down into a dark, circular pool below. Over time the damp passage of water had smoothed curves and gullies into the rock and spawned a patchwork of olive and lime-coloured moss on every surface; velvety soft, slippery and compelling.

All these aspects conspired to provide a tranquil, almost magical atmosphere, right there in the heart of the woods, but it was the statuary which really made this particular grotto distinctive.

It was Mel who discovered the first one. The interior of the walls were heavily draped and curtained in a mix of Virginia creeper, brambles and ivy, making it easy to mistake the protruding shapes for buttresses, positioned as they were at regular intervals around the periphery of the room. But they were not simply wall supports, they were plinth-mounted statues; figures sculpted from stone and startlingly pale, having been protected and hidden from view for so long.

The excitement and delight in Mel's expression drew me straight to her. Shrugging off her coat she pushed up the sleeves of her dress and together we worked side by side, carefully tearing away the overhanging foliage in great handfuls at a time, to reveal a beautifully crafted, female nude, nearly two metres tall. She was portrayed in mid-step; parting intricately carved clumps of water reeds with her body as if fleeing from something or someone, though the expression on her face was perfectly serene.

Bracing herself against me, Mel reached up and ran her hand up the smooth white thigh of the nude before us, searing my already-warm body with a different kind of heat. The gesture was seemingly innocent but intensely erotic, adding fuel to the desire that raged inside me. Unable to resist Mel in such close proximity, I dropped my mouth to the bare patch of skin between her shoulder and her neck and kissed her, luxuriating in her tantalising scent. She shivered at my touch, her head falling sideways and presenting me with more naked skin. As I trailed kisses up to the sensitive place behind her ear, she shuddered and sighed, swaying slightly on her feet.

'Sorry, I couldn't resist,' I muttered, my voice hoarse as I stepped back away from her. Tipping her head back Mel gazed up into the face of the statue, without turning around, and I moved over to the next hidden plinth, clearing my throat. 'Let's see what the rest of these are like…'

At length we uncovered three more female nudes, each one more openly seductive than the last. Mel made no attempt to communicate her thoughts to me in words; she didn't write me notes or send any texts, but as we progressed I began to suspect that she was deliberately caressing the figures' curves with her fingers; purposely brushing against me; intentionally teasing and provoking me, while I struggled and failed to keep my mind pure.

The four sculptures were arranged in opposing pairs, lining two sides of the grotto, leaving one last overgrown mass lurking behind the spring-fed pool at the far end. It was with an increasing sense of anticipation that we approached this last work of art. It was set higher up the wall than all the others, and at Mel's gestured suggestion I lifted her up onto the plinth base so that she could reach the top.

Before long an imposing, faun-like figure was revealed; with the hind legs, hoofs and curved horns of a goat, and the arms, head and torso of a bearded man. But his hirsute, muscular build was not the only thing marking him out as male. Jutting out from between his fur-covered thighs was a large erect penis, which, frankly, put my trapped hard-on to shame.

Mel gasped when she stumbled across the impressive phallus, her cheeks flushing with heat and her eyes darkening as they darted to mine.

'I guess being trapped in a room with four naked beauties will do that to a man,' I muttered.

Mel's face split into a huge smile and I shook my head in mock despair, unable to help smiling in return.

'Maybe it's time to find out who these guys are supposed to be.' In a bid to distract myself from my own lascivious thoughts I retrieved my mobile and commenced a Google search. With Wikipedia's help it didn't take long to find the information I was looking for.

'Right, I believe this is the god Pan, from Greek mythology – see the reed pipes he carries in his hand...' I glanced up and caught Mel running her hand slowly across Pan's chest. Clearing my throat I returned my eyes to the relative safety of the small screen. 'He was the god of shepherds and flocks, woods and mountains, fertility, lust and rampant male sexuality...' I paused to swallow, but didn't dare raise my eyes from the screen. 'He was known for actively pursuing nubile young nymphs and goddesses, heedless of the consequences...' Was this a joke?

I slowly looked up to find Mel caressing Pan's big hard cock with one hand, her eyes intent on mine.

'Please don't do that,' I muttered, unable to look away, my mouth dry.

Mel withdrew her hand, and dropped down until she was seated on the edge of the plinth before me, her legs dangling and her head level with mine. I kept my eyes on hers, but in my peripheral vision I could see she was slowly hitching her dress higher up over her thighs.

'Melody...' I warned, my cock throbbing in my pants, but still I couldn't turn away. Trailing the fingers of one hand up the inside of her leg she then touched herself, like I had once before. Her eyes dilated, her breathing shallowed and her cheeks pinked as she began to pleasure herself, her gaze fixed on mine.

It was too much. The whole world was conspiring against me. How could any hot-blooded male be expected to resist temptation like that? Mel was my own personal nymph; virginal yes, but definitely not innocent – the woman was hell-bent on seducing me.

Casting my phone aside I cupped her face in my hands and claimed her mouth in a kiss.

Chapter Thirty-six

Oh how I'd missed Liam's kiss; his touch; the musky warmth of his skin and the protective feel of his rough hands on me. Slipping my hands underneath his T-shirt I wrapped my arms and legs around him, urging him closer into my embrace and relishing the solid mass and weight of his body against mine.

I knew all about the god Pan and his carnal desires – I'd read a book once – 'The Brinkworth Guide to Ancient Myths and Legends' – and could recall Pan's attempts to seduce various women; the water-nymph, Syrinx, and the moon goddess, Silene. That these mythological figures had been hiding here in this garden all along was extraordinary, but right now all I could think about was the unbridled lust the stories represented and the living, breathing, hot-blooded man before me. Liam may not be a god, but he certainly had the power to bring me to life or, I suspect, destroy me completely.

Withdrawing, he used his hands to loosen my grip on him. His physical size and strength made it impossible to prevent and intense disappointment lanced through me. But instead of moving away he pulled off his T-shirt, dropped to his knees with the defeated groan of a felled tree, and looked up into my face.

'Do you trust me?' his voice was unusually husky.

I nodded and he moved his hands up beneath my dress to my hips, braced himself, leaned forwards, and placed a soft kiss on the birthmark on the inside of my thigh. The seemingly innocuous gesture was as welcome as it was unexpected, giving me goosebumps, while his eyes roamed across my face assessing my reaction. Encouraged by whatever he saw there he proceeded to press a long, lingering kiss to the damp cotton between my thighs and my whole body thrilled and ached with delight. Liam began to ease my knickers down and I shifted up off my bottom to make it easier for him. He sat back on his heels to gently unhook them from my feet and I flushed with heat as he gazed at me there; my most intimate parts spread open and exposed. But the sober expression on his face and the hungry look in his eyes made my insides clench with excitement.

Rising back up onto his knees, he gripped my hips and brought his face in towards me, and I closed my eyes. Pressing his mouth to my sensitive flesh he began to tease me with his tongue and I was overwhelmed by a rush of emotion. Was there ever a sensation naughtier or more heavenly? Trembling all over and fighting for breath, I clutched at his hair, near-delirious, as he quickly worked me up to a dizzying peak; my pelvis flexing back and forth with a drive of its own and my muscles tensing all over in anticipation.

Because this time I understood what was happing to me; I'd longed for another orgasm for weeks. My sheer desperation left no room for embarrassment as I greedily rubbed against him...

And then he made a sound; a low moan similar to the noise he made when enjoying good food, and the vibration tipped me over the edge into that incredible shattering sensation I so craved; my body shuddering in great waves from head to toe; my lungs gasping; my blood pounding in my ears and the roof of my mouth.

As I began to drift back to Earth I realised he had risen to his feet. I opened my eyes and his gaze locked on mine – dark and burning. As incredible as my orgasm was, I now wanted more; I wanted *him* in the most carnal of ways. I wanted to see him naked; give him pleasure; feel him inside me and see him come. Without taking my eyes from his, I reached out and unhooked the button at the top of his trousers. He stared back intently, but didn't try to stop me as I began to lower the zip of his fly. Before I'd even reached the bottom the heavy length of his cock sprang forwards into my palm, still concealed in his boxers, but hot and throbbing. He closed his eyes and shuddered as I wrapped my fingers around him and gently squeezed.

'We don't have to do this,' he muttered, though whether he was trying to convince himself or me, I couldn't be sure.

Afraid that he might stop me, I tugged his trousers down from his hips with both hands. And to my delight he proceeded to finish what I'd started; kicking off his boots, peeling away his socks and then removing both his trousers and boxers completely. My breath caught in my throat at the sight of him – feet planted, shoulders back and penis unashamedly erect; thick and swollen with need. He did not look vulnerable without clothes. On the contrary, he looked handsome, virile and powerfully masculine.

Swallowing hard I visually feasted on him, my blood humming in my veins. How long had I been waiting to see this man naked? Many months, though it felt like years. Without looking down I rummaged around in the concealed pockets of my dress until I found the condoms I'd stashed there. He raised an eyebrow when he saw them.

'You came prepared huh?'

I nodded and he smiled.

'Not up here,' he said, gently taking my spare hand and helping me down from Pan's plinth. Scooping my coat up off the floor, he led me over to a smooth moss-covered boulder, about the size of a twin bed, and spread my fur coat out over it. Sitting down on one end, his cock jutting up to his belly button, he gazed at me where I stood between his knees.

'We have to take this slowly, OK? I don't want to hurt you.'

Nodding, I pressed the condoms into his hand. With his teeth he ripped one open and I watched, fascinated, as he efficiently rolled it down over his length.

'I want you to go on top so that you're in control,' he explained, shifting himself further backwards. 'Come straddle me.'

He offered me his hand and without hesitation I scrambled up onto the fur-covered rock, hiking up my dress and kneeling with a knee either side of his lap.

'If you want to stop me at any time, for any reason, I want you to slap me across the face, exactly as you did before, OK?' He lifted my palm to his cheek for added emphasis and I nodded, bemused by his concern. 'I'm serious, Mel, it's important that you are able to say no – don't hesitate, just hit me and I'll stop, OK?'

I appreciated his consideration, but at that moment it was frustrating; the longer he delayed the more I wanted him. Pulling my dress up and off over my head I threw it aside, thrilled to be completely naked with him at last. Liam's penis lurched and he groaned as his eyes roamed over my bare breasts; my nipples tightening under his gaze.

'God, you are beautiful,' he muttered, gripping my thighs and trailing hot kisses from my neck down to my chest. As he took my nipple into his mouth, pleasure spiked through my body making me convulse.

He looked up at me. 'Jesus, Mel, I don't know if I can do this; I'm ready to come already.'

Too late to back out now, Liam Hunt. Bracing my hands on his shoulders I shuffled closer to him so that his sheathed erection pressed against my opening. Leaning back on one elbow he gripped himself in his other hand and rubbed the head slowly back and forth along my labia, making my whole body tremble and ache with yearning.

His breathing became laboured as I leaned forwards and began to press down and ease onto him, slowly, a centimetre at a time, holding my weight in my thighs and maintaining a gentle rocking motion with my hips. He stared intently at my face – his jaw clenched and his brow furrowed with concentration as he lightly skimmed my clitoris with the pad of his thumb, creating a warm, fluttering sensation inside me, and helping me to relax. It was uncomfortable as he began to stretch me open; my body gradually accommodating him, little by little, and yet I revelled in the intimacy of the moment; the intense ardour in his eyes. I wanted more, and patience had never been a virtue of mine. With one long exhale I sat up, letting myself sink right down onto him, taking the rest of him inside me in a sudden, sharp rush so that we were skin to skin in his lap.

'Oh fuck,' he breathed, collapsing back onto both elbows and squeezing his eyes tight shut as he fought to maintain control. 'Are you OK?' he said, re-opening them and pinning me with a fresh look of determination.

Grinning at him I nodded and the tension in his expression softened slightly with relief. I felt victorious sat there astride him, part of his body encased in mine, and as I ran my hands over the tanned muscles of his abdomen and circled his navel with my thumb, the pain ebbed away to be replaced with a satisfying fullness; a gratifying ache and an urge to move. Experimentally I circled my hips, feeling him there inside me; solid and pulsating, and he collapsed flat onto his back with another groan.

Leaning forwards I pressed a kiss to his lips. He tasted unusual though not unpleasant, and I realised it must be myself I was tasting. Bracing my hands on his warm, downy chest, I slowly lifted myself up along his length and then pushed down, letting him fill me again; causing a delicious ripple of pleasure to spread out through my core.

'Jesus, Mel, you have no idea how amazing you feel...'

Reassured, and confident that the painful part was over, I started to move on him with a steady rhythm. Watching as Liam closed his eyes, gritted his teeth and clenched his fists, only turned me on more. Being able to ride him like that; affect him so much; excite and pleasure him with my own body, was intensely liberating and as I gazed down at him I could feel another climax rising up inside me.

As I got close I held onto his forearms, viciously digging my fingernails into his skin, and this time he came with me – his large hands gripping my hips, his face contorting and his body bucking deep inside mine as he groaned my name.

Chapter Thirty-seven

There was blood on the condom afterwards; proof, as if I needed it, that I had deflowered an angel. And yet, weirdly, it felt more like *she* had taken *me*. I'd never experienced sex like it. The woman could turn me on with a look, so seeing her naked and taking possession of me like that... it had required a monumental amount of effort and concentration to hold back from coming too soon. But by God, Mel was worth it.

She stared as I removed the condom, tied a knot in it and set it aside, and I wondered what she was thinking.

'I didn't hurt you too much did I?'

She shook her head and settled down close beside me, tucked into my sweaty armpit, one arm and one leg thrown casually, but possessively, across my body. Together we lay in silence, looking up at the pale patch of sky bordered by skeleton trees, listening to a blackbird singing. The sun had moved further over to the west out of view and the air was cooling, but Mel was warm against my side. Stroking her hair with one hand, I lightly circled her right nipple with the other. I'd never felt so content.

After half an hour or so her skin began to goose-pimple and I knew it was time to get dressed and go back to work. Our clothes were slightly damp from where we had abandoned them on the mossy floor as we gathered and pulled them on, one by one. Despite the haze of post-coital bliss, or perhaps because of it, I had a keen urge to be honest with Mel. Her gift of virginity had created a new level of intimacy between us, and I wanted her to be able to trust me in return. I didn't want there to be any secrets between us.

'The other day, when you asked me why I don't drink…'

Mel stilled and looked up at me, her wide eyes fixed on mine.

'I didn't tell you the whole truth.'

She didn't move a muscle, not even to blink, as she waited for me to continue with my confession.

'Alcohol makes me aggressive.'

Her brows lifted in surprise.

'Lester drinks, and it doesn't seem to make him angry or anything, but I… I turn into a monster. It had the same effect on my mum; she was a violent drunk. She hid it well, so you couldn't always tell, and my dad bore the brunt of her wrath more than Lester and me, but… it wasn't good. I don't want to be like that; I don't want to be the way she was, so I try to avoid it altogether – alcohol I mean…'

Retrieving her phone from her coat pocket Mel tapped out a one word question: Was?

'She died of a heart attack when I was nine.' My voice broke at the end of my sentence, betraying the raw emotion I kept locked down inside. This was why I never talked about my mother.

Taking my hand Mel encouraged me to sit down by patting the rock we'd made love on. As soon as I was seated she made herself comfortable in my lap, and I cradled her in my arms, pressing my face into her hair and

192

fortifying myself with the reassuring feel of her. Drink corrupted my mother, there was no denying that; it made her mean, volatile and easy to hate. But on the rare occasions she was sober, she was someone else; someone calm and kind. On those days she was my mum and I loved her. Reconciling my feelings for her was always difficult, but losing her, especially at such a young age, was even harder. Part of me would never get over it. Would she have approved of Mel? I liked to think so. I imagined Mum might have admired her inner strength and determination.

The memory of how turned on I was when Mel slapped me reared up unexpectedly in my mind, and I quickly pushed the unwelcome thought away. Retrieving her phone, Mel tapped out a message.

I can't imagine you hurting anyone.

I swallowed heavily, glad that she couldn't see the guilt that was no-doubt written on face. But I'd started this, and I wanted her to know everything. 'When I was at University I almost killed someone. I didn't know him very well, he attended the same lectures as me but... anyway, we were at the pub one night and we'd both had a lot to drink and we got into a stupid argument about nothing... but I got really riled up. He threw the first punch but once I started hitting him back, I couldn't seem to stop. They had to drag me off him. It took five of them. He was taken to hospital with facial injuries and a severe concussion and I was cautioned by the police. I don't know why he didn't press charges; he should have; it was a complete over-reaction and I deserved to be punished.'

So you stopped drinking?

'Yes, and I haven't hit anyone since. Not even my brother, even though he deserves it sometimes.'

Raising my hand to her mouth she tenderly kissed my knuckles; as if offering her acceptance or a silent blessing.

I was glad to have confided in her; getting everything off my chest felt cleansing, healing in some way. And, feeling closer to Mel than ever before, I couldn't resist asking her the one question I'd held in check for months: 'Will you tell me how you lost your voice?'

She went rigid with tension in my arms and immediately I wished I could take the words back. But after a brief hesitation she typed out a response and showed me the screen:

`I think I stopped talking when my mother died. I was 6.`

'God, Mel... I'm so sorry.' My heart swelled with grief as I pictured her as a small child. Losing a parent was tough enough at nine, but at six it must have been near impossible to make sense of.

She shrugged and I tightened my arms around her and kissed her forehead.

'Do you remember it?'

`No. I don't remember her at all, but I think I have bad dreams about her.`

'I'm so sorry.'

She looked up at me, but there were no tears in her eyes. Softly I kissed her on the lips.

'So...' I was keen to know more, but afraid of upsetting her, yet she raised her eyebrows; silently encouraging me to go on. 'Your muteness is psychological rather than physical?'

Yes, but it feels physical to me.

I recalled how she hadn't called for help when she was drowning, or spoken when delirious with fever, or cried out when she came, and I realised her trauma must be deeply ingrained.

'Didn't your dad take you to see someone – get you treatment; therapy of some kind?'

He thought I'd grow out of it and when I didn't, I refused treatment.

I raised my eyes from the small screen in surprise. 'But why? Don't you want to be able to talk?'

She shook her head.

'Why not? Isn't it frustrating not being able to speak your mind? Don't you sometimes want to scream and shout and sing...?'

Abruptly she hopped off my lap and I knew I'd said too much.

'I'm sorry, I'm just trying to understand...'

Without a backward glance she stalked out of the grotto with her arms crossed angrily across her chest.

'Don't go, Mel...'

As she stormed away from me, yet again, I mentally chided myself for being insensitive. Should I respect her right to walk away and give her space, or should I chase after her this time? Her body language implied I should keep my distance, so I let her go with a sigh.

The woman was obstinate, proud, unpredictable and infuriating, and sometimes she wielded her silence as a weapon, or more accurately, a shield to hide behind. But that was almost certainly down to her unusual upbringing – that and the fact that she'd been living in isolation all her life, instead of receiving the help and support she needed. Sinclair had a lot to answer for. Single parent or not, in my eyes he had failed his daughter. Given the circumstances it was a miracle that Mel was as well-rounded, passionate and funny as she was. And despite, or maybe *because* of her eccentricities, I loved her.

*

I was halfway through a Chinese take-away when the doorbell rang. Back when Cally was living with me I cooked every day, but lately it had lost its appeal; my culinary efforts seemed excessive when there was only myself to feed. And after a long day at work – involving alfresco sex with my client's virginal daughter; confiding my darkest secrets; upsetting her, and then finally admitting to myself that I'd fallen in love with her – it seemed sensible to simply order in.

'Bridget?'

'Surprise! Sorry to turn up like this, but I'm back. I happened to be in Wildham, and I wanted to apologise in person for how busy I've been…' She kissed me on the cheek and patted my arm as I automatically stood back to let her in.

'You don't have to apologise…'

Her hips swaying and a bottle of wine clutched in one hand, she walked through to the kitchen. 'Oh I've interrupted your dinner, how rude of me!' Eyeing the food cartons on the counter she turned on her heel. 'Do you want me to go? We could always catch up another time…?'

'No, it's fine, I… I need to talk to you actually.'

196

She grinned at me from across the room. 'Great, do you mind if I open this bottle and pour myself a drink while you finish eating?'

'No, I...'

My words were drowned out as she rummaged in my cutlery draw in search of a corkscrew. 'Would you like some? I know you don't usually drink but this looks like a particularly good Spanish Rioja – it was a gift from Marguerite...'

'No, I won't, thanks.'

'Sit down! Don't let me stop you – your food will get cold.' Moving over to the table I looked at the remaining food congealing on my plate, but I'd lost my appetite.

'I've finished actually – I might save the rest for tomorrow.'

While I set about transferring the leftovers to the fridge and pouring myself a glass of water, Bridget settled on the sofa with her wine and launched into tales of her research trips abroad. Her glass was almost empty by the time I'd summoned enough courage to say what I needed to.

'I can't see you anymore, I'm sorry.' The joy faded from her features and I rushed to fill the awkward silence. 'It's not you – you're lovely, really, and it's not because you've been away or anything – in fact I'd like to stay friends if that's possible, but, well... I've met someone else.' Her eyebrows rose as she stared at me. 'It may turn out to be nothing, but it wouldn't be fair to keep seeing you if...' I trailed off, unsure how to finish my sentence without sounding offensive. 'I'm sorry,' I added again, wishing the armchair I was sat in would swallow me whole.

Bridget licked her lips and leaned forwards, displaying a generous V of cleavage as she carefully set down her glass. Clearing her throat she returned her eyes to mine while I waited, nervously, for her to speak.

Chapter Thirty-eight

Liam wanted me to speak! I'd been comfortably mute since I was six years old but now he's decided I should want to talk – just like everybody else. Why had I expected him to be any different? Why should he understand when no-one else ever had? Why couldn't he accept me the way I was? Why did he have to go and ruin everything just when things were getting interesting? Stupid man.

I'd spent the whole morning trying to proofread a debut author's novel. It was a period romance, not my sort of thing at all, and littered with spelling and punctuation errors, grammar mistakes and awkward sentences, many of which, in my professional opinion, should have been caught and corrected at the editing stage. The ending was rubbish too – the heroine was whisked away to a faraway country by the hero and she was pathetically grateful, even though she had a perfectly good home already. Unfortunately it was not my job to suggest plot changes; I'd been told off for that before.

Liam spent the day working somewhere in the grounds and I deliberately stayed away to punish him; for suggesting I should want to use my voice; for wanting to change me; for letting me down. But even though he was out of sight, I was distracted by thoughts of him. If I was really honest with myself, it wasn't what he'd said that had upset me, it was realising how much I'd fallen for him.

He made me happy. He was warm and kind and he was my only friend, and now we'd had amazing sex. Tantalising flashbacks of his naked form, his electric touch and the way he felt inside me, tormented me relentlessly. Now that he'd opened up my mind (and body) to pleasurable sexual possibilities, there were a hundred different dirty things I wanted to try out with him. And I'd tried to keep my emotions out of it, I really had, but it had been far more incredible and meaningful than I'd been expecting; connecting with another human being on a physical level like that.

The terrifying truth was, I'd fallen in love with the man. If he now decided he no longer wanted to hang out with a strange, stroppy, stubborn mute... what would I do? How could I go back to my dreary black and white existence when being with Liam Hunt was vivid Technicolor?

I spent the afternoon whiling away the time, listening to Paloma Faith's 'Only Love Can Hurt Like This' on repeat, and irritably re-painting my fingernails three times over.

Eventually the distant but familiar snarl of Liam's van starting up roused me from my wallowing, and a glance at my watch confirmed it was five-thirty. He always left promptly on Tuesdays to get to rugby training. But with his departure imminent I suddenly regretted avoiding him all day. Racing downstairs I flung open the front door, but I was too late and he was gone.

Cross with myself I slumped down to the tiled hall floor. I was pushing him away because I was scared he would leave. Even I could see that was bananas. So what should I do about it?

Tonight Liam would be hanging out with his friends again; drinking in that pub with that pretty redhead who, instead of avoiding him and giving him the silent treatment, would flirt with him like a normal person.

Bitch. Was it her he really wanted? Was I just going to sit back and let her have him?

Forty-five minutes later, dressed all in black, I'd wolfed down a cheese sandwich and cycled out the front gates, on my way to Wildham rugby training ground. The sun had set and the night was quickly shrouding everything in shadows, but I was used to cycling around town in the dead of night, and grateful for the camouflage.

By the time I reached the club I was warm from frantic pedalling, except for my hands and face which were frozen stiff. The pitch smelled damp and earthy and was floodlit in an eerie white light, which cast the surrounding world into even denser shade. But there were few spectators around. One or two observed from the warm comfort of their cars while a couple of men in tracksuits and padded jackets lurked near the door to a squat, single-storey building. There was no sign of the redhead, and my arrival went unnoticed.

On the windowless side of the clubhouse I stood in the shadows astride my bike, quietly picking at the pebble-dashed wall, while on the field the coach barked instructions. The team practised endless drills in varying permutations – passing the ball back and forth; running in and out between lines of cones on their tiptoes, and tackling each other whilst wearing cushions of padding.

Balls, cones and cushions aside, the imposing size and speed of the men coupled with the powerfully synchronised lines they moved in, made them seem more like an invading army rather than simply players in a game. But then maybe war was a game of sorts; a senseless game with devastating consequences. Rugby was infinitely preferable.

Liam was easy to spot when standing, because he was taller than everyone else, and I enjoyed watching him move; practising rugby with the same focus, skill and confidence that he applied to everything else he did. But I grew chilly just standing there and was relieved when they finished for the night.

As they piled into the clubhouse I retreated and cycled on ahead to The White Bear, relishing the pump of blood in my muscles. It was only as I drew up to the cold, dark garden, that it dawned on me that Liam and his friends would be seating themselves *inside* the pub, where I would not be able to observe them.

Fiddlesticks. I just wanted to check if there was anything going on between Liam and that redhead. I was new to this whole love and relationships thing, and I'd already given Liam my body. If I was going to give him my heart, I needed to know that he felt the same; that he was different with me than with other women; that I could trust him. Was I brave enough to go in there and hide somewhere at the back? What was the alternative? Freeze to death lurking outside? Give up and go home?

I was no quitter.

The pub wasn't as crammed full of bodies as I'd anticipated but it contained enough tables, chairs, pillars, nooks and corners to create a labyrinthine effect. Once inside I feared I'd never find my way out again, but the welcoming warmth and the reassuring scent of furniture wax was enough to draw me in. I could feel heads turning and eyes following me as I walked straight up to the bar and smiled widely at the woman serving, hoping to mask my discomfort.

'Hello there, what can I get you?'

I pointed at the nearest beer tap, still smiling and grateful that there was enough background music and chatter to obscure my silence.

'A pint of Fosters?' she said, frowning slightly, and I nodded, beaming at her to make up for my complete absence of Ps and Qs.

She fetched a clean glass and pulled my pint without further comment and I started to relax until I realised I'd forgotten to retrieve my purse from its hiding place. Smiling awkwardly at the old guy sitting at the bar next to me, I bent down and unzipped my right, knee-high boot. The black leather peeled back like a banana skin, revealing the purse stuck to my naked calf before I quickly zipped it up again. As I straightened up my face burned but the man didn't say anything, and the barmaid simply told me the price as she set my pint before me. It was almost three times the cost I was expecting, compared to supermarket lager, but I paid it without hesitation and hurried over to a small table tucked in a shadowy corner.

My drink had spilled down my arm but I tried not to think about it as I settled myself in a seat with my back to the wall. I'd taken several gulps of the cold fizzy liquid to calm my nerves, before discovering I didn't like lager at all. No wonder Gregory never drank it. Releasing a few furtive burps under my breath, I finally lifted my eyes and risked a glance at my surroundings. To my great surprise and relief nobody was looking in my direction.

Bar and beer aside, the interior of the pub wasn't so bad. It had an eighteenth century feel about it with an abundance of varnished wooden surfaces, a large open fireplace, and cushioned velvet upholstery. My heart rate had almost returned to normal by the time Liam and his friends started piling in through the door. They were jovial and noisy and greeted by several of the regulars before finally settling themselves and their drinks around a cluster of tables clearly marked 'reserved'.

Keeping my head down I surreptitiously peeked at them over my pint, pleased to see Liam seat himself between two other men and not facing in my direction. Irritatingly the redhead, whose name I'd overheard was Poppy, had positioned herself directly in front of my man, where they could easily make conversation. What kind of name was Poppy anyway?

By now I was starting to put names to the others, too: Liam's older brother, Lester, was not as tall but shared the same prominent brow and still had a tell-tale limp from his accident in the summer; and I figured that the attractive pregnant brunette with him must be Liam's Irish sister-in-law, Maire. The younger, dark-haired, good-looking guy that Liam talked to the most was presumably his best mate James, but try as I might I couldn't recall the name of his slightly reserved but leggy girlfriend.

On the rare occasions when Liam spoke to Poppy or any of the other females in the group, I studied his profile intently, but could detect no obvious difference in the way he interacted with them, other than that he was marginally more polite. Several of the men frequently told jokes with filthy punchlines, which made me smile and made the other women roll their eyes.

I deliberately sipped my drink slowly to make it last and to avoid a repeat trip to the bar – it tasted even worse warm – but soon the bottom of my glass was in sight. The rugby crew had sunk several rounds in the same period of time, but were showing no signs of leaving, and I wasn't sure how long I could stay unnoticed without at least a drink for cover. I was considering slipping out the back door, retrieving my bike and heading home, when a vibration in my left boot alerted me to a text message. Liam was the only person in the world who had my number.

Across the room he was talking to James, but I could see he had his mobile in his hand beneath the edge of the table. Warmth spread through me at the idea that he was thinking of me. Reaching down I unzipped my boot, retrieved my phone and clicked open the message:

Would you like to join us? X

My head shot up and I stared at him but he wasn't looking in my direction. Did he know I was here? Had he known all along? Of course he had – how humiliating.

Glancing back at the screen I re-read Liam's message, my fingers tingling with adrenalin. He'd added a kiss – he'd never done that before – it was a tiny thing but it made my heart beat faster in my chest. And he'd covertly texted me. He could have just shouted my name across the

pub; exposing me as a freak on first sight, but he hadn't;
he wasn't; he was giving me a choice; an out.

And I was grateful for that.

But was I ready to meet all his friends?

Chapter Thirty-nine

My whole body ached with the urge to go to her. It no longer mattered if Melody Sinclair was wrong for me – I'd fallen under her spell. The crazy beautiful woman had seduced me, gifted me her virginity and then denied me her company for a solid twenty-four hours. It was unbearable. Every little thing made me think of her; from the piece of slate Adam's burger was served on – it was the exact colour of her eyes when she was angry – to the butterfly pendant Kat wore – the shape of her birthmark. Mel was all I could think about. The hold she had over me was so strong that staying away from her, especially when she was so near, was almost painful.

After last night's confession, Bridget had let me off lightly. She didn't get angry, upset, stroppy or difficult; she didn't even push me for a more detailed explanation. It was a testament to her sensible and forgiving personality that she calmly departed with a polite wish to remain friends, taking the rest of the wine with her. Her generous understanding was more than I deserved, and a huge relief. And now I was completely free to pursue Melody.

But if Mel had wanted me to go to her, she wouldn't be hiding in the corner of the pub – dressed all in black, complete with boots and dark make-up – and spying on me from afar, would she? Or would she? Really I had no idea – the woman was a complete mystery. I didn't want to frighten her away, so I'd sent her a text inviting her to join us, and now I was on tenterhooks awaiting her reply...

No. My heart sank.

Can I ask why?

I don't want to embarrass you.

You won't embarrass me.

They'll think I'm weird for following you here and not speaking and you'll feel ashamed of me. I'd rather leave.

Without further consideration I pushed back my chair and strode over to where she sat. She looked startled and rose to her feet as I closed the gap between us.

'I could *never* be ashamed of you,' I hissed, cupping her face in my hands. The words came out more forcefully than I'd intended, but I'd reached my limit. I was done trying to resist her. Leaning down I kissed her on the mouth and after only a second's hesitation she returned my kiss with all the passion she tried so hard to hide; her body pressing into mine and her arms binding possessively around my waist. She bit my lip, hard enough to draw blood, and the sting of pain only made me want her more.

But as consumed by her as I was, I was also aware of a curious audience behind me.

'C'mon let's get out of here,' I said, wrapping one arm firmly round her shoulders, turning and steering her swiftly across the room. 'Everybody, this is Melody. Mel, this is everybody,' I said, pocketing my phone, grabbing my jacket and ignoring all the stunned faces around the table. 'Goodnight all.' With that I guided a shocked Mel straight out the front door before anyone could express a word.

The night air was crisp and refreshing after the stuffy warmth of the pub. Pausing on the pavement I helped Mel into my jacket. It swamped her completely and hung down past her knees, but she slipped her phone into a pocket and gazed up at me with bright eyes and an amused smile hovering on her lips.

'See – no-one said anything at all,' I said lightly.

Mel's grin broadened and she reached up on the tips of her toes to kiss me again. Now that we were alone, our kiss deepened, our tongues wrestling with mutual impatience for more. I groaned, pausing to catch my breath. In my back pocket my mobile was vibrating with incoming, no-doubt-nosey texts from my mates, but I ignored it.

'I don't suppose you want to come back to mine? It's nearer than yours…'

She nodded, but then tried to lead me into the undergrowth beneath the trees.

'Where are you going…?'

Understanding came when she wheeled her antique-looking bicycle out of the bushes and into the light of a street-lamp.

'You cycled here?'

She nodded and looked up at me expectantly.

'Do you have a helmet? You should really wear a helmet – I'll have to get you one if you're riding around on the roads…'

She shrugged.

'Right.' Swinging one leg over the frame I settled myself on the cracked leather saddle. It squeaked under my weight but thankfully didn't buckle. The bike didn't have any extra gears, but the tyres were plump with air and the brakes appeared to work when I squeezed them. There was no luggage rack over the rear wheel but there was a large wicker basket mounted on the handlebars which, when jiggled, seemed sturdy enough to take her weight. 'Hop on then,' I said, patting the basket.

With her arms crossed, lips pursed and one eyebrow raised, she looked at me, unimpressed.

'What? Don't you trust me? My house isn't far, I promise.'

Rolling her eyes she swung one booted leg across the back wheel behind me, braced her hands on my shoulders and then stepped up to perch on the pegs which protruded from either side of the rear axle.

I chuckled. 'Or that might be more comfortable…'

We wobbled a little as I set off, Mel's fingertips biting into my shoulders – it had been a while since I'd ridden a bike – but once I'd got my balance we were flying; the wind stinging my face and the girl I loved, warm at my back.

We reached my front door in a matter of minutes and I was quick to get us inside. Darting around the lounge I switched on the electric fire, drew the curtains, tidied away the local papers, straightened the cushions and moved a dirty mug into the kitchen. I hadn't been expecting company and I was anxious to make a good impression.

Casting off my jacket she gazed around the room and then stepped over to warm her hands in front of the artificial fire. The dark dress, heavy black eye-liner and purple nail-polish she wore made her skin, hair and eyes seem paler than usual, and for all her small stature, Mel made a striking, seductive, almost unreal impression on my ordinary little living room.

Clearing my throat I moved closer to her and she turned towards me.

'Can I get you a dr—'

She pounced; her hands cold and her kisses searing. Her tongue sought out mine and her fingers wormed beneath my shirt and jumper, her short nails clawing at my back. We only stopped kissing long enough to tear off our clothes, neither of us wanting to break physical contact for any longer than was strictly necessary.

Collapsing onto the rug, I took her down with me and she insisted, in her own silent and persistent way, on having me right there and then. Her skin was flushed, her nipples erect, and she was gloriously wet between her thighs. As she urged me flat on my back and straddled my lap, I only just managed to get a condom on. Holding my eyes with hers she positioned her body at the perfect angle to take me, and this time I pushed up inside her with relative ease; the tight heat of her making me moan. Lying beneath her, at her mercy, I matched her thrust for thrust as she rode me, and as she pinched my nipples hard enough to leave bruises, we both came fast and hard; bathed in sweat, gasping with exertion and trembling with sweet, sweet release.

Afterwards she flopped down onto her back beside me and I rested my head between her soft, bare breasts, listening to her heartbeat while she idly stroked her fingers through my hair. As much as I'd enjoyed losing myself in the moment, I now wished I'd been able to last longer, go slower and make love to Mel the way she deserved to be made love to.

'I love you,' I confessed.

Her fingers stilled, her breathing halted and her heart-rate stuttered in her chest, but there was no taking it back now, so I ploughed on.

'That's what I should have said yesterday – that regardless of whether you ever find your voice or not, I love you, Mel.'

After a few minutes, when she still hadn't moved, I summoned up enough courage to lift my head and look at her face. Smiling tightly she looked away and I silently cursed myself for being a reckless fool.

'Coffee?' I said.

Chapter Forty

His house was tiny – a dolls-house – especially with him taking up all the space in it. The ceilings were low, the living room was the size of my bathroom, and his kitchen was little more than a cupboard. It smelled faintly of Chinese food. I was conscious of his neighbours living just the other side of the walls, as if in the next room, when in fact they were in a separate dwelling. It was a peculiar concept to get my head around.

As Liam filled the kettle I pointed quizzically at the small washing machine tucked between the sink and a tiny refrigerator.

'What? There's nowhere else for it to go – we don't all have laundry rooms...'

There was amusement in his eyes as he explained, and no trace of reproach in his tone, but it occurred to me that it might be insensitive to point out all the differences between his house and my own. It didn't change how I felt about him. Presumably most of the population of Great Britain lived like this; it was my situation that was abnormal, not his. Even so, it seemed unfair that a man as tremendous as Liam was constantly forced to bow, stoop, and sidle in the place he called home.

Leaving Liam to make drinks I drifted back into the only other downstairs room. The weirdest thing, once I'd gotten over the compact scale of the place, was how plain everything was. It wasn't so much the absence of clutter – collecting and displaying precious artworks and ornaments was a particular obsession of Cornelia's, one that Gregory had avidly preserved and continued in her memory – I hadn't expected Liam to share the same compulsion. No, it was the overall mutedness of the interior décor which surprised me – cream walls; boxy furniture; beige synthetic furnishings... no real colour, or pattern or personality. Was this house decorated to his taste or someone else's? An ex-girlfriend perhaps...? Above the fireplace was an empty picture hook and I stared at it as if it might provide some sort of clue. Then my eyes landed on a wine glass by the mantelpiece. There was a trace of dark liquid left inside and a smudge of pink lipstick at the rim; tiny, minor, details that clawed painfully at my eyes as I turned away.

The plain décor extended up a narrow flight of stairs and into a clean, compact bathroom. I had a thorough nose through the cupboard below the sink and the medicine cabinet behind the mirror, but was relieved to find a complete absence of feminine products. I took my time touching his things – weighing his heavy electric razor in my hand; sniffing his deodorant, shower gel, shampoo and aftershave; committing it all to memory. I wanted to know him; be a part of him; keep him for myself. On impulse I put his toothbrush in my mouth; partly to taste him and partly to leave a trace of myself behind.

Across the carpeted landing the bedroom door was temptingly open and I slipped inside and switched on the light, aware that downstairs the kettle had already boiled. The large bed was neatly made, but I was relieved to see an unruly stack of gardening books piled on one bedside table and a colourful jumble of potted plants competing for light and space on the window sill – reassuring evidence of the Liam Hunt I knew.

The wardrobe door creaked traitorously as I inspected the interior, but only Liam's clothes hung inside, alongside dozens of empty hangers. Pressing a sleeve to my cheek, I inhaled the comforting scent of his washing powder as my gaze fell on a large cardboard box half hidden in the bottom.

'Mel? You OK?' Liam called up the stairs.

Realising I was almost out of time, I quickly lifted the box flaps and scanned the contents. There were books, CDs, a collection of feminine hair things, a mug bearing the name 'Cally' and a small teddy bear; none of which I had time to properly investigate, because I could hear Liam starting up the staircase. What really captured my attention was a framed black and white photograph showing Liam with his arm around his ex.

Cally was dressed plainly; the sort of woman who was beautiful without having to wear flashy clothes or draw attention to herself. Tall, dark and elegant, she was everything I was not. And they looked happy in the picture; young, relaxed, content. Why had she left him?

Jealousy churning in my stomach I quickly closed the box, slammed the wardrobe shut and turned to face the bedroom door just as Liam came into view. Wearing only a pair of boxers and a smile, he had to turn his large bare shoulders sideways to duck inside the room. His hair was still ruffled from my fingers and I was immediately conscious of the bed between us; a renewed throb of desire pulsing between my thighs.

'Hey. I just wanted to check you're alright,' he said. 'Look around as much as you like – I've got nothing to hide…'

He was always so understanding; so forgiving; too good to be true, and here I was snooping through his things. What was I searching for? An excuse to ruin things between us? So what if he chatted to women in the pub? So what if he'd lived with a woman before? He clearly didn't anymore. And it was me, Melody Sinclair, standing here in his bedroom now, wearing nothing but his shirt.

And he'd just said he loved me…

But that was only the sex talking, wasn't it? The heat of the moment? I was pretty sure *I* loved *him*, but could he really feel the same way? About me of all people? It seemed unlikely.

'I've made coffee; are you ready to come downstairs, or… I mean, I could bring it up…?'

I shook my head and moved towards the door and he carefully, politely stepped aside to let me pass; as if we hadn't just fornicated like animals on his living room floor.

He followed me back downstairs and when I perched on the sofa he brought me a plain, white mug full of steaming decaffeinated coffee. It was black and no doubt full of sugar, exactly the way I liked it.

'Is everything OK?' he asked, taking the nearby armchair.

I nodded, averting my eyes from the wine glass I was trying to ignore, and burned my tongue as I took a large gulp of coffee. It felt weird between us all of a sudden and

I knew that was my fault. Back at the pub Liam had kissed me right in front of his friends and even introduced me to them, albeit briefly. He wasn't ashamed of me, and that concept alone was amazing, but love... what did I even know about love?

Without looking I could sense Liam scrutinising me. Retrieving my phone from his jacket pocket he passed it to me. 'Talk to me, please.'

Setting aside my coffee I looked down at the phone in my hand and then back at him, unsure what to say.

'I meant what I said before – about loving you – and I don't expect you to feel the same way, but I *do* need to know if I've freaked you out, or scared you off or anything... you look so confused,' he added softly, lifting his warm fingers to the side of my face and smoothing back my hair.

I tapped out a question and showed it to him: Isn't it just sex?

His face paled as he read my words, the light dying in his eyes as he looked back at me. It occurred to me that I might have wounded his pride with my careless use of the word 'just' so I tagged on a few extra words for emphasis: Really great sex.

He smiled at that, but not properly; the light didn't return to his face.

'Not to me,' he spoke so quietly that I almost missed it. He cleared his throat. 'It's more than really great sex to me, Mel – I care about you; I like being with you; I—'

Standing up, more abruptly than I intended, I cut him off and almost tripped over the coffee table as I jerkily picked up the offending wine glass to show him. His expression quickly morphed from surprise to comprehension to worry as he registered the evidence trembling in my hand.

'Oh God, Mel, that's nothing.' Standing, he took it from me and set it aside. 'Bridget dropped by unexpectedly yesterday for a drink, and I told her I couldn't see her anymore – that I was seeing you. She's the woman I went on a couple of dates with ages ago, but nothing ever happened between us, I swear. It was nothing like you and I...' The anxiety in his voice was obvious, but his eyes were earnest and sincere. 'You do believe me, don't you? I wasn't keeping it from you deliberately; to be honest I'd forgotten all about her visit...'

And the redhead?

He stared at the screen, and then at me, and then back again, mouth opening and closing, utterly confused.

Impatiently rolling my eyes I elaborated: From the pub.

The perplexed expression on his face would be comical if I wasn't so concerned about what his reply was going to be. 'Do you mean Poppy? Adam's sister...?'

I nodded, watching him closely for tell-tale signs. Signs of what, I wasn't quite sure.

'Why...?' The greatest actor on Earth couldn't have bettered the pure incredulity on Liam's face at that moment. It was immensely reassuring and I realised that I was being unfair to him. 'Poppy's an events planner; very friendly and bubbly; but she's like a little sister to me; to all of us. I don't... there's nothing...'

OK.

He still looked concerned. 'And I know you found some of Cally's stuff upstairs but things have been over between us for months. She's moved on, I've moved on...' He held my gaze so openly that it was hard to doubt him. 'There's only you, Mel...'

Regardless of what I'd read about most men only caring about one thing, and despite my own fears and reservations, I believed this man; I trusted him.

Liam Hunt loved me.

At this realisation an excited kind of joy surged up in my chest making my fingers shake as I typed: I lobve you too.

He laughed, as much with surprise and relief as at my typo. 'You do?'

Nodding I stretched up and kissed him, and he gazed at me, still disbelieving.

'Really...?'

I nodded again.

'You're not just saying that to make me feel better?'

Can I be your girlfriend?

He laughed again; a deeper chuckle rumbling outwards through his chest as he took my head in his rough palms.

'Yes – absolutely – nothing would make me happier.' He pressed his mouth to mine and I wrapped my arms around his big warm body, drawing him closer to me.

'I want to make love to you,' he muttered against my lips.

Hesitating, I shook my head and let go of him.

'What's wrong?' he said, searching my face as I returned my attention to my phone.

Not here.

'No, OK, let's go upstairs, it will be far more comfortable…'

He took my hand, but again I shook my head. As much as I wanted to be with him, and as glad as I was that Bridget and Poppy were not an issue, that bed upstairs was still his and Cally's. I accepted that whatever they'd had was over, but her name still echoed in my ears, her perfect image lingered in my mind, and her spirit still lurked up there in the wardrobe. If I was going to completely exorcise that particular ghost I needed to know the full story of their relationship. But not right now; not tonight; I didn't think I could take it. All of this love and potential happiness between Liam and me was so strange and new and fragile, and I didn't want to spoil it.

It's late and I'm tired, I'm going to go home.

'Oh. OK… I'll drive you home in the van – we can put your bike in the back.' He looked disappointed, and I gave him my most reassuring smile. 'I haven't said or done anything to upset you have I?'

I shook my head and kissed him again for good measure.

'I guess we'd better get dressed then.'

Chapter Forty-one

I was kicked awake by a small foot jabbing at the back of my knees, and when I failed to respond quickly enough, the foot was joined by a tiny fist prodding between my shoulder blades. Rolling over I squinted at Mel and smiled.

'Morning, beautiful.'

She pressed a warning finger to her lips and scowled. So far, waking up beside the girl of my dreams was not as idyllic as I'd imagined. Shoving her *Swatch* watch under my nose she tapped at it impatiently. It was gone 9 a.m. but I was exhausted. Mel hadn't wanted to stay over at my place last night, so I'd driven her home in the early hours of the morning and accidentally fallen asleep in her over-the-top four poster bed.

'Shit, is that really the time?'

This time she pressed a finger to my lips to silence me and held up a piece of paper between us. The message scrawled in black eye-liner read:

Mrs Daly's here, you must get out before she realises you're in the house.

'Mrs Daly?'

She rolled her eyes impatiently and scribbled: *Housekeeper.*

'Oh right, OK.' Propping myself up on one elbow I blinked at her. 'Can I steal a kiss first?'

Her whole face softened and she smiled and nodded as I leaned in and pressed my lips to hers. She had smudged

221

panda eyes, hair stuck to her cheek and stale breath, but she was soft, warm and beguiling and I loved her and she loved me. As she pressed her near-naked body against mine, my morning wood begged for attention.

Pulling her head back she silently giggled, brushing her fingers over the stubble round my lips by way of explanation.

'Does it tickle?'

She nodded and I gently rubbed my cheek along her jaw and down her neck, luxuriating in her intoxicating scent as she writhed against me. As I found her breast through her thin nightshirt with my stubbled lips, she gasped and shuddered, goosebumps spreading out across her skin.

'Mmm,' I whispered around her nipple, 'I think I've just got time to make love to my girlfriend before I go…'

Grabbing my hair she yanked my head back, hard, so that I was looking at her face. Her cheeks were flushed with pleasure and her pupils dilated, but she had a steely look in her eye as she shook her head.

God she was sexy. Sighing I let her push me over to the edge of the bed where I sat up and pulled on my jeans, shirt, socks and jumper from the day before. If I couldn't have Mel this morning I'd settle for a shower, a shave, a clean set of clothes and breakfast, but it seemed all that was out of the question. Wrapped in her dressing gown, Mel jotted down clear instructions for leaving the house unseen and escaping into the grounds.

'I could do with going home first – half my tools are there and…'

Mel shook her head, adamantly, her eyes glaring. *She's seen your van – it will look suspicious if you go and come back again – you'll have to pretend you arrived early this morning*, she wrote.

'Well I kind of did…' I said, shrugging into my jacket and picking up my shoes.

She smiled, despite her worries, and I kissed her again before turning to leave.

I must have looked ridiculous; a man of my size tiptoeing about in socked feet, but I successfully made it to the far end of the house, out the front door and into the stables without drawing attention to myself. It was a cold morning and while the kettle was boiling I pulled my waders on over my jeans, to keep myself warm as much as to protect them. Thankfully I'd left a sweatshirt behind in the summer, so I swapped it for the collared shirt and jumper I was wearing, in order to look less conspicuous.

Why was Mel so nervous about the cleaner discovering our relationship anyway? It was none of her business, and the fact that she'd informed me when Mel was ill implied that she already knew at least something about us. That arse Sinclair would have to find out about us eventually. Maybe I should be trying harder to get him on side…

I was busy sanding the weathered timber walls of the boathouse when Mel came to find me later that afternoon. She crept up behind me and tried to push me into the lake, but wasn't physically strong enough and lost her balance, almost falling in herself. As we laughed she reached up to tenderly brush dry flakes of paint and dust from my hair and clothes, before realising that we might be seen from the house. With one hand she dragged me inside the boathouse out of view, where I pulled her against me and kissed her. She was wearing a thick, oversized, cream-coloured knitted jumper as a dress. It was cinched in at her waist by a shiny blue belt, with the cuffs rolled up to reveal her hands. Below the knitwear she wore an opaque pair of lacy white tights and a set of traditional Dutch wooden clogs on her feet. She looked like some sort of pixie, but no less sexy for all that.

'Hey beautiful, what's in the bag?'

Slipping a faded chintz carpet bag off her shoulder, she delved inside with one hand and presented me with a shrink-wrapped stack of sandwiches and a grin.

'Oh, you star, I'm starving, thank you.'

A small rowing boat took up most of the interior space in the shed, raised and mounted a foot off the ground in a sturdy metal frame. Stripping off my waders I climbed inside, and once I'd seated myself in the stern, Mel settled herself opposite, our knees gently touching. While I tucked into the sandwiches she talked to me via the screen on her mobile. She had questions about the rugby session she'd witnessed the day before, but really I think she was curious about my friends from the pub.

'James, Adam and I all went to school together – Lester and Maire too, but they were a couple of years above. James owns Southwood's Garden Centre, y'know; the one on the edge of town…?'

Mel shook her head.

'Well it's full of pretty plants; I think you'd like it there; I'll take you sometime.' Mel pulled a face. 'I think you'd like James's girlfriend, Kat, too.'

Why do you say that?

'Because she's kind and plain-speaking and she's not as loud and gregarious as Poppy.'

Doesn't mean she'd like me.

'Of course she would! What's not to like? All my friends will love you if you give them a chance.'

Melody looked distinctly unconvinced and uncomfortable, but before she could change the subject I plucked my phone out of my back pocket and clicked through to my messages.

'Look – ever since I introduced you in the pub yesterday I've been bombarded with excited texts from my friends – they all want to meet you properly…'

I kept eating and watched Mel intently as she clicked and scrolled through my inbox. Most of the messages were from Adam, Lester and James; vaguely rude, back-handed compliments like: "You sly dog!" and "Get back here you pussy, and let us meet her!" and "Are you ashamed of us or what?" and "No wonder you've been keeping Melody to yourself – she's way out of your league mate!". Poppy had texted: "I can't believe you've been seeing someone in secret! She's gorgeous! When can I meet her??" and Maire had said: "I'm so happy for you – the two of you look great together, you must come for dinner soon."

Once Mel had read them all, some of them twice, she passed my phone back to me and picked up her own.

Aren't they all friends with Cally?

'Yes… but we had a fairly amicable break up, so it's not like they have to choose sides or anything, and anyway Cally has been living in London – I don't think anyone's seen much of her for months.' While Mel tapped out something else, I balled up the cling-film, tossed it back in her bag and took a swig of orange juice from the carton she'd brought.

Were you together long?

'A few years. But when I look back on it now, it was more like a friendship than a romantic relationship – it was nothing like this – you and me. The way I feel about you is… huge; all-consuming; life-changing…'

Leaning forwards Mel kissed me, and I cradled her face in my hands and tried to kiss her back with all the truth of my feelings for her; I wanted her to understand that she was *it* for me; my one and only, and that no-one else could ever compare. By the time she withdrew she was flushed but smiling.

On the surface she seemed to be coping amazingly well with all my baggage, especially when you considered that relationships as a whole were so new to her. But I was afraid of pushing her too hard too soon, so I changed the subject.

'The weather forecast is set to be fair for the next week or so; cold but dry,' I said. 'I wanted to make the most of it so I've arranged for Olly to come and help me glaze the glasshouse on Monday – I just wanted to warn you…'

She shrugged and smiled.

'You sure you don't mind? I know you don't like him being around…'

Maybe he's not so bad - I don't know him.

'He's a walking, talking headache, is what he is, but I'll try not to let him get on your nerves too much.'

226

I'd been stroking her leg, almost unconsciously, but the unexpected discovery that her tights were in fact stockings was arousing. With my fingers I explored the smooth bare skin of her thighs and traced the lacy edge of her knickers with my thumb. Between her legs I could tell she was already aroused and she shivered with anticipation as she reached for my fly.

'We can't. Unless you have any more condoms on you…?' I said, hopefully.

She looked disappointed and shook her head.

'I meant to bring some, I'm sorry.'

I was uncomfortable inside my jeans and it was a relief when she continued to free me; her hand wrapped snugly around my shaft. But then she released me to tap out a message on her phone, leaving me exposed.

I want to watch you. She stared at me expectantly as I read the words.

'Watch me? You mean…?'

She nodded.

'You want to watch me… masturbate…?' Her request was surprising but as she made me say the words I throbbed in my hand.

As her burning gaze dropped to my lap I began to work my length slowly in my palm. I'd only ever jerked off in private before, and it seemed shameful to be doing it here, in this boathouse, in front of a lady. But the way Mel brazenly lusted after me and bossed me about with barely a word turned me on beyond all belief.

Her eyes never leaving my lap, she spread her legs wider and began to touch herself, making me groan. For someone so new to sex, Mel was an accomplished seductress. Sitting there in that boat, working myself in my fist, I watched, mesmerised, as she swiftly brought herself to a shuddering climax.

'Jesus, Mel, I want... I need...' I was incapable of finishing my sentence.

Still recovering, and breathing hard, she abruptly stood up over me, and yanked my head back by my hair. As she forced me to look at her, darts of pain shot straight from my scalp directly to my groin and I erupted in my hand with a groan, shooting semen all over her stockings. How did she know? This glorious, extraordinary woman – how did she know exactly what I wanted; what I *needed*, when I hadn't even known myself?

Loosening her grip, she perched herself delicately on my knee and pressed a tender kiss to my lips; as if, in her own quiet way, she hadn't just conquered me entirely.

It was several minutes before I recovered the power of speech. 'Sorry about your stockings,' I said at last.

Shrugging, she produced a wodge of paper serviettes from her bag and cleaned up her legs and my hand. Smiling impishly, she kissed me again and stood up.

'You're not going...?'

Shouldering her carpet bag she picked up her phone and I waited while she tapped out a reply.

I love you, but you have work to do - this boathouse won't sand itself.

Laughing I shoved my fingers into my hair, wincing slightly at the lingering burn in my scalp.

Did I hurt you?

'A little, but nothing I can't handle.'

She smiled, reaching out and tenderly smoothing down my hair with her fingers.

'Why do you do it?' I said, on impulse.

What? she mouthed.

'Deliberately hurt me like that.'

She studied my face for a moment, giving me just enough time to regret my question while she tapped out a reply: `Because you like it.`

The blunt truth of this statement was like a punch to the gut, flooding me with shame. 'And it doesn't bother you? That I like it?'

`Why should it?`

'Well... a shrink, a psychiatrist, might have something to say about it...' I tried to ignore the uneasiness in my stomach as she typed.

`So what? You're not sleeping with a shrink, you're sleeping with me, and I love who you are.`

Her acceptance was more than I could have hoped for and more than I deserved; I was pathetically grateful for it and kissed her hard. 'Thank you,' I whispered against her lips.

Smiling, she withdrew and returned her attention to her phone once more:

`You're welcome. Now get back to work.`

I laughed and shook my head as I read her parting words, and she smirked as she flounced out the door.

Chapter Forty-two

From the warmth and safety of the house I observed, my breath condensing on the windows, as Liam and Olly arrived to meet the delivery of new glass. The men worked together to carefully unload it from the truck before gingerly carrying each piece round to the walled garden, pane by pane.

Olly didn't stop talking the whole time.

It was only about five degrees outside. There had been a frost overnight, and although the sun was now shining on the green patchwork landscape, the light had a milky quality and was yet to thaw those parts of the grounds still in shade. The old me would simply have stayed indoors; tucked up in my warm room above the kitchen, especially with a relative stranger hanging around. But Liam had been gone all weekend, working on someone else's garden, and now my desire to be close to him was more powerful than my reluctance to face Olly.

A good part of my weekend had been spent in the grotto sketching the five naked statues – Pan and his harem – from various different angles, and thinking about my boyfriend. Since Liam had opened my eyes and awakened my body, the human obsession with sex – as illustrated by the Victorian sculptures – no longer seemed so ludicrous or so dirty. My mind was opening up to a whole new world of kinky experiences and possibilities .

And I loved him. I loved his kindness and his patience; I loved how big, strong and powerful he was, and how safe and protected I felt in his arms. But I also loved how willingly he handed me control. Turned out he liked a little pain with his pleasure and trusted me enough to let me see it. I imagined that not all men would be prepared to do the same.

I could have texted him over the weekend and begged him to come back and spend the night with me, but I was too proud; this was all too new to me, and Liam was too much of a gentleman to invite himself over. Damn him. Instead I'd visited the pawn shop to exchange more of my unwanted jewellery for cash, which I then took straight to the large and imposing supermarket on the main road. Thankfully they now had computerised, self-service checkouts – no speech or embarrassment required on my part – and I was now in possession of enough condoms to put a prostitute to shame. The next opportunity we had to be alone together, I would be ready. And until then I would simply be satisfied to spend time in my new boyfriend's company – I was not about to let one loquacious teenage boy stand in my way.

At midday I ventured into the kitchen to make tea and sandwiches for three. Ignoring Mrs Daly's mocking expression, I threw on a jacket and boots and carefully carried everything out on a large tray towards the walled garden.

Liam was up a ladder as I arrived, fitting a large pane of glass into the timber-framed roof with his large and capable gloved hands. Olly was stood below holding the base of the ladder steady; providing a stream of vocal support that Liam could probably do without.

'Yeah, that looks great from here – sweet – must be the right piece of the puzzle after all. If you need more clips, I've got them here. Do you think the next pane will be the same size? Shall I go find it...?' He started backing away.

'Just hold the ladder, Olly.'

'Oh yeah, right, sorry.' Abruptly Olly grabbed hold of the ladder again, making Liam wobble and then sigh.

It was Liam who sensed my presence first, but his glance of surprise alerted Olly, who immediately abandoned his hold on the ladder again. Studiously ignoring them both I concentrated on setting the heavy tray down on the end of a raised bed.

'Hello there,' Olly said, trotting towards me with a huge grin. 'What's this? Lunch...? For us...?'

In my peripheral vision Liam was descending the ladder, but I looked at Olly and nodded while he peeled his gloves off. He was a few inches taller than me, despite being three years younger, but even with all the bulky layers he was wearing, he nowhere near matched Liam's impressive size. Blue eyes sparkling with warmth from behind his floppy fringe, his huge grin was unnerving.

'It looks great, thanks.' Olly helped himself to a cherry tomato and popped it in his mouth. 'I didn't catch your name before...?' he added with his mouth full.

'Olly, this is Melody – Mel, meet Olly,' Liam said, calmly walking up behind Olly, slapping him on the back and seamlessly rescuing me from the threat of another awkward silence.

'Good to meet you, Melody,' Olly said, glancing from Liam to me.

'You didn't have to bring us lunch,' Liam said.

I shrugged and he smiled, one of those special smiles that warmed my blood, and I knew that despite the physical space between us, he was still mine.

'I'm gonna help myself if that's OK? I'm starving,' Olly grabbed a sandwich and stuffed it into his mouth with an appreciative moan as he sat beside the tray.

Liam shook his head in despair, taking a mug of tea and a sandwich for himself and sitting on the raised bed opposite. I stayed where I was, on the other side of the tray, sipping anxiously at my tea, while bracing myself for the onslaught of questions that was undoubtedly coming my way.

I didn't have to wait long.

'So, what's it like, living in a mansion?'

With a roll of my eyes I typed a response on my phone and held it out across the lunch tray for Olly to read.

'It's like living in a house, but more spacious,' Olly said, reading my reply aloud with a puzzled expression. 'Can't you talk?'

I shook my head.

'Serious? Why not?'

I shrugged non-committally.

'That's cool. I had a mate once who was deaf. He could lip-read so well that people didn't even realise he was deaf most of the time.'

I tapped out another text and thrust it beneath his nose.

'I'm not deaf,' Olly read aloud. Clearly he was unable to resist speaking, but at least it made Liam privy to our conversation. 'No, I know, I'm just saying… but, like, it must be annoying sometimes when you can't say what's on your mind, right…?' I texted again. 'At least I don't give people ear-ache,' Olly read out, making Liam laugh. 'Yeah, OK, very funny,' Olly muttered, taking another bite of his sandwich.

I hid my smile behind my mug of tea as I warmed my hands on it and Liam winked at me across the path.

I was actually enjoying myself.

Chapter Forty-three

Mel was a marvel. I'd assumed she'd keep her distance while Olly was around, but each day she came out and had lunch with us, freely making conversation with Olly through the text function on her mobile as if she'd been doing it all her life. Today she looked as delightful as ever in a long embroidered corduroy skirt, a warm, fitted velvet jacket and a quirky feathered hat. Though he teased her, Olly wasn't fazed by Mel's unusual appearance, and she gave as good as she got. It was immensely gratifying to see her interacting with someone else with such ease, and to witness her confidence growing day by day. Her courage both inspired and aroused me, especially when she was deftly putting Olly in his place with a look, or a few carefully chosen words.

But a small, petty, jealous part of me missed having Mel all to myself. We'd not been alone together for almost a week. She never invited me back or suggested I return after I'd dropped Olly off home each evening, and I didn't want her to feel pressured into coming to mine. Of course it was sensible to take our relationship slowly, and time apart from each other was probably healthy, and yet, as I witnessed the friendship developing between Mel and Olly, I began to feel absurdly desperate to be close to her; claim her for myself.

With only three years between them, Olly and Mel were much closer in age than she and I were. Olly was young, fun and single, and he could be charming when he set his mind to it. What if she preferred him to me?

Unsettled by this idea, I promptly lost my appetite. Picking up my paintbrush I returned to today's task of painting the boathouse, leaving Olly and Mel to continue their lunch and conversation behind me on the deck.

'Have you heard of Bad Bears' Picnic?' Olly asked. 'They're a London-based rock band – they're really good. They're playing at The Barfly on Saturday night if you fancy coming to see them…?'

Olly had stopped reading Mel's texts aloud, so I could no longer hear her replies, but I refrained from turning around and making eye contact with her. Wasn't this what I'd wanted all along? For Mel to make friends with people her own age and discover the world out there beyond her home? This was her opportunity, and as much as I didn't want to lose her, I wouldn't be the one to hold her back. Bracing myself for Mel's response I forced myself to stay calm and kept painting; focusing on broad, even strokes of the brush.

'You have a boyfriend?' Olly said with obvious surprise. 'Who?'

The brush stilled in my hand and my eyes closed as her slender arms slipped around my waist from behind. Her warm body pressed up against mine as she squeezed me in a tight, possessive hug. God I'd missed her touch. Swallowing the lump of emotion in my throat, I dropped the brush in the paint pot and turned in her arms to face her. Her silvery eyes were defiant as she stared up at me, and a smile hovered on her lips as I cupped her up-turned face and pressed my mouth to hers. I kissed her deeply, releasing my fear, relief, and intense gratitude in an effort to communicate all my love, without words.

'Shit...' The expression on Olly's face was comical as we pulled apart and looked at him. 'You two are together...?'

Mel nodded as she turned towards him, and I couldn't keep the smile off my face.

'You've been together this whole time...?'

She nodded again, drawing my arms firmly around her as she leaned back against me, discretely hiding my erection which was now pressing into her lower back.

'You sly dog,' Olly said, walking up to us and punching me on the shoulder. 'You kept that quiet,' he added, with a shake of his head. Picking up the can of paint at my feet, he retrieved the brush and started scraping off the excess. I'd never seen Olly Dent lost for words before.

Glancing up at me, Mel urged me away from Olly, across the decking, and beyond the lake.

'I'll just carry on with this shall I?' Olly called after us as Mel led me into the trees.

'Yes please,' I said over my shoulder, 'I'll be back in a minute...'

Dragging me out of view behind the trunk of the nearest oak tree, Mel pulled my head down to kiss me with greater urgency. It was wonderful to have her in my arms again; to be enveloped in her deliciously scented warmth and fervour. As I hoisted her up into the air she wrapped her legs tightly around my hips, her body clinging to mine. Maybe she'd been missing the physical side of our relationship as much as I had.

237

As she scraped her teeth along my jaw, followed by her hot tongue, I muttered her name under my breath, feeling near-delirious. Stumbling forwards I braced her gently against the trunk of the tree, and she burrowed beneath my clothes and unzipped my fly. As she took hold of me and sucked on my tongue, I tried to stifle a groan. The fresh air was cool on my skin, but no match for the throbbing heat Mel generated in my body. As I rucked up her skirt and slid my hands beneath her, I discovered that she wore absolutely no knickers at all. Her eagerness only ramped up my own arousal and I kissed her again. Extracting a ribbed condom from her pocket, she rolled it on over my straining length while I continued to stroke and caress her.

'Are you ready?' I whispered, conscious of Olly not far away.

Nodding she shoved her hands into the back of my pants; scoring my skin with her nails, grabbing my bum, and giving it a decisive squeeze. She gazed intently into my eyes as I shifted her up into position and filled her, her body capturing and claiming mine. But I was close; too close. Holding her still I savoured the feel of her around me, the warm sunlight filtering down through the trees and the natural music of the birds singing. Did life get any better than this?

She began a rocking, flexing motion with her hips, clenching and massaging rhythmically around my shaft, deep inside her, until I could take no more and was forced to move. Cupping her bottom in my hands I lifted her up so that I could thrust back inside her, stealing her breath, before repeating the action; driving inside her again and again. On the third thrust she began to fall apart; her body spasming with the force of it and her fingernails digging in hard enough to draw blood. With two more drives inside I was joining her; grunting with my own explosive, leg-trembling release.

As she covered my face in kisses I collapsed against her, pinning her to the tree with my body and breathing hard.

'God I've missed this,' I muttered, nestling my face in her hair. 'Are you OK?'

I sensed her nod and smile, and then her body shook with silent laughter.

'What's so funny?' Drawing my head back I looked at her.

'Holy shit, are you guys doing it?' Olly's shocked voice rang out through the trees.

'Get back to work, Olly,' I growled, not taking my eyes off Mel's face and hoping I was preserving her modesty with my own body.

Olly muttered under his breath as he stomped back the way he'd come, kicking dead leaves out of his way as he retreated. Mel continued to quietly chuckle as I withdrew, set her back on her feet and made myself decent.

'I'm glad you find it amusing. I'm his boss; I'm supposed to set an example... I'm never going to hear the end of this...'

Mel tried and failed to stop smiling, her cheeks flushed and eyes alight with mischief, as she grabbed a handful of my sweatshirt and pulled me in for another kiss. She had never looked happier or more beautiful and I was overwhelmed with pride that she was mine. In that

moment I realised that I would forgive this woman for
anything.

Chapter Forty-four

It was half past four on Friday afternoon when Olly rang the bell at the front door. Mrs Daly was there immediately, as if lying in wait, and Olly's loud, cheerful voice carried right through the house as I hurried to meet him.

'Hello, I'm looking for Melody, she about?'

'No she's not, and you set one muddy foot inside this house and I'll have you arrested for trespassing.'

'Er, right, OK…'

I glared at Mrs Daly as I reached the door.

'He's not coming in this house,' she muttered. I waited for her to retreat further down the hallway before turning my attention to Olly.

'Sorry, I just wanted to let you know I'm off now – my mate, Boz, is picking me up at the gate and we're heading into London for the weekend to see that band and get wasted. You sure you don't wanna come?'

Olly's offer amused me, but in my haste to reach the front door, I'd neglected to bring anything to communicate with. I smiled as I shook my head.

He shrugged dramatically. 'I tried. Laters, Mel…' he yelled as he trudged away into the twilight.

I was surprised that the light was already fading, but then October was almost over, the clocks had gone back and tomorrow would be Halloween. Not that the occasion meant much to me – I knew all about it from the internet and horror movies, but I'd never had an opportunity to celebrate it. Trick or Treaters were not admitted through the gates, and dressing up as a witch, purely for my own benefit, simply didn't appeal. But maybe it would be different this year – now that I had a boyfriend – maybe we could do something...?

Liam wasn't visible from my bedroom window, but his location was marked by a plume of grey smoke rising above the trees in the far north-east corner of the grounds. Having changed and found myself an old pair of heels, I followed the silvery ribbon of path through the encroaching darkness until I came to the clearing.

The bonfire was the size of a car and impressive in its ferocity. The pyramid-like structure was composed of broken palettes, rotten fence posts, and a tangle of twisted branches. The woody autumnal fragrance tickled my nostrils even at a distance, the shifting orange flames mesmerising as they danced. I took a moment to admire the fine architect of the inferno as he stood with his back to me, silhouetted against the blaze; broad and imposing. A shiver of excitement ran the length of my spine as he turned, alerted to my presence by a sixth sense. He didn't say anything and I couldn't see his face, but I knew he was smiling.

Slowly I walked towards the bonfire, as if unaffected by Liam; as if I wasn't desperate to be near him and aching for his touch. Stopping beside him, I gazed into the flames, savouring the tense crackle of anticipation between us as heat and light bathed my face and hands. When I could wait no longer I looked up at him and his eyes caught mine, burning with an intensity of their own.

'Alone at last,' he said softly, raising his hand and stroking the side of my face with one rough fingertip. I rose up onto my tiptoes as he took my chin between finger and thumb and bent down to kiss me, his lips soft and rousing. As his tongue found mine I sighed with pleasure and he used his arms to gather my now-limp body securely up against his. We kissed for a long time, revelling in the taste and feel of each other's mouths; lost in the luxury of it.

At length we paused to catch our breath and I basked in Liam's smile.

'You look like some sort of wild animal in this big furry coat.'

I stepped back away from him and he reluctantly loosened his hold on me with an unspoken question in his expression. Without taking my gaze from his, I began to unbutton my coat, starting at the neck and slowly working my way down. His reaction made me smile; his eyes widening and his jaw dropping as he began to see that I was entirely naked beneath, except for my shoes. The coat slipped from my shoulders and crumpled to the ground at my feet and he cursed under his breath.

His gaze roamed all over my body, bright and hungry; warming my skin along with the flames. Gently placing his big hands on my shoulders he looked deep into my eyes.

'I'd like to make love to you, Melody' he said hoarsely, making my hair stand on end. I nodded my consent and then watched as he picked up my coat and spread it out on a large pile of dry leaves. It provided a soft, comfortable mattress as he helped me to lie back, removed my shoes, and then knelt to straddle my legs with his own.

'Are you warm enough? We can move closer to the fire if…?' I shook my head and silenced him by sitting up and pushing his jacket from his shoulders. Removing it he then tugged his jumper and shirt off over his head all in one go. His naked torso was stunning in the firelight – the shifting light and shadows burnishing his skin and emphasising the sculpted lines and planes of his muscles.

Kissing me, he urged me to lie back again, and surveyed me with steady concentration as he began to run his warm, callused fingertips lightly down my body. He started at my neck; tracing the outer curves of my breasts and my ribs, always skimming past my erect nipples which strained tightly, desperate for his touch. Tenderly he continued on down, softly circling my belly and my hips, and by the time his knuckles were grazing my thighs I was a mess of tingling, sensitive flesh. His gentle patience, combined with the clear bulge in his pants, had me aching and quivering with anticipation.

Once he'd reached my toes he stretched his long body out beside mine, supporting himself on one elbow, as he re-traced the same route but this time with his mouth; quietly trailing kisses down from my neck, pausing only to blow air over each breast and dip his tongue inside my navel. I writhed and squirmed beneath his lips, fisting the fur beneath me as his hot mouth brushed tantalisingly close to my entrance, but shifted softly to the trembling inside of my thighs. He kissed, licked, and nipped at them as I bucked beneath him; silently urging him to move higher. What new kind of torture was this? How could such a big, strong man be so gentle, attentive and teasing? As Liam worked to prove his love, he imbued my body with so much pleasure that I felt deliciously molten; as if my bones were melting with desire from the inside out. But I wanted, needed, more; I wanted him inside me; to consume me.

Sensing my growing desperation, he climbed to his feet, retrieved a condom from his back pocket, and kicked off the rest of his clothes. I waited at his feet; feverish and panting with anticipation, while he stood over me, naked before the flames, and sheathed his jutting cock.

As he lowered himself on top of me, supporting himself on his arms, he dipped his head, returned his mouth to mine and flexed his hips; rubbing himself between my thighs. Deep in his chest he groaned and I shuddered in response, wrapping my legs around his hips and plundering his mouth with my tongue; begging him to take me. At last he did so, and I stared into his eyes, mesmerised by the ardent, almost pained, expression on his face as he pushed up inside me; burying himself from root to tip and making me whole again.

He paused there for a moment, regaining control, before withdrawing and re-entering me with a long, slow thrust which made me gasp and sigh. Soon he was rocking back and forth inside me; his chest pressed to mine, his muscles flexing beneath my fingers, and his abdomen repeatedly rubbing my clit in a delicious rhythm. My insides trembled and tightened as he drove me higher and higher and I dug my nails viciously into his back as I clung to the edge of my sanity.

'Oh God, I love you, Mel,' he muttered with a ragged breath, his words pushing me over that edge. With one last thrust he emptied himself inside me, moaning, as I shattered and convulsed beneath him; overwhelmed by the sheer intensity of our love.

Withdrawing he collapsed to one side of me, to avoid crushing me with his weight, and I nuzzled my face in his chest as our breathing started to return to normal.

'How dare you!' The cold condemnation cut through the night, turning my blood to ice as Liam stilled beside me.

No! How could he be here – he wasn't due back till next week…

Liam was quick to pull the edge of the fur coat up over me, a seemingly instinctive and belated attempt to preserve my modesty as I lay frozen in shock. Reaching for his clothes, Liam staggered to his feet and attempted to pull his jeans back on while I looked for the source of the voice.

Gregory was standing at the edge of the clearing, partly obscured by shadows now that the flames of the bonfire had abated. He wore his heavy black winter coat over his suit, his hands fisted tightly at his sides as he stared at me, his face ugly with barely controlled rage.

'Get back to the house,' he said sharply.

I glanced at Liam, who was tugging the rest of his clothes on, while I slipped my arms into the sleeves of my coat and pulled it tight around me. I was now wearing it inside out; the fur soft against my skin but little comfort.

'Now, Melody,' Gregory barked, taking a threatening step closer.

I was reluctant to leave the two men alone, but defying Gregory now would only make him angrier. As I stood and pushed my feet into my shoes, Liam and I exchanged a look in which he tipped his head in the direction of the house, encouraging me to go. And with that I was walking back the way I'd come; avoiding Gregory's eye, but holding my head high and any tears of frustration firmly in check.

Chapter Forty-five

Shit. How could we have been so careless? My need for Mel blinded me to all common sense and now I was going to suffer the consequences. Sinclair, her gaoler of a father, looked about ready to kill me, and as I shoved my feet back into my boots I fervently hoped he wasn't armed.

'You really are the lowest of the low,' he said, taking two angry steps towards me.

'Look, I'm sorry you had to find out this way–'

'Don't you dare try to tell me you're sorry, you filthy son of a bitch! I give you a job, good money, and this is how you repay me? By seducing my precious girl right under my nose; taking advantage of her special needs–'

'Special needs...?' I interrupted.

'She can't speak, you idiot, or hadn't you noticed? She's entirely reliant on me; she's vulnerable and innocent and she's mine, damn you, you will not take her away from me!'

Bewildered by his outburst I held my hands up in a placating manner. 'Are we talking about the same person? She may be mute but Mel seems pretty independent to me, and she's old enough to–'

'Don't lecture me on my own wife, you ungrateful bastard–'

'*Wife*!' I was stunned; I could feel my heartbeat changing, the back of my neck prickling with sweat. 'What do you mean wife? I thought–'

'Of course she's my wife, what did you think? What did she tell you? You didn't believe any of her lies did you...?' he sneered.

My confusion congealed into a painful sense of shame and despair as his words rang in my ears. Hadn't I known all along that something wasn't right about their relationship? Hadn't I avoided asking her more questions because I didn't want to hear the answers? I'd chosen to believe Mel when she said Sinclair was her father, because I'd *wanted* to believe her; because I loved her and coveted her for myself.

'She's a dreamer; a fantasist; she lives in her own little world and lies all the time,' Sinclair said. 'You can't believe anything she's told you.'

'I'm sorry,' I muttered.

'I don't want your apologies, just leave, go on. I don't ever want to see you around here again!' Spittle sprayed from his mouth as I passed him. He stank of whiskey and cigars; of a wealth and influence that seemed to mock me.

It started to rain, and that wretched man followed me all the way back to the house, ranting about how he was going to make sure I never got any decent employment ever again. His words barely registered. My mind was filled with Mel; all the months we'd spent together; all the moments we'd shared; the stolen looks, texts and kisses; the way we'd made love... was it all lies?

An immense pressure was building in my chest and I had a pressing urge to get as far away from Wildham Hall as possible. As the rain grew heavier I didn't bother to stop at the stables to collect my things. The same, familiar gaze penetrated deep into my bones from the windows of the house as I passed, but I studiously avoided looking up. Snatching the key-fob which activated the front gates from the dashboard of my van, I chucked it at Sinclair before climbing in and slamming the door. As I executed a jerky three-point turn, narrowly missing the Merc, the rain hammered down on the wind-shield like a manifestation of my misery. Aggressively I took off down the drive, almost colliding with the still-opening gates at the other end, before accelerating away into the black, wet night, with a scream of burning rubber.

Chapter Forty-six

I waited for Gregory in his study, with my sleeve pushed up and my first question scrawled in Biro up my arm: *What did you say to him?*

He ignored me as he entered, poured himself a large scotch, downed it, and then poured himself another. His hand was shaking, but whether with rage or something else I couldn't be sure. Upon finding us in the clearing his reaction had been worse than I'd imagined – I'd never seen him so riled up – and I needed to know what had transpired after I left. But still Gregory made no reply. He was a master at using my own silence against me.

Storming towards him, I yanked the tumbler out of his hand and whiskey slopped onto the floor. He looked at me then, with glazed eyes, and I realised he'd already had a skinful.

'How could you?' he said, his voice dangerously smooth. 'How could you let that Neanderthal touch you?'

He went to put his arms around me and I shrugged out of reach, pointing again at the question on my forearm.

'How could you let *him* touch you, and not *me*...? It should have been me,' he added, this time grabbing hold of me with greater determination. 'I thought you'd changed... started dressing differently – more provocatively – for me, but all along...'

I twisted away, but he pulled me back against him and his erection jabbed at my behind. A shudder of revulsion swept through me, the glass slipping from my hand and spilling amber liquid all over the carpet. As he pressed a kiss to the side of my face my stomach churned with nausea. Furious and frightened, I stamped on his toes with the heel of my shoe; launching myself out of his grasp as he recoiled in pain. Without turning back I fled through the house towards my bedroom, horrified by Gregory's behaviour and wondering if I was somehow to blame.

There had been moments, particularly in the last year or so, where I'd caught him looking at me oddly and he'd certainly been more attentive recently, but I'd hoped it was all in my imagination; I hadn't wanted to consider what it might mean. Who would want to believe that of their own father? But then I hardly knew him as a person at all; he was someone I occasionally shared a house and a meal with. He might be blood, but in every way that counted he was a stranger to me. Who knew what he might do?

I was surprised to pass Mrs Daly on the back stairs, I had forgotten she was there, but perhaps it was as well that there was a witness present, should I need one. Even so, I wasn't about to stop and listen to her crow at me. In the nursery I switched on the light, grabbed the nearest sheet of paper and a pen and wrote in large letters: *What are you doing? I'm not her! I'm not your wife – I'm your daughter!*

I was holding it up in front of me like a shield by the time Gregory reached my doorway.

'You think I don't know that?' he growled, snatching the paper from my hands. 'You're nothing like her; you never could be. She was perfect... she was everything to me... *everything*...' With this admission he sagged, the anger draining from his features and his eyes dropping to the floor. Witnessing his grief was almost as uncomfortable as fending off his lewd attentions, and so I turned away. I still needed to know what he'd said to Liam. He'd sacked him for sure, and probably said plenty of nasty things, but the way Liam left, without even acknowledging me had me worried. Why had he looked so upset? Did he still love me? Would he keep his word and come back for me...?

'What the hell's this?'

I turned back to find Gregory staring open-mouthed at a phallic rendering of Pan in his hand. In my haste I'd scribbled my message on the back of a grotto drawing by mistake.

It was in that moment that Mrs Daly, who must have been hovering nearby, chose to exact her revenge.

'Oh that's one of those statues from the garden, isn't it?' she said, casually depositing a pile of clean washing on the end of my bed. She had never brought me clean washing before.

'What statues?' Gregory demanded.

'You know – in that grotto garden, or whatever it is, in the woods behind the walled garden...'

'The fernery?'

'That's the one – the gardener's been restoring it and it's full of rude figures,' she said smugly, eyes gleaming.

Stunned, I watched this exchange, helpless to interrupt. I had no idea that Mrs Daly ever ventured into the grounds, let alone explored the grotto. Holy crap, had she witnessed Liam and I having sex there? The hideous notion made me flush with humiliation.

'There were always rumours about that garden,' Gregory said, his eyes returning to mine. 'That's why it was locked up – it was considered to be dangerous; a celebration of sin and debauchery; corrupting…' His gaze dropped to where my coat was gaping open at the collar and I clasped it tightly closed around my neck, nauseated once again by his eyes on my skin. 'I'd always assumed it was old-fashioned prudishness, but now I come to think about it, Cornelia was always afraid of that place. She never wanted me to open it; never wanted me to see what was inside. She used to say: "Sin spreads like a disease from generation to generation; infectious and all-consuming…"'

I shook my head. I could scarcely make sense of what he was saying, but he must be wrong. His eyes narrowed and slid around the room alighting on the mobile phone I'd carelessly left out. No! Before I could move, he swiped it up from the night-stand, glaring venomously at me as I stepped towards him, palms up in an openly begging gesture, pleading with my eyes.

Ignoring me, he rounded on Mrs Daly. 'You knew didn't you! You knew what was going on between the two of them and you never said anything…?'

'No I… well I suspected, but I… it wasn't my place to…' I recognised the panic that flared up in her eyes, but she was on her own – she'd dug her grave and I, for one, would not be writing a single word in her defence.

'Get your things and get out,' Gregory said, balling up my drawing and discarding it on the floor.

'Mr Sinclair, you can't–'

'I just did,' he snapped.

'But it's her… she's possessed by the devil,' she said, pointing a crooked finger in my direction.

'You could be right about that,' Gregory said with a grim smile as he shoved my phone into his trouser pocket. 'But that's by the by – it seems none of my staff can be trusted and I'm sacking the lot of you.' Stepping aside, he let her pass. 'Be gone by the time I get back.' Mrs Daly marched stiffly out of the room without another word. 'And you…' he said, turning back to me, '…you do not leave this room. Is that understood?'

I stared blankly at him and he took an angry step towards me.

'Is. That. Understood?'

Knowing that it was not a good time to push him, I nodded, and he slammed the door behind him as he left.

For a while I paced my room, too restless to sit, my mind a cacophony of emotions as I tried to process everything that had happened. Hearing the back door slam down below, I observed from the window with a growing sense of unease as Gregory went to the stables and re-emerged a few moments later with a battery-powered torch and what looked like a large sledgehammer. What had I done? Following the intermittent torchlight with my eyes, I miserably traced his progress through the trees as he went to destroy the compelling mythological figurines that had helped bring Liam and I together. I was grateful that Gregory wasn't taking a sledgehammer to Liam himself. But upon hearing the first crashing blow in the distance, I had to switch on my music, and turn it up loud.

Chapter Forty-seven

'Another round,' I said, tossing a tenner onto the bar.

Wendy was busy rinsing glasses and hesitated, her gaze flicking from me to James and then back again. 'You sure that's a good idea?'

Giving her a hard stare I raised one eyebrow.

'You boys have been hitting it rather hard tonight, that's all...' Her misplaced concern pissed me off, but James jumped in before I could argue:

'Aw go on, Wendy, pour him another pint – he's a big lad, he can handle it.'

She hesitated again and James flashed his most charming smile. 'Right, well, there'd better not be any trouble or I'm holding you responsible, James Southwood.' Positioning a clean glass beneath the beer tap she began filling it with lager.

Wendy set my pint and change before me, called last orders and moved to the other end of the bar where are large group of punters were dressed up for Halloween.

'So, are you ready to tell me what's going on, big guy?' I took a large gulp of cold beer, but this time James wasn't going to let it drop. 'Has this got something to do with Melody?'

Simply hearing her name made me angry and I banged my glass down on the bar, harder than I'd intended. James pretended he hadn't noticed.

'I thought things were going well with her, y'know, since she came along to The White Bear and everything… you looked good together…'

'Appearances can be deceptive,' I muttered.

'Look, if you've had a falling out, I'm sure it can be resolved, you just need to talk to her about it. Isn't that what you've always told me in the past…?'

Great. Now my best mate was throwing my own relationship advice back at me.

'Whatever it is, whatever has happened, I don't think drinking is—'

'She's married.'

'What…?'

James's prolonged silence gave me an opportunity to escape to the men's room. There was a guy in there using the urinals dressed up as The Joker in a lurid purple suit. He smirked at me, but exited before I had a chance to react. As I washed my hands I avoided my reflection; I didn't need to see myself to know I was a fool.

When I emerged from the gents I noticed that most of the other punters had left and the staff were clearing up for the night. I staggered slightly on my way back to the bar, but I wasn't yet drunk enough by half.

'Did you know she was married?' James launched straight back in.

Reclaiming my drink I shook my head. 'She lied to me.'

'I'm sorry, mate, that's harsh; really harsh. But… is she happily married? I mean, she can't be, can she? So, maybe she'll leave him…?'

'She lied to me,' I repeated. 'I loved her – I really...
for the first time I really... but it was all lies...' I could
feel anger building inside me; my stomach churning like a
kettle on the boil, but that sensation was preferable to
feeling hurt and used. Downing the last dregs of my pint I
left the empty on the bar. 'Where else is still serving?'

James got to his feet beside me and pulled on his
jacket. 'Nowhere round here. I might have something we
can drink back at mine if—'

'What about an offy? There's one across the square
isn't there?'

It was cold outside and peeing with rain; the wet
pavement reflecting the orange glare of the street-lights in
a disconcerting manner. As we approached the off licence
a bloke was coming out and rudely shouldered James
aside.

'Easy, mate,' James muttered, but the guy didn't turn
or offer any sort of apology. I recognised him as the same
Joker who'd smirked at me in the gents and my irritation
peaked.

'Hey, what the hell was that?' I said to the back of his
mop of green hair.

The bloke turned around and grinned at us; the effect
exaggerated by his heavy make-up. 'You should watch
where you're going,' he said with a shrug. Something
inside me snapped and I grabbed him around the throat
and slammed him against the nearest wall.

'Whoa, Liam, just leave it, OK?' James said, behind
me.

'Yeah, tough guy, listen to your girlfriend...' The
Joker jeered.

Blood pulsed in my ears with rage. Still holding him suspended a foot off the ground with my left hand, I pulled my right fist back level with the little shit's head and the smirk finally fell from his face. 'Apologise,' I growled.

'Fuck you,' he spat.

'Don't mate, he's not worth it,' James muttered.

'C'mon you pussy, do your worst, you ain't gonna hurt me!' The Joker was smiling again – a mocking grin that only made me angrier. I wanted to hurt him; teach him a lesson; make him sorry; make him bleed and my knuckles tightened in anticipation.

Suddenly there was a blur of motion and Mel's face was before me. For a second I thought I was seeing things; that I'd drunk far more than I'd realised, or finally cracked, and I blinked hard.

James cursed and grabbed hold of my shoulders from behind. 'Stop! Melody, get out of there...' He was panicked and I realised that he could see her too.

I experienced a weird sense of Déjà vu and a flashback to when Mel had thrown herself between a tree and my chainsaw. But this time it wasn't an ancient magnolia tree she was protecting, it was some arsehole I wanted to beat to death with my bare hands.

'Who the fuck are you?' The Joker said from behind her.

'Move,' I said, narrowing my eyes at her.

She stared back at me without even flinching; fearless, silent, and achingly beautiful. I hated her for what she'd done to me.

James tried to grab Mel's arm but she twisted out of his grip, without taking her eyes from mine.

'Move or you're going to get hurt,' I warned.

My arm trembled with the need to lash out and inflict a measure of the pain I felt inside, but she merely crossed her arms and raised her chin and James cursed again.

'Look if you're gonna hit me, just hit me, you fucking pussy...' said the guy pinned to the wall.

Silent tears had welled up in Mel's eyes and spilled freely down her cheeks, unnerving me completely. Why was she crying? In truth I didn't hate her and I could never hurt her – she was my reason for getting up each morning; the only person who really got me; and I loved her – secrets, lies, husband and all.

Abruptly I released the piece of shit squirming in my hand, grabbed hold of Mel and kissed her. She collapsed into my arms as I desperately tried to kiss away all her tears. Behind me, James exchanged insults with The Joker, who was cocky and triumphant as he took off, but I wasn't listening, not now that I had Mel in my arms; her scent in my nose; her taste on my tongue.

'Right,' James sighed. 'Are you two going to be alright getting home...?'

*

I woke with the hangover from hell; my mouth dry, head thumping and stomach churning. I only just made it out of the bedroom and across the landing before heaving bile into the toilet. Lying naked on the cold bathroom floor, I groaned as events from the previous night elbowed their way painfully into my conscious mind. I'd nearly killed someone – a snotty little kid in the wrong place at the wrong time, but I'd wanted to kill him. And I would have if... Mel! Sitting up too fast I clutched my head as pain lashed through my skull and my stomach heaved. Where had she come from? She'd appeared out of the blue and, as if by magic, stopped me from ending up in court on an ABH charge. What did it mean...? Wait, how did I get home?

With great effort I dragged myself to my feet and started down the stairs, and that's when I had another flashback – she'd helped me up the stairs. I'd staggered home with her tucked under my arm, using her like a walking crutch, and then I'd made a pathetic attempt to seduce her. Unsurprisingly she wasn't keen. God what an idiot.

Unfortunately the rest of the night was a blank. Was she still here? Hope surged in my chest as I checked the living room and kitchen, but there were no signs of Mel at all. She was gone.

With another groan I slumped on the sofa. Of course she was gone. Last night she'd witnessed the very worst side of me – the violent drunk I usually kept so carefully concealed. What woman in her right mind would want to be around that kind of a monster? No wonder she'd run back to her husband.

But then again, why was she in town in the first place? Was she looking for me? Was she planning to leave Sinclair, like James suggested? Was that what she'd come to tell me? Did she love me after all...? Oh God, what if I'd hurt her...?

Once I'd gone back to the bedroom and pulled on clean boxers, I stumbled around the house in search of my phone before finally locating it in a trouser pocket. I sent her a text begging her to let me know that she was OK and that she'd got home safely. And then another saying I was sorry and that I loved her. And then, before I could get carried away and ring her, simply to hear her breathing, I headed to the kitchen for coffee.

Chapter Forty-eight

How could he? Gregory had clearly lost his mind. He'd locked me in my bedroom and then driven away, and I had no idea when, or even *if*, he'd be back. I hadn't even been aware that he possessed a key to the nursery, and now I was an actual prisoner in my own home.

He was punishing me. During the night I'd sneaked out while I thought Gregory was asleep. I'd gone to find Liam to make sure everything was alright between us. But he'd been drinking heavily, he was angry and he wanted to murder some idiot in a crazy Halloween costume. Thankfully I'd managed to diffuse Liam before he did any damage, but I was unable to get any sensible conversation out of him before he passed out.

When I crept back home and returned to my room, I found that Gregory had taken away my computer and replaced it with a can-opener and a stack of tinned foods from the pantry. It was while I was standing there in complete shock, in the murky early hours of the morning, that he had callously closed and locked the door behind me and ran away. The coward.

So here I was; reduced to breathing stale air, eating cold soup from a can, and drinking water straight from the tap; with no means of escape or communication with the outside world. Gregory had clearly postponed Yvette's visits (if he hadn't sacked her permanently) so I had only one hope, and the last time I'd seen him he was passed out drunk.

But he would come for me.

He would.

Wouldn't he?

On the first day of my incarceration I repeatedly kicked and hammered at the door and windows and hurled tin cans across the room in frustration, but it had gotten me nowhere. The heavy door wouldn't budge, the leaded windows remained sealed shut, and the cans were only more tricky to open once dented.

The time dragged, and without my computer I couldn't work, or even email the agency to explain why. The publishing world was all about deadlines and what use was a proofreader who couldn't be reached or relied upon? Chances were I'd be fired, if I hadn't been already. In retaliation I set about destroying every stuffed toy Gregory had ever given me – ripping their heads off, pulling out all the stuffing and gouging out every last beady, glass eye. But the stuffing got everywhere; the cobwebby fibres clinging to the bed, the carpet, the curtains and my clothes; only increasing my sense of suffocation.

As the hours dragged by, I slept and read books and took long baths – anything to keep the panic at bay. I even smoked the rest of the joint I'd kept hidden for years, because, why not?

But on the morning of the fourth day, when Gregory had still not returned, real fear set in. There wasn't much food left and I was hungry. Eyeing the clock I sized up the last few remaining tins with growing anxiety; obsessively counting and re-counting them and mentally calculating how long my rations might last. I had no idea how much longer I might be trapped here. How long did it take for a person to die from starvation? Was it very painful? And what did I want my last meal on Earth to be; tinned tomatoes or kidney beans...?

Where was Liam...?

I hoped he wasn't still drinking. He wasn't wrong when he'd said it didn't agree with him. He'd apologised repeatedly all the way back to his house and sworn he would sober up, but what if he hadn't managed it? And as I'd helped him up to bed he'd told me that he still loved me, but was that just the drink talking?

Given my current predicament I now wished that I'd left Liam clear written instructions to come over here and get me, but then how was I to know that Gregory was crazy enough to pull something like this?

*

Winter had crept in overnight. I sat at the window, wrapped in a blanket, and watched as the pale sun rose over the horizon. With the fresh, foot-deep snowfall, a hush had settled over the landscape so profound that I believed I might be entirely alone in the world. It weighed heavy in the naked boughs of the trees and the meshed top of the fruit cage and iced the formal lawns and terraces so that they resembled the tiers of a wedding cake.

But my thoughts could never do justice to the changing seasons. I wanted to hear Liam's take on it all. It was like poetry when he talked about the landscape; about the trees, the wildlife and the cycle of life; the way in which we were all connected. He made me feel a part of something when he talked like that; he made me feel special.

Where was he…?

Why didn't he come?

By eleven a.m. the rumbling in my stomach had become too distracting and I devoured the last of the peach slices as if it were the finest caviar. It was as I got up to rinse out the tin that I became aware of how chilly I'd become. With a trembling hand I pressed the main light switch on the wall, staring in disbelief when nothing happened. Then I tried the bedside lamp, the radiators, and even plugged in my hair-dryer before finally accepting reality: there'd been a power cut. Aside from the oil-powered range down in the kitchen, everything had stopped working. The temperature outside was about zero degrees and the room was getting colder. Would the residual heat leaking up from the room below be enough to keep me from freezing to death? Come nightfall, at around four-thirty this afternoon, I was going to be imprisoned in total darkness.

Liam…?

Chapter Forty-nine

This was too much. It had been five days. I'd tried being patient; tried to stay away to give her and Gregory time to sort out whatever they needed to. But she hadn't replied to any of my texts, emails or phone calls – in fact her phone seemed to be permanently switched off – and I felt like I was going completely bonkers. I couldn't sleep, or eat, or sit still for more than a few minutes at a time, and I was so distracted during rugby training that I was a bumbling liability.

I needed to know that she was safe; that she'd forgiven my drunken loutishness; that she still wanted to be with me; that she loved me, even half as much as I loved her. I had too many desperate questions and no answers, and my hope and optimism were depleting day by day.

During the night a minor snowfall had taken out two power lines, leaving half of Wildham without electricity. I'd always loved waking up to a crisp, snowy landscape. They were infrequent in this part of the country, often fleeting, and evoked a childish sense of glee. There was something about the fresh white shock of it which always had me spellbound. But not this time; not without Mel.

James, Lester, Olly and I had spent all morning helping salt and clear access to those homes cut off from the main roads; checking on those pensioners who lived alone, installing generators and delivering supplies. But now my feelings for Mel were overriding all other fears.

Let Gregory have me arrested; I didn't care; I was going to go and see her.

I no longer had the means to open the grand entrance gates, and they were far too high and spiky to climb over, but that wasn't going to keep me out. I now knew the Wildham estate like the back of my hand. Where the estate bordered the road the boundary consisted of solid steel railings backed up by a dense prickly hedge, but beyond that, where the grounds bordered farmland, a 1.5 metre high timber post and rail fence, designed to deter sheep and cattle, was all that stood in my way. Parking my van outside the front gates, I skirted along the snow-piled road edge until I came to a farmer's gate and made light work of hopping over it before trudging cross-country back towards Wildham Hall. My tracks through the snow clearly marked my trespassing, but that couldn't be helped. Nothing was going to keep me from Mel now.

Approaching the house under the relative cover of the trees I made my way round to the drive, and was relieved to find that the Merc was absent. Quietly I walked right around the house, but the power appeared to be out – there were no lights on, no sounds, and no signs of life from within. Not wishing to sneak up on Mel, or Mrs Daly for that matter, I traced my footprints back to the large front door and rang the clunky bell. I waited before ringing the bell again. Twice. But no-one came to the door or even a window, and anxiety crawled through me. Mel couldn't have left, could she...?

No. She had to be here. She wouldn't leave – not without at least saying goodbye. Unless... unless that was why she'd come to find me in town? As far as I could remember she hadn't conveyed a single word that night – neither written, typed or mouthed. But then that wasn't unusual for Mel – we'd gotten so close; we understood each other so well that often words weren't necessary between us.

Oh God, had she been trying to say goodbye…?

Stomping back around to the far side of the house I craned my neck to get a look at her bedroom window. At the sight of her I thought my heart might burst out of my body with relief. She was swaddled in her bed covers and slapping the window with her palms, her eyes wild.

'You OK?' I shouted up.

She shook her head and slapped a paper sign up against the leaded glass and I deciphered the words: *I'M LOCKED IN!*

That bastard. That was it. Married or not, there was no way in hell I was leaving her with Sinclair now. En route to the back door I picked up a spare brick and when the door wouldn't open I simply smashed a laundry room window, reached in, and unlocked it from the inside. Even in my fury and my eagerness to get to Mel, I paused long enough to brush aside the broken glass and kick off my snow-covered boots on the mat before striding through the cold, mausoleum-like house to the nursery. It took three attempts to break open the door with my shoulder, but I had all the strength and motivation I needed.

Mel leapt up into my arms and kissed me and I immediately felt restored; as if I could breathe again; as if the last few days had been nothing but a bad dream. Holding her close, I let her fill my vision and breathed her deep into my lungs, revelling in her very existence while she covered my face with sweet, smiling kisses.

'Are you OK, baby, did he hurt you?' She shook her head and I glanced around at the blizzard-like carnage in the room. 'Where's your phone, did he take it?'

Scowling she nodded.

'And your computer?'

She nodded again.

'Bastard,' I muttered. 'When's he coming back?'

She shrugged and I released her back onto her feet.

'Hey, isn't that my watch?'

The wristwatch my mother had given me for my ninth birthday was lying amid an assortment of other items on the bed. Retrieving it I scrutinised it carefully, but there was no doubt it was mine; I'd recognise it anywhere. 'I lost this months ago, where did you find it?' Mel was blushing when I looked at her; a sheepish expression on her face. 'You took it didn't you?'

She mouthed the word 'sorry', anxiety clear in her eyes and I shook my head in disapproval, while she blinked up at me like a contrite child. But in all honesty her little act of thievery didn't annoy me. In fact, I loved that she'd wanted a piece of me so soon after we first met. Regardless of whether it was to punish or provoke me, it was flattering.

'I'll have it back now if that's OK,' I said strapping it back onto my wrist. She nodded and we exchanged a smile.

Grabbing a notepad and pen she led me back downstairs, her bed covers trailing behind her like a train.

'What's with all these taxidermied animals?' I said, ducking slightly to avoid the protruding tusks of a wild boar.

G likes to hunt, Mel scribbled down on her notepad. *Someone should shoot, stuff, and mount him on the wall – see how he likes it.* Her comment amused me, and I made a mental note never to get on her bad side.

Once we reached the kitchen, Mel opened the pantry and, after much rummaging about, helped herself to a large packet of biscuits. I searched several cupboards for a backup generator but could find no evidence of one. Only the large Aga was still functioning. While I filled the kettle, set it on the hotplate and set about making two cups of tea, Mel seated herself cross-legged at the table in her nest of blankets, spilling biscuit crumbs as she munched.

'Please tell me he didn't lock you in without any food?'

She shook her head, picked up the pen and jotted down: *I was rationing myself.*

'Jesus. He shouldn't have locked you in at all – it's abuse.' She made no move to either agree or disagree and I bit back my frustration. 'What about Mrs Daly, hasn't she been?'

Sacked. Mel wrote the one word without remorse and I set our tea on the table, pulled out a chair and sat down opposite her.

'Sorry there's no milk – it's gone off.'

She smiled sympathetically and I sighed and rubbed my face with my hands. There was so much we needed to talk about; so much I wanted to know; hundreds of questions had been circulating in my head for days, but now that she was here in front of me, it was hard to begin.

'I want to apologise for the other night – I shouldn't have started drinking – it was stupid and I'm sorry you had to see me in that state. I'll understand if you want nothing more to do with me, but… you can't stay here, Mel. I don't care if he's your husband, he can't treat you this way.'

She stared at me for a moment and then launched a chocolate chip biscuit at me like a missile.

'Ow,' I said as it connected with my nose and broke into pieces across the table top. 'What was that for?' She was already writing, so I took a fortifying gulp of tea before reading her response.

He's my FATHER you idiot.

'That's not what he says.'

And you believe him over me?

'I don't want to believe him, obviously… but why do you always refer to him by his first name? Why not call him 'Dad'?'

She shrugged and wrote: *We've never been close.*

'OK. So why did he tell me you were his wife?'

She grimaced. *Because he wants me for himself.*

Biting back the sudden urge to vomit, I took her hand and she laced her fingers through mine. 'You do realise how wrong that sounds?'

She nodded, and simply stared into my eyes as I tried to digest this new information and internally wrestled with a growing sense of anger. After a while she collected up the notepad and rose to her feet, and I followed her back upstairs.

Mel led me into her mother's room; the opulent bedroom of a woman who had been dead and gone for fifteen long years. Not that you could tell. The cluttered space was a veritable monument; a shrine to the deceased, and it cast Sinclair's dodgy state of mind into sharp relief. Mel handed me a framed photograph of her parents' wedding day – a plain registry office affair in which her mother looked regal and her father looked impossibly young. If anything Gregory and Cornelia looked more like mother and son than husband and wife, but their happiness was clear to see. Going by the date they must have had Mel less than a year later.

'How did she die?'

I don't know – G won't talk about it.

The revelation made me hurt for her and for the grief and confusion she must have suffered as a child – no wonder she'd stopped speaking. Before I could assemble any words of sympathy, Mel was writing again.

I think G blamed me for her death for a long time, but lately he's changed – become more attentive.

I knew precisely what she meant by 'attentive' – it made my teeth clench and my hands ball into fists with angry revulsion, but I held it in check. Relaxing my hands I placed them on Mel's shoulders and turned her to face me.

'He hasn't hurt you, has he? Physically I mean – he hasn't touched you in any way he shouldn't…?'

She held my eye as she shook her head and I believed her, though I was still too angry to fully embrace my relief.

'You were definitely not responsible for your mother's death, understand? I don't care what Sinclair thinks, says or does, no six-year-old has that kind of power, OK?'

Mel didn't look as emotional as you might expect somebody in her position to be – perhaps she'd never had a chance to feel close to either parent, and was used to their absence; maybe she had buried her feelings on the subject very deep, or perhaps she had simply dealt with them. Either way she gently put a hand to the side of my face and nodded her understanding with a serene smile – as if I was the one that needed comforting.

I'd believed Mel over Gregory Sinclair from the moment she'd thrown a biscuit at my head and called me an idiot, but this extra insight into her family background laid any further doubts to rest for good. Mel was unmarried and she loved me… now if I could only convince her to leave with me.

'It's getting cold in here and it might be a while before the power's back on – how do you fancy a trip to The White Bear?'

Chapter Fifty

For once I was glad to leave the house. Liam insisted on boarding up the broken window and clearing away the glass in the laundry room before we left, but he was swift and efficient with his big, capable hands, and soon they were wrapped warmly around mine as he led me away.

The White Bear was a welcoming prospect as dusk fell, with its glowing lights, roaring fire and hot food, despite the smell of wet dog. The place was crowded with local people and their pets, all taking refuge from the power cut, and I was glad to have Liam at my side. He knew many of the patrons personally and stopped to greet them, introducing me by my first name as we stripped off our bulky layers of outer clothing and made our way to the bar.

Across the room I spotted Poppy sitting at a small table with her brother, Adam. Anxiety brewed inside me while Liam bought our drinks, but the siblings enthusiastically waved us over with matching grins, and when Liam asked me if I was happy to join them, I found myself nodding.

As Poppy introduced herself she stood up and flung her arms around me in a hug, almost spilling my drink. The unexpected onslaught made me stiffen like a board in her embrace, but the cashmere jumper she wore was wonderfully soft against me cheek. Her hair smelled of cranberries, and as she withdrew, the warmth in her smile was so genuine that it was infectious.

'It's so good to finally meet you,' she said. 'I was just telling Liam the other day that he was selfish to keep you all to himself. There are so few women in our social circle – we need to stick together – and we're long overdue for a girly get-together.'

Liam gave my left hand a gentle squeeze as we took our seats; I realised my nails were digging into his skin, and tried to relax my grip.

'This is Adam,' Poppy said.

'Great to meet you, Melody,' Adam said, reaching across the table and shaking my hand. 'Big guy has hardly stopped smiling since he met you. What's your secret?' he added with a wink.

'Adam!' Poppy admonished, elbowing him in the ribs. 'Just ignore him – he's always got his foot in his mouth.'

Liam shot a warning glare at Adam over the rim of his pint of orange juice, but Adam just grinned back.

'So is the power out at the Hall as well?' Poppy asked. 'Is that why you're here?'

I nodded.

'Oh, wait,' she said, placing her hand over mine with a concerned expression. 'Do you have something to write with? I don't want to be asking you loads of questions when you can't answer them...'

Her consideration was surprising; Liam must have fore-warned her about my muteism. Had he told all his friends about me? The idea of him talking about me behind my back was unsettling, but actually, it was a relief not to have to explain myself for once. Taking the notepad and pen from my pocket I laid them on the table and Poppy smiled.

'Liam said you're a proofreader, is that right?'

I nodded, took a sip of water and picked up the pen. *Yes, but I'm thinking of going into copywriting.*

'Wow, really, why?' Poppy said.

I think I'd be better at it than some of the copywriters I work for.

Poppy snorted with laughter and showed what I'd written to Adam, who grinned at me.

'Adam's a copywriter for a website developer,' Liam whispered in my ear.

I bit my lip and Adam shook his head, smiling ruefully. 'You're probably right – I've read some appalling copy over the years.'

'You should get Melody to do some proofreading for you,' Poppy suggested. 'At least you'll get an honest opinion on your writing.'

'I'm not sure I'm brave enough,' Adam said, pulling a face. 'But our company is always looking for good copywriters, so I might be able to get you a foot in the door…?'

That would be amazing, thanks, I wrote, surprised and relieved that I hadn't offended him too badly.

Adam picked up his bottle of beer. 'I'll have a word with my boss and find out what they're looking for,' he said as his lips pressed against the top of the bottle and he drained the contents.

'Just imagine – you could end up working together!' Poppy smiled warmly, and I understood why everyone was so drawn to her.

Adam glanced at his watch and then up at his sister. 'I'm afraid we should be going.'

'Yeah, I guess,' Poppy sighed. 'I wish we could stay and get to know you better, but we said we'd take some food home for Mrs Kenmore, our neighbour.'

OK.

As Poppy hugged me goodbye I was reluctant to see her go. I was glad to have Liam all to myself again, but we had difficult things to discuss – like what to do about my father – and my brief conversation with Adam and Poppy had left me feeling too exhilarated to be serious. Were all Liam's friends that nice and easy to get on with? Gregory had always insisted that meeting new people would be traumatic for me – that others would be intolerant of my condition, that they'd be cruel. But I was starting to realise that Gregory was wrong about a lot of things.

'Are you hungry?' Liam said when they'd gone, tenderly brushing his thumb across my lips.

Nodding I stretched up and kissed him on the mouth – right there in the crowded pub – and he went to find a menu with a broad smile on his face.

Once we'd devoured two portions of cheesy chips, I licked the salt from my fingers, eyed the puddle of water that had leached from my boots, and waited for Liam to say what he wanted to say.

'Mel... I know we haven't been together very long, but I *do* love you... and, well... with things being the way they are... I wondered if you would consider moving in with me?'

I'd known it was coming. And I should be flattered. I *was* flattered. Only...

'I realise it would be a big change for you,' he continued, 'I know you're used to having your own space and everything, but we could find a bigger house to rent... and I can stick most of my stuff in storage...' The earnest expression on his face made my heart ache. I loved him, and I loved the idea of sharing my life with him; falling asleep in his arms every night; waking up to his smile each morning. But...

Picking up my pen, I wrote slowly, agonising over each word: *I love you too, and I want to be with you, but it doesn't seem fair that I should have to leave my home just because G is behaving like a loon.*

'You're right – it isn't fair. But it's his house isn't it?' I nodded. 'And you can't stay with him after everything he's done... everything he might do...'

What if I get him to leave me alone?

'How are you going to do that?'

Threaten to go to the police or something.

'But you still couldn't trust him, surely? I wouldn't feel comfortable leaving you alone with him.'

It was humiliating to think that I might need protecting from my own father. He was a pompous ass and he had an unhealthy obsession with his dead wife which was now, by extension, making him inappropriately possessive of me. But he was spineless and essentially harmless, wasn't he? *Maybe you could move in with us?* I wrote.

Liam's eyebrows shot up in surprise. 'Even if your father agreed to that, which, frankly, is highly unlikely, I still wouldn't be there all the time to protect you.'

I can handle Gregory myself, I don't need protection.

'Mel, he's physically bigger and stronger than you, and he's clearly unhinged…'

Irritated by Liam's calm, common sense I shoved my notepad aside, stood and pushed my way through the over-crowded pub to the ladies toilet. It was vacant as I entered, which was lucky since Liam was right behind me and followed me inside.

I glared at him and crossed my arms as he bolted the door shut behind us.

'Are you getting stroppy with me?' he said cupping my face in his large hands and peering into my eyes. 'Because I'm not letting you walk away from me anymore. I don't care how cross you get, you're stuck with me now.'

Stupid man. Couldn't he see I needed to be by myself? Twisting out of his grasp I surveyed the small space. I'd not been in many public bathrooms before, and this one was surprisingly quaint and clean, with just the one toilet and a sink unit that resembled a traditional dressing table mounted on a raised platform along one wall.

'You have every right to feel angry and frustrated, Mel – tell me what I can do.' I turned back to Liam and he smiled, unfazed by my wrath. 'You wanna hit me? Go on, do it, I can take it and it might make you feel b—'

I punched him in the stomach, the muscles in my hand and arm jarring at the sudden impact. Liam didn't flinch.

'Hey, don't hurt yourself – look, like this…' Taking my hand he gently tucked my thumb behind my other knuckles, '…and try to throw your arm out level with your shoulder.'

I jabbed him again and he smiled.

'Good, that's better, how did that feel?'

Damn I loved him. Grabbing his head I kissed him, revelling in the taste of him, lightly seasoned with salt. He grew hard as I pressed myself into the warm, solid contours of his body, and he groaned. His primal response to my kisses never failed to excite me. I wanted him to fill me with his patient strength; make me feel invincible the way only he could. When I gave him a squeeze of encouragement he grabbed my bottom and lifted me up into his arms.

'Is this your way of avoiding the matter at hand?' he said, kissing along my jaw to my earlobe and down my neck. I unbuckled his belt and fly and he walked me backwards and set me on the counter beside the sink. 'You really want to do this here?'

I nodded, hopping down and hastily pushing down my leggings and knickers. He muttered something unintelligible as he caught a glimpse of my naked parts, quickly producing a condom and rolling it on. Up on the platform I turned my back to him and re-established eye contact in the mirror. His gaze was dark with desire as it connected with mine. Bracing my hands on the counter-top, I leaned forwards, lifting my hips, and tipping my bottom up towards him.

'Oh Jesus, you want me to…?'

I nodded slowly, the ache between my legs growing in direct response to the need in his expression. Maybe Mrs Daly was right; maybe I did have the devil in me – or perhaps the great god Pan had corrupted me. Either way I didn't care. This lust; this craving for sexual pleasure was something Liam and I shared, and I wanted to celebrate it.

Slowly and deliberately he entered me, one hand on my hip and the other pressed to my clitoris. The moment was intensely intimate against the background hum of the crowded pub – Liam with his trousers round his ankles and me with my head almost pressed to the mirror, our eyes locked…

We both jumped guiltily as someone tried the door handle, and then smiled at each other with relief that the door was locked. Wasting no more time Liam took me exactly as I needed him to. With a smooth and faultless rhythm, he steadily drove away a week's worth of fear and frustration; gradually increasing the pace with thrust after measured thrust; skilfully winding my insides tighter and tighter until I was floating somewhere near the ceiling. I came with an almighty judder and he let go inside me, stifling a low, guttural moan in the base of my neck.

We left the ladies toilet separately – Liam ducking out first and then waiting for me outside the door so that we could weave our way back to our table hand in hand. But as we passed the community noticeboard near the door, Liam did a double take and stopped dead in his tracks. Releasing my hand he used a finger to lift the corner of a leaflet advertising window cleaning from where it obscured a poster beneath. As he stared at the board his whole body tensed, and unease unfurled in my stomach. What was it? What was wrong? Ripping the poster from the wall he turned to me, his face pale and his eyes uncharacteristically hard.

'He's not your father,' he said.

What? It was hard to hear him against all the chatting and laughter and the chinking of glasses behind the bar Had I misheard?

'That must be what all your bad dreams are about – he's not your real father,' he said.

His words still made no sense and I cast an eye over the missing persons poster that he was thrusting at me. It was about a five-year-old girl who'd gone missing one summer, sixteen years ago. She'd last been seen wearing a white cotton dress with a rose motif and matching pink tights. I couldn't see what relevance it had to anything, but when I looked up, Liam was still staring at me in shock, so I returned my eyes to the poster. Next to the picture of the little girl was a second image, but of a woman who, at a second glance, was vaguely familiar. The caption below stated that it was a digital approximation of how the little girl might appear today and added that she had a distinguishing birthmark – shaped like a butterfly – on her right thigh…

The cheerful voices of the other people around me had become deafening, like a roaring in my ears and the whole planet seemed to shift under my feet. Stumbling to the door I propelled myself outside into the snow, my legs giving way as I opened my mouth and silently screamed into the night.

Chapter Fifty-one

I caught Mel a split second before she hit the ground, and as I tried to embrace her she pummelled my chest repeatedly with her fists. It was a reasonable reaction, considering she was unable to scream, shout and swear like anyone else would in her position. She was getting good with her fists now – I would have bruises – but I took it all willingly.

I regretted letting her see the poster like that, but I'd been in shock; I was still shocked. Why hadn't I made the connection sooner? I was sixteen when little Melanie Crowe disappeared from a summer fête in a neighbouring town – her face had been everywhere for weeks; every newspaper, telegraph pole and noticeboard in the county – the whole country knew her name. But with her gappy grin and pigtails, I hadn't associated that little lost girl with Melody Sinclair, until now.

Before long the beating of her fists ceased and she sagged in my arms, drained.

'I'm so sorry,' I whispered, pressing kisses to the top of her head. She didn't react and I waited as her breathing calmed. 'Are you ready to go back inside?'

Gazing down at the now screwed up poster clenched in her fist, she shook her head.

'OK. Will you wait here while I go back and get our things?'

She nodded absently and straightened up as I released her. Afraid to leave Mel alone, even for a second, I was quick to retrieve the notepad and our coats, scarves, hats and gloves, but when I returned she hadn't moved a muscle – she was still standing, staring at the paper in her hand, lost in thought.

We trudged back to the estate without discussion of any kind. Mel was distracted; presumably contemplating her past; silently struggling to accept the idea that she'd been kidnapped and lied to her entire life; that she might be someone else entirely. I worried about how it might affect her and what it meant for our future.

Now that night had fallen the temperature was plummeting and the snow melt was hardening into ice, making it treacherous under foot. But we reached Wildham Hall without incident and I was relieved to find Sinclair still absent and the electricity supply restored.

Mel went straight upstairs and I followed her into what I took to be Sinclair's bedroom. She no longer seemed angry, upset or even anxious; on the contrary, she was unusually serene. My skin prickled with apprehension and I feared I was experiencing the eerie calm before a storm, but I was reluctant to ask either how she was feeling or what she was doing. I suspected she wouldn't stop to answer me anyway.

With growing unease I looked on as she lifted a section of panelling out of the bottom of Sinclair's wardrobe, but rather than a magical passage to Narnia, a solid-looking safe was revealed. As Mel settled herself cross-legged on the floor before the locked, fifteen inch high door, I couldn't shake an impression of Alice in Wonderland from my head. Were the clues to her lost childhood inside?

Finally letting go of the poster in her hand, Mel smoothed it out on the carpet so that she could clearly read the details. Taking a deep breath she carefully entered the six digit date of Melanie Crowe's disappearance into the electronic keypad. The loud click made me jump as the locking mechanism released, and the safe door slowly, silently, swung open.

Chapter Fifty-two

Inside the safe were stacks and stacks of cash; great pink bricks of the stuff; neatly banded wads of fifties in such mint condition that it could be play money. It was in my way, so I pulled it out, carelessly chucking it aside.

'Jesus,' Liam muttered, squatting beside me, picking up a bundle and flipping through the end with his thumb. 'There must be thousands of pounds here…'

With the money removed I could focus on the slim manila files that had been buried underneath. Dragging them out into my lap I flipped them open one by one, flicking through the contents, scan-reading them and then discarding them each time my patience got the better of me. There were piles of bonds; documents pertaining to various stocks, shares, investments and savings accounts; numerous insurance certificates, and I even found the original deeds to Wildham Hall. That file seemed to include ancient-looking plans of the grounds which would be of interest to Liam, so I passed it to him before turning my attention to the last folder in my lap.

This was it; the proof I'd been looking for. The file held several papers but on top was a slim envelope with '*Melody*' written across it in Cornelia's distinctive handwriting. As I turned it over in my fingers I saw that it wasn't sealed; Gregory had no doubt read the letter inside. He had always implied that Cornelia's death was my fault and I was in no particular hurry to have that theory confirmed, so I carefully set it aside.

Beneath the letter was a creased and faded missing persons poster from mere days after Melanie had disappeared. Laying it out on the carpet beside the recent version Liam had found, I noted that in sixteen years, though the design and format of the poster had changed, the scant few details had remained the same.

The last remaining scraps of paper in the file were old news cuttings relating to the disappearance, neatly extracted from the local papers with a pair of nail scissors. Reading through the articles I mentally sifted the facts from the conjecture, and then studied the black and white photograph of Mr and Mrs Crowe sitting side by side. The couple looked dazed but otherwise ordinary. Scrutinising their features I searched for signs of my own, but the image was too grainy for me to draw any conclusions one way or the other. So these were my real parents...

'You OK?' Liam said softly.

Nodding I offered a half-hearted smile, but in truth I didn't know what I was, or even *who* I was for that matter.

'Did you notice that these deeds are all in the name of Melanie Crowe? It looks like Cornelia transferred ownership right before she died. Wildham Hall, the grounds, everything belongs to you – it has done all this time...'

Even if I could speak, I wouldn't know what to say to that. Returning my attention to the safe I realised there was still something lurking inside; something tucked right in the back corner, so reaching in I dragged it out.

Liam cursed under his breath as I stared at the little white, rose-printed dress in my hands, waiting for it to trigger a blinding flash of recognition or memory. But there was nothing – only a vague sense of sadness and a growing certainty that I was once someone else: I was once Melanie Crowe.

'This is unbelievable,' Liam said, as I neatly folded the dress and set it to one side. 'What do you want to do? What can *I* do? Can I get you anything? A cup of tea? Something stronger…?'

I properly looked at Liam for what felt like the first time in hours. He was sat right there on Gregory's bedroom floor beside me; solid and substantial; his low voice and patient concern deeply reassuring. On instinct I crawled into the warm comfort of his lap and he wrapped his strong arms around me; burying his face in my hair and rocking me as if I were a child. Maybe I was still a child inside – a lost one.

'So…' he murmured, '… do you want to go to the police now or in the morning?'

I looked up at him, startled. Police…? It hadn't even occurred to me.

'Here, talk to me,' he said opening the text function on his phone and handing it to me.

I'm not going to the police.

'Mel, it's a crime what they've done to you – how much more evidence do you need?' He waved a hand over the accumulated items on the floor around us. 'And your parents – your *real* parents – must have been going through hell. They need to know that you're alive.'

Not yet.

'I'll go with you – you don't have to go through this alone…'

I jabbed his phone at him.

'OK, not yet, I get it – we'll go in the morning. I guess it's getting late anyway. Do you want to stay here tonight or come back to mine?'

Stay here.

'OK.' He kissed my temple. 'Probably a good idea; the roads are icy.' I stood up and he staggered to his feet beside me. 'You sure I can't fix you something to help you sleep – a hot chocolate or something?'

Just take me to bed.

'Yes ma'am.' With that he swept me into his arms and carried me to my room.

At my insistence Liam made love to me, repeatedly, late into the night. He didn't speak of what we'd discovered or pester me with questions; he simply let my body do the talking; let my wandering hands, erect nipples and moist thighs be his guide. And I was grateful for that.

But in the early hours of the morning I woke from the same old nightmare, the one I now realised was based in fact. It may have all happened too long ago for me to remember the specifics, but the raw emotion – the upset and confusion of being snatched away from everything, and everyone, I knew and loved – had shadowed me all my life.

For a while I lay there watching Liam sleep; letting his slow, steady breathing calm and console me, then I crept out of bed, retrieved the envelope with my name on it, and tiptoed over to the nursery windows. It was a clear night and the icy landscape below sparkled in the moonlight; reflecting back enough silvery light to read by. My hands shook as I unfolded the letter from Cornelia, but it was time to find out what she had to say.

My dearest Melody,

Please know that I love you and that I am sorry for all that I have done. I should never have taken you from your parents; it was a selfish act, especially when I have first-hand experience of the terrible agony of losing a child. All I can offer in my defence is that I was not in my right mind at the time. I fell in love with you on first sight; immediately and completely. I wanted you for myself and I was convinced I could give you a better life.

I see now that I was wrong, but I cannot simply take you back, for fear of jeopardising Gregory's position. Neither can I live with this guilt. It grows heavier with each passing day. I pray you will forgive me for my weakness.

As I write this I console myself with the knowledge that Gregory will be a wonderful father to you and love you as I do. I've made sure that you will be well provided for. My only wish is that you live a long and happy life, have children of your own one day, and do not judge me too harshly.

Sincerely yours,

       Cornelia Sinclair.

Her words were nauseating and I bit back the urge to vomit as I balled the letter up in my fist. But I already knew I hated her. What was worse was how much I now hated myself. How had I let the Sinclairs do this to me? It was deeply humiliating. Somewhere along the way I'd simply accepted Gregory and Cornelia as my parents; I'd never questioned it; never once tried to fight back or run away. What a fool I'd been – how utterly gullible – I felt ashamed of myself.

Shivering, I stared at the fragmented ghost of my reflection in the window. In all good conscience could I really inflict this ridiculous, ugly mess on someone as wonderful as Liam? Didn't he deserve better?

Chapter Fifty-three

Mel was already up and dressed when I surfaced, and she was armed with a note:

I need you to go. I need time to get my head around everything.

'What time is it?' I said, rubbing my face and then extending my arms out into a full-on satisfying stretch and yawn.

She held up her bedside clock and I was surprised to see it was almost eleven a.m. but my newly reinstated watch confirmed it.

'I thought we were going to the police station this morning?'

She held up another sheet of paper which read: *I'm not ready to go to the police yet.*

'OK, but you can't stay here alone; what if Sinclair comes back?'

She shrugged and held up another prepared note. Clearly she had already anticipated everything I was going to say. This one said: *He's a coward. He doesn't scare me anymore.*

'Mel, the man abducted you and essentially kept you prisoner for sixteen years! Last weekend he locked you in your room with barely enough food to eat... coward or not, he can't be trusted.'

Her next note read: *Please respect my wishes and go.*

Her last words hurt. Needing to close the distance she was putting between us, I pulled her into a hug, but her body was tense and unyielding against mine. 'Look, I can't pretend to understand how you must be feeling, but please don't shut me out. I'm here for you; let me help you.'

It seemed she had run out of prepared notes, so she picked up a pen and wrote on the back of one: *I need to do this by myself. Please.*

'Do what?'

Rolling her eyes with irritation she clamped her mouth shut in a hard line. There was no point arguing with her, she was too stubborn, and considering everything she was going through, I didn't want to force her into anything.

'He's still got your phone – how will you contact me when you need me?'

I can email you from G's PC.

I sighed heavily in defeat, and she rewarded me with a fleeting peck on the lips before leaving me to dress alone.

Something was different this morning; something had changed. Last night Mel and I had been about as intimate as it was possible for two people to get – our bodies melded and synchronised in an orgy of intense love-making powerful enough to arouse and stimulate all the senses and block everything else out. It seemed to be what she needed and I was happy to oblige. But today something was off. Mel was calm and collected again, but something had altered in her demeanour that I couldn't put my finger on. And her insistence on being alone worried the hell out of me. I wanted to respect her wishes, of course I did, but there was no way I was abandoning her now.

I said goodbye and let her watch me leave Wildham Hall. At home I showered, changed, and filled a rucksack with supplies before turning around and sneaking back onto the grounds, unseen. The air had turned milder and the cloudy sky now matched the last of the dirty grey slush underfoot. But at least I no longer left tell-tale footprints behind everywhere I went.

In the stables I made myself a moderately comfortable base, from which to keep an eye on the woman I loved. I had food and drink; blankets and a hot water bottle to stave off the cold; a powerful but lightweight pair of bird-watching binoculars; and a book to help pass the time. By positioning myself in a chair to one side of the window I could observe the house; monitor the windows and the back door and listen out for anyone approaching along the driveway, all without being seen. It occurred to me that our roles had now been reversed and where Mel had once stalked me, it was now my turn to stake her out from the shadows. But my motives were pure – regardless of her past, Mel was the most precious person in the world to me – I would do anything to protect her and keep her safe. If it came to it I'd die for her, it was that simple.

Chapter Fifty-four

Once Liam was safely out of the way I set about tidying up. Gregory had been gone seven days now and I figured he'd return soon. I would be ready for him when he did.

I started in his bedroom. I didn't bother putting anything back in the safe – I figured the contents belonged to me – but I closed and locked the door and eased the wooden panelling back into position; hiding all outward signs I'd been near it. As I passed his en-suite bathroom I paused to eye the electric fan he kept up on a shelf in the corner. It had a cable long enough to extend to the bath and should be easy enough to switch on and chuck in. But that plan would involve me bursting in on Gregory while he was naked, which was not an idea I relished. Shaking my head I closed the door.

I carried the cash, the files and the dress upstairs and stashed them in an old chest in the eaves of the house, where he would not find them. As I was about to descend from the top landing I pondered the possibility of pushing him down the stairs. But I would need to lure him there first and take him by surprise, and even then he may not fall far or injure himself badly enough for my liking...

Safely back on the first floor I turned my attention to the wrecked nursery. There was nothing I could do about the broken door lock; the timber frame had splintered with the force of Liam's entrance, but I cleared all the shredded teddy bear remains into bin bags, laboriously hoovered up every last stray wisp of stuffing, and made the bed. Eyeing the prison-like windows I mentally ran through all the other bedroom windows, assessing whether any of them were suitable for pushing Gregory out of. But we had no balconies and none of the upper windows reached the floor, so forcing a grown man out of one would be near impossible. I abandoned that idea.

The sealed nursery windows were a fire hazard and I made a mental note to see if Liam could get them unsealed. I didn't dwell on thoughts of setting Gregory alight for long though. It was far too risky – the whole house might go up – and it would create a horrible smell.

As I carried the five remaining cans of food back down to the pantry I calculated how hungry I'd be by now, if Liam hadn't come to my rescue. That bastard hadn't left me nearly enough food. But of course locking Gregory up and starving him to death, although fitting, would take far too long.

In the kitchen I did the washing up and then sharpened the set of chef's knives; methodically running each blade back and forth across the stone until they glinted ominously beneath the overhead lights. While I was at it, I fetched Gregory's letter-opener from the study and honed that too, just in case I couldn't get to the kitchen when the time came. Tucked inside the desk drawer I found my confiscated mobile phone, so I switched it on and plugged it into the wall to charge, deliberately ignoring the influx of old text messages that arrived from Liam.

In the laundry room I perused the rat poison and the bottles of bleach, reading the warning labels and weighing up my options. Would he smell this stuff if I popped it in his whiskey? If possible I would like him to suffer before he died, but I was conscious of not allowing him enough room to retaliate; getting the dosage right would be tricky.

A loud bang like a gunshot made me jump and I glanced out the window in time to see a burst of green light sparkle across the sky, closely followed by another and then another. Of *course* – I could shoot him – what could be more appropriate than for Gregory the hunter to become the prey? And it was the fifth of November; every night this weekend would be filled with loud cracks, bangs and whistles. No-one would identify a rifle shot for what it was, until it was all far too late…

Chapter Fifty-five

I was stiff with cold and pacing the tack room in an effort to keep my blood flowing when I heard the subtle clank of the front entrance gates opening. Pressing my face to a crack in the door I swept an eye over the house; searching for a glimpse of Mel whilst straining my ears for any sounds more local than the exploding fireworks overhead. I could just identify the purr of Sinclair's Mercedes as it crawled up the drive, the wheels crunching on the gravel. He was back.

I was about to make a run for the nearest trees and sneak through the shadows to get a view of the front of the house, when a movement caught my eye. My hair stood on end and a surge of adrenalin flooded my veins as Mel stepped out the back door with a large gun in her hands.

Like me she was dressed all in black, but with her long leather boots on and her fiery red hair concealed inside a dark hat. The hunting rifle looked unnaturally long and cumbersome against her tiny frame as she quietly pulled the door shut behind her, tiptoed over to the tree line, and began picking her way through the shadows towards the drive.

Barely breathing I followed several paces behind her, grateful that the noisy detonations overhead covered my heavy tread. Was that rifle loaded? Was she really intending to kill him or purely hoping to scare him? It would certainly get Sinclair's attention. But then why had she come outside? Why not confront him inside the house? After what had happened at the garden centre with James and Kat, I'd seen enough gun violence to last me a lifetime – I really didn't want to witness any more.

Both Mel and I paused as lights went on in the windows up above. I got a brief glimpse of Sinclair as he darted from room to room, presumably searching for his missing prisoner. Eventually he came back downstairs to the study – which lit up like a stage set as he entered the room.

Light spilled from the large bay window but didn't reach far enough to expose those of us loitering beneath the trees. We both looked on as Sinclair helped himself to whiskey from a decanter, opened his briefcase and lifted several files of paper out onto the desk. Sitting down in the window with his back to us, he was blind to our presence and in perfect view; an easy target. My body tensed with anticipation as Mel slowly lifted the barrel of the rifle in her hands and began to take aim.

'Please don't,' I whispered.

Despite the fireworks detonating loudly in the sky above, my voice made her flinch. Thankfully the gun didn't go off.

'Don't do this, please. There'll be no coming back.' Rolling her eyes Mel glared at me and I offered up a notepad and pen. 'Talk to me, please.'

She cast a glance back at Sinclair, but he wasn't going anywhere; he'd picked up the phone to make a call. With a sigh she lowered the rifle to her side and I realised it must be heavy for her. Transferring it into her left hand, she snatched up the pen and scrawled *GO AWAY!* on the pad in my hand.

'You do this; you kill that bastard, and he is free of any guilt or punishment; he gets away with what he's done and *you* become the criminal! Please, that isn't you…'

I could almost hear her teeth grinding together as she held back tears of anger and frustration. *Who am I then? Because I don't know anymore*, she wrote across the page.

Lifting my hand I went to caress her face but she jerked back away from me, her hand tightening around the rifle. 'You're the same person I fell in love with. You are smart and funny and brave and beautiful and none of this shit has to change that. Not if you don't let it.'

She stared at me for several seconds, her face tinged alternately red, green and blue beneath the fireworks before she re-employed the pen in her hand. *I don't even know what my name is anymore.*

My heart ached. For all her spirit, courage and obstinacy, she was still a girl lost. 'Well,' I said, quietly clearing my throat. 'You're free to choose – or you can give yourself an entirely new name if you want to – change it by deed poll. You're an adult – you have money – you are free to be whoever you want to be…'

Turning back she contemplated Sinclair through the window. He was still talking on the phone and shuffling papers on his desk, full of his own self-importance and oblivious to the fact that his life hung in the balance.

'Whoever you decide to be, you don't want to spend the rest of your life in prison, surely? Not because of that fucking bastard in there…?' Slowly she shook her head and I took it as a good sign. 'Can I have the gun?'

She glanced down, as if she'd forgotten it was there, and I shoved the notepad into my jacket pocket so that she could pass the rifle to me. My pulse thudded with relief as I disarmed it, removing and pocketing the cartridges for good measure. With a shiver Mel wrapped her arms around herself. 'Come back to the stables and we'll work out what to do next,' I said, offering her my free hand.

Shaking her head she retrieved her own mobile from her pocket.

I'm going to confront him and I need your help.

'I'm not sure that's a good idea... wouldn't it be better to leave it to the police?'

Mel's mind was made up, that much was clear as she added: I need you to make sure he listens.

It was no small thing that she was asking for my help. Despite the challenge in her demeanour, her request was a plea from the heart. She was determined to go in there and face Sinclair, alone if necessary, but if he chose to ignore her or lock her up again, she would be powerless to make herself heard.

Regardless of my reservations, Mel deserved to have her say; a chance to confront the man who'd taken everything from her. And I loved her – I would be whatever she needed me to be.

'Lead the way.'

Chapter Fifty-six

'Melody – there you are – how did you get out? Where have you been? Where have all the things gone from your room?' Gregory's voice was somewhere between irritation and genuine panic as I stepped into the study. His eyes widened as Liam filled the doorway behind me. 'What are *you* doing here? I thought I told you to leave.'

'You locked Mel in a room and left her without enough food to eat; did you really think you would get away with that?' Liam's voice was low, calm and steady, and all the more effective for it.

Gregory blanched. 'It's none of your concern what goes on in this house.'

'Mel is my concern. If it was up to me you'd already be in prison by now, so I suggest you sit down and read what she has to say.'

'I'm not going to be threatened by a mongrel like y—'

Liam moved around me, the rifle held casually in one hand and took two menacing steps in Gregory's direction. Instinctively Gregory shifted back behind his desk and abruptly sat down. His eyes darted nervously between the gun and the empty space in his cabinet as Liam gently rested the rifle by his feet.

Approaching Gregory's desk I tapped, `You're not my real father`, into my mobile phone and showed him the screen.

'What's that supposed to mean?' he muttered.

`You kidnapped me.`

His eyes widened further, his face taking on an unhealthy grey tinge. 'Don't be ridiculous,' he said, with a tremor in his voice. Liam moved up behind me in a show of silent support, his shadow looming across the desk while Gregory shrunk into his chair.

You stole me from my real parents when I was 5.

Sweat broke out on Gregory's forehead. 'That's crazy – I don't know what you're talking about.'

How could you? What kind of sick person does that?

He shook his head, trembling. 'You don't understand; it wasn't me; I didn't want to; I only went along with it out of love...'

Cornelia.

'Yes... yes... I'm sorry...' Gregory started weeping, hiding his face in his hands as his shoulders began to shake. It was pathetic. It was nauseating how quickly he had broken down and admitted to being complicit in ruining my entire life; so far his pitiful confession hadn't given me any sense of satisfaction at all. Glancing up at Liam, I was unsurprised to see my own disgust reflected in his features. He turned away and went to sit in a chair across the room, seemingly confident that Gregory posed no threat, and I returned my attention to the small screen in my hand.

Tell me what happened.

Gregory drew a handkerchief out of his pocket, wiped his face and blew his snivelling nose.

'She... she wanted a child so badly... you can't begin to understand... she'd had five miscarriages and two still births and I couldn't bear to see her go through any more. I loved her so much... I just wanted her to be happy...' He paused to blow his nose again and took a few shaky breaths. 'She just brought you home one day. I tried to talk her into taking you back, but she was a changed woman – so happy – so utterly smitten – and I could never refuse her anything, not really. She cut your hair and dressed you up as a boy at first; so that no-one would recognise you. But then she fired all the staff and started dressing you up in wigs and frilly dresses; like you were a doll. And she kept you safely within the grounds and stopped you from speaking to anyone but her. It was like her own private world, just the two of you; she even shut *me* out. I tried not to mind too much because she was happy – really happy – for a while. But it didn't last. She knew what she'd done was wrong and the guilt started to eat away at her. She couldn't give you up, but neither could she live with what she'd done to you; to your parents...' Gregory sighed heavily.

She killed herself.

Gregory glanced at my mobile screen and nodded forlornly. 'Sleeping pills.'

So why didn't you take me back to my parents?

Gregory shrugged avoiding my eye.

WHY? I shoved the mobile in his face, tempted to hit him with it.

'How could I? I'd have been arrested and it would have destroyed Cornelia's good name...'

You could just have left me somewhere with an anonymous note!

He shook his head. 'I couldn't take that risk…'

I stared at him, appalled. `Coward.`

He bristled at the insult. 'It's not like you've had a bad life – I never felt like I was your father, but I still tried; I've provided for you; protected y—' His head snapped back as I punched him as hard as I could. There was a crunch as my fist connected with his nose and blood sprayed across his shirt front. 'Argh, my nose!' he yelled, clutching his face.

Liam was beside me in an instant. 'Nice,' he commented, positioning himself protectively between us, but Gregory was too concerned with his own face to think about physical retaliation.

'Ah shit, that hurt,' Gregory muttered, gingerly pressing his handkerchief to his nose and tipping his head back to stem the blood.

My hand tingled with urge to hit him again, but Liam was in my way, his arms crossed over his broad chest.

'Look, I'm sorry OK?'

'So what are you going to do about it? Liam said.

Gregory glared at Liam and then at me. 'I'll make it up to you, Melody, I can give you money; lots of it; I'll even sign the house over to you if—'

'The house already belongs to her, we've seen the deeds,' Liam growled. 'Try again, arsehole.'

'Oh… right, OK…' Gregory stammered. 'Then I'll go to the police – that's what you want, isn't it? I'll hand myself in – I'll tell them everything…'

Liam turned to me. 'What do you think?'

Truthfully I was disappointed. Gregory and Cornelia had taken away my family, my freedom; even my voice.

I'd hoped that by confronting Gregory, hurting him and making him squirm, that I'd feel better; that I'd feel triumphant or relieved, but it didn't change anything. I still despised myself for having been a victim all my life without even realising it. I nodded my agreement, weary of the whole thing.

'Hey, are you OK?' Liam's voice was quiet as he gently cradled my face with one hand. His warm touch was familiar and soothing, and I closed my eyes as I leaned into his palm with a sigh. How was this wonderful man still here at my side; kind and comforting, after everything he'd found out about me; after everything I'd said to him? Would I ever be worthy of this gentle giant? He leaned down and pressed a tender kiss to my forehead, and I could hear Gregory shifting uncomfortably in his chair.

When I opened my eyes Liam's steady gaze held mine. 'Shall we all go to the police station together?'

I nodded.

'Do you mind if I tidy myself up first? I've got blood all down my shirt,' Gregory was as vain as ever and amazingly calm under the circumstances.

'Don't take too long,' Liam warned, without taking his eyes from mine.

Liam wrapped me in a warm hug and we stood in silence listening to Gregory as he made his way upstairs, moved about in the bedroom and ran the taps in the bathroom above. After a few minutes there was a loud thump followed by an ominous stillness. Drawing apart we exchanged a look before simultaneously making a dash for the stairs.

Liam reached Gregory's en-suite bathroom before me, and swore as he took in the sight of Gregory's body slumped on the floor; convulsing with a hideous gurgling, choking sound amid a spreading pool of dark liquid. Grabbing a towel and quickly dropping into a crouch over the body, Liam tried to stem the blood, but the gaping red slit at Gregory's throat was deep and rapidly decanting his life force like wine across the tiles. With one last spraying cough, Gregory stopped moving, the ugly, wet sound replaced by a sickening silence.

As Liam retrieved his mobile from his back pocket and dialled 999 he distractedly wiped his fingers down his jeans; the same way he always did, except this time it wasn't mud he was wiping off his hands. The rusty metallic smell of the blood was overpowering in the confined space. A cacophony of fireworks started up again; whistling, cracking and reverberating across the sky outside the window – an exuberant display of celebration at odds with Gregory's unseemly demise. I felt light-headed, as if I might float right out of my body, as I stared at the recently sharpened letter-opener lying glinting at me from the bathroom floor. I'd done it – I'd killed him – I was a murderess now.

Chapter Fifty-seven

It was mere minutes before sirens started up in the distance, but no matter how quickly the emergency services arrived, it would make no difference to Sinclair now. Leading Mel back into the bedroom, I made her sit down with a brandy while I set about getting the entrance gates and the front door open. Concerned by how still and pale with shock she had become, I quickly returned to her side, but she didn't move.

I was totally unprepared for how aggressive the police were as they made their entrance. I called out to let them know where we were, but they swarmed through the house fully armed and clad in body armour as if taking down a lethal terrorist cell, rather than responding to a suicide. One forced me down onto my knees at gunpoint yelling at the top of his lungs, while the others spread out, quickly checking the body in the bathroom and rapidly assessing every other room. With my hands up and my face pressed to the carpet I tried, unsuccessfully, to explain the situation, but they didn't appear to be listening – their priority was to get me in handcuffs.

Once various officers throughout the house had conveyed their discovery of a suspicious firearm and declared an 'all clear' over their network of radios, a senior, plainly-clothed officer appeared in front of me. I was granted enough space to sit back on my heels and tried to keep my irritation out of my expression as I raised my gaze to meet his.

'Liam Hunt?' he said.

'Yes, it was me that called you—'

'Detective Inspector Fletcher, Hertfordshire Police.'

'Right, are the cuffs really necessary?'

'Liam Hunt, I'm arresting you on suspicion of the murder of Gregory Sinclair. You do not have to say anything—'

'Are you kidding me? He killed himself!' The detective carried on cautioning me regardless.

'A week ago Gregory Sinclair reported you for harassment. Now he's dead and here you are in his house covered in his blood,' he said.

I stared at him in shock. 'What? But... I tried to help him—'

He cut me off. 'Two months ago you were involved in a fatal shooting at Southwood's Garden Centre—'

'Oh come on, I wasn't *involved*, I just happened to be there – it was nothing to do with me!'

'—You also have a known history of violence.'

'I was cautioned *once* when I eighteen but I was drunk—' I said, staggering to my feet.

'When you've been a police officer as long as I have, Mr Hunt, you stop believing in coincidences. You can explain down at the police station.'

'No, stop!' Mel's voice rang out as clear as a bell, making every hair on my body stand to attention. The fireworks outside had ceased and everyone turned to look at her as her words hung in the air.

The sound was even more beautiful than I'd imagined and instantly brought a lump to my throat, while my body burned with the need to hold her. A female officer was trying to lead her away, but Mel stood firm with her fists clenched at her sides, her beautiful grey eyes determined and locked on mine. 'It was me – I killed him,' she said.

Chapter Fifty-eight

They swept me away in the back of a patrol car to the police station where they photographed, swabbed and printed me and took away my clothes. I sat in an ugly, over-sized, grey marl tracksuit, in a small, featureless room, on an uncomfortable moulded plastic chair, at a table with three strangers. Nothing seemed real. But I opened my mouth and I told them everything.

I started by describing my life at Wildham Hall and the fact that Gregory spent most of his time abroad, and then skipped ahead to my relationship with Liam and the events of the past week. When I mentioned the proof I'd discovered of my abduction, it materialised on the tabletop in front of me, each item neatly labelled and sealed inside clear plastic bags for me to identify. I spoke about wanting to kill Gregory; about contemplating poison; loading cartridges into the rifle and sharpening the letter-opener on his desk. I told them how I made him cry, made him confess, called him a coward, broke his nose, and then let him go upstairs alone... and I described the horror we found next.

I had no idea where my voice had miraculously come from – I didn't recognise the sound and it felt more like vomiting up words than speaking – but I needed to get it all out. For the most part DI Fletcher, and the other people in that room – a female police officer and a duty solicitor – simply let me talk and talk and talk for hours, with barely any interruption.

I was exhausted by the time I'd finished; my mouth dry and my throat raw. The female officer took me to a cell where I curled up on my side on a hard bed, too drained and numb to cry or worry or even think, and simply fell asleep.

Several hours later I was woken and delivered back to the same interview room, where I retook my seat across from DI Fletcher, apprehensive about what he might say. This man with his pock-marked skin, receding hairline and penetrating eyes, could feasibly have me locked away for good, or even worse; have Liam locked up. Strong, gentle, loving Liam. Thoughts of him filled my head, blurring my vision and choking my airway. In that moment I could only hope and pray that I'd said enough to keep him safe.

'It's clear to me that you are the victim in all this, Melody. Your fingerprints confirm that you are indeed Melanie Crowe; the girl who went missing in July sixteen years ago. We could find only minor traces of the deceased's blood on you, and so far all the evidence backs up what you've told us.' Slipping a pair of reading glasses out of his breast pocket, he perched them on his nose and flipped open a file. I recognised an upside-down photograph of Cornelia clipped to the first page.

'Cornelia Sinclair's medical records suggest that she suffered from various mental disorders all her life, and that she did indeed have several miscarriages in the years before she committed suicide. It seems highly probable that it was she who abducted you, but without any witness testimonies that may be difficult to prove.'

I wanted Fletcher to stop talking, but the words, the voice, that had come to me so easily the day before, had gone back into hiding.

'So far our investigation into Gregory Sinclair suggests that he too was a disturbed character. He had a chequered childhood – I won't go into all the details, but he was almost certainly a victim of abuse himself – and we have evidence that points to more than one instance of fraud...'

I missed a lot of what the detective was saying, as my mind grappled with everything that had happened. Closing my eyes I tried to take deep breaths, silently wishing this could all be over.

'... It's safe to say Sinclair had a lot to hide, not just your abduction, and he'd have known that once you reported and exposed him, it would all come out. Faced with that prospect it's possible he was motivated to commit suicide... but either way, we are ruling you out for his murder.'

As I studied the detective's expression, I hardly dared to believe what he was saying.

'It's understandable that you wanted to hurt him, Melody, but we don't believe you are actually to blame for his death.'

'And Liam?' I croaked.

'I'm afraid preliminary forensics are more damning where Mr Hunt is concerned. He has a history of violence and he certainly has motive. He'll remain in custody until we've established whether or not he should be tried for murder.'

I stared at him. 'But he's innocent; he didn't do anything; I've told you!'

Fletcher closed the file, removed his spectacles and pushed them back into his pocket. 'We're releasing you today without charge. Is there anyone you'd like us to call for you? Someone who could bring you a change of clothes or—'

'I'm not leaving here without Liam.'

He pursed his lips. 'Melody, your parents – Carol and Stephen Crowe – have been informed that you've been found – they're on their way here now...'

'I don't want to see them,' I said. They might be my flesh and blood but they were strangers to me, and the idea of having to face them now, while Liam was still locked up, was too much.

'You don't have to see them, of course; that's your right, but they've waited a long time to find you... surely they deserve to see for themselves that you are alive and well...?'

I stared down at my hands in my lap. I'd never felt less alive and well. I wanted to crawl into the warmth and safety of Liam's arms and sleep for a year.

'Obviously we can arrange for you to speak to a counsellor first – that's standard procedure in cases like these...'

I wished he'd shut up. I didn't want to be a case, I just wanted Liam back.

'And I should warn you – we've taken precautions, but even so – there's a good chance the press will get wind of your story sooner or later and they'll want statements, interviews...'

I shook my head, desperately trying to tune out what he was saying. 'I only want to see Liam, no-one else, just Liam…'

He started to speak again and I covered my ears with my hands, squeezed my eyes shut and began humming loudly, aware that I was finally losing it.

Chapter Fifty-nine

What on earth had possessed her? Why had Mel confessed to a murder that she clearly didn't commit? When I think back to all the times when she *should* have used her voice – to defend herself or to call for help, like when she almost drowned in the lake for example, and instead of screaming she'd stayed resolutely mute – and now she'd finally spoken up only to incriminate herself. Would I ever understand the eccentricities of Mel's mind?

The nightmarish process at the police station seemed to go on forever – the prying, the prodding, the poking and the relentless questions; the same information repeated over and over again, approached and re-hashed a hundred different ways. Yes I loved Melody, and yes we were both angry and upset about what Sinclair had done to her; but no, we didn't kill him.

I was confident they wouldn't find my prints on that letter-opener, I hadn't touched it, but would they find Mel's? Would that be enough to charge her? Surely not. Even so the situation looked bad. People didn't just suddenly slit their own throats – slaughter themselves like animals – did they? I wouldn't have even thought it possible if I hadn't seen the evidence with my own eyes. Statistically speaking it couldn't be a common method of suicide, you'd have to be pretty crazy to even try it, and yet, he had, the stupid bastard. Was Sinclair deliberately hoping to frame us? My only hope was that the autopsy and blood analysis results would support the truth.

Yesterday they'd granted me a phone call and I'd used it to call my brother. He was shocked to say the least, but he'd contacted Will Cranston, our family solicitor, on my behalf, who in turn had provided a clean set of clothes, a toothbrush and two packaged sandwiches, along with his legal advice.

But I was more worried about Mel than myself. They wouldn't tell me anything about what was happening to her. I had no desire to end up in jail, but at least I was physically big and strong enough to look after myself. Mel was so vulnerable in so many ways and she had already suffered so much; I couldn't bear the thought of her in prison. If it came to that, I would confess to murder myself. Cranston wouldn't like it, but tough shit. I wasn't going to leave the woman I love to rot in a jail cell.

By Sunday morning I figured that I must be nearing the thirty-six hour mark of my detention. Unless a judge granted an extension the police would have to charge or release me soon. A solemn face appeared at the hatch in the door to my cell, before it was unlocked and opened.

'Come with me,' said one of the two uniforms standing in the corridor. I was tempted to ask what was happening, but I didn't want to give them the satisfaction of withholding the answer, so I simply ducked through the doorway after the first officer whilst the second followed close behind.

We navigated the utilitarian maze of corridors in near silence, my mind racing. Was this it? Had all the forensic test results come back? Was I finally going to be charged with murder? Was Mel...?

318

As we reached the doorway to Interview Room 2, the officer in front paused to speak to a colleague, and my attention was drawn to the far corner of the room. A small figure was hunched in a chair, head down, feet drawn up and arms wrapped tightly around their knees. At first I thought it was a child; the standard police-issue grey tracksuit swamped their tiny frame and hid their hands and feet completely. But then, sensing my presence, the figure raised their head, a pair of eyes peeking out from beneath lank strands of hair, and my legs almost gave way with an agonising stab of recognition.

Mel…?

Chapter Sixty

Liam...? Was that really him? He looked stooped and haggard, half of his face disguised under nearly three days of stubble, but his eyes, his lovely hazel brown eyes were unmistakable, locked on me and widening with surprise.

Leaping up I darted across the room, tripping over my wretched tracksuit bottoms as I went, but he took two powerful strides towards me and caught me up in his arms; clutching me to his chest as if I was a part of him gone too long. The warmth and reassurance of his embrace as I was engulfed in his familiar scent was overwhelming, triggering tears I hadn't realised I was holding back.

'God, Mel, what have they done to you? Are you OK?' he asked as I sobbed into his matching sweatshirt. 'Look at me, baby, are you OK?'

As I dragged my gaze up to his he stroked my hair back, anxiously searching my face. I wanted to reassure him, but couldn't speak past the knot of emotion in my throat, so I reached up and kissed him with all the energy I could summon. After days of bad food and stale coffee, nothing tasted as good as he did right then.

Someone cleared their throat in the doorway and we broke off our kiss, dragged back to the reality of our surroundings with a bump.

'Take a seat, both of you,' DI Fletcher said. Liam lowered me to the ground with obvious reluctance, but kept a firm hold of my hand as we sat down across the table from the detective.

'You'll be relieved to hear that we're releasing you without charge Mr Hunt.' I pressed my face into Liam's shoulder, shaking with relief.

'What about Mel?' Liam's voice was deep and urgent as it rumbled through his chest.

'She was released yesterday, but she wouldn't leave here without you,' the detective said.

'Jesus, baby,' Liam muttered, pressing a kiss to my head and stroking my hair.

'The coroner has ruled Gregory Sinclair's death a suicide, so we won't be pursuing any further action. You're both free to go. I'll give you a minute alone and then you'll need to see the custody sergeant to reclaim your personal effects...' I tuned the detective out as I focused on trying to calm down. Were they really letting us go? Was it really over?

Once we were alone, I wiped my eyes and nose on my sleeve and Liam urged me to look at him.

'Did you hear that, Mel? We're free. Everything's going to be OK, I promise...'

His earnest expression made me want to melt with love for him – my gorgeous man. I swallowed hard, focusing on the feel of my vocal chords and the words I'd wanted, needed, to say for so long.

'Liam, I love you.'

A huge smile split across his face. 'You have no idea how good it is to hear you say that. I love you too,' he said, leaning in to kiss me.

Epilogue

'Can we go swim in the lake now?' Ferne says.

'Yeah, can we, Uncle Lim?' Aster tugs my trouser leg and cranes her neck to squint up at me. Six-foot-six is a long way up when you're just four years old.

'Only if Mummy and Daddy say it's OK,' I say glancing over at Maire who is already helping Ferne strip down to a spotty pink bathing costume.

'You'll need sunscreen, Aster,' Maire says, tossing a plastic bottle in Lester's direction. Catching it he uses it to beckon Aster towards him.

'Come here, sausage.'

'Maybe we should all go down to the lake? I'm up for a paddle,' Dad suggests.

'Aye, I can't wait to dip my swollen feet in there,' Maire agrees.

'You sure you can waddle that far, sweetness?' says Lester, while smearing sun cream across my niece's scrunched up nose.

Maire pulls a face at him. 'I'm not a duck! My walk is all swagger, I'll have you know. Anyway you're coming with us, husband of mine; you can carry me if I get tired.' Lester sighs heavily but can't keep the grin off his face. He never could refuse Maire anything, even before she fell pregnant with his third child.

'Yes, let's all go,' my mother-in-law says, gathering plates from the table.

'Just leave that, Carol,' I say. 'We can clear up later. Do you know where Mel's gone?'

Stephen breaks off mid-conversation with my dad. 'She wandered off into the trees in that direction,' he says, pointing. 'I asked her if she wanted any company but she said she needed to stretch her legs and wouldn't be gone long...'

I nod with what I hope is a reassuring smile. The Crowes were reunited with their lost daughter seven years ago now, but Mel's parents still get anxious whenever she's out of sight, and with Mel being the free spirit that she is, that's frequently. 'You guys head on down to the lake and I'll go find her.'

I watch for a while, waving off assorted family members as they abandon the remains of the picnic and wend their way down through the grounds, chatting and laughing as they go.

Time to find Mrs Hunt.

As I head into the cool shade of the trees, I can't help counting my blessings. Thinking of Mel as my wife still gives me a rush of pleasure. It's been three years since our modest town hall ceremony and the intimate family picnic reception that followed afterwards, here in the grounds of our home. It was such a wonderful day that the party warranted repeating. We've held the same picnic each summer since, and it's fast becoming a tradition.

From the moment Mel told me she loved me in the police station that day, I wanted to marry her. We were both worse for wear at the time, having spent most of the weekend locked in separate prison cells, fearing the worst. But my relief at being reunited with her again, and the look in her eyes as she declared her love for me, with her very own voice, well, that was it for me – I wanted her to be my wife. Mel, on the other hand, perhaps understandably, was not sold on marriage and took longer to come around to the idea.

Even without a media furore, the Crowe family reunion was always going to be tough on Mel. After sixteen years of quiet solitude and self-dependency, the sudden raw and unconditional love and devotion of two parents she barely remembered was hard to accept. And the scandal of her childhood abduction and subsequent reunion with her parents was big news in a place as small as Wildham. With the help of my friends, my family and my solicitor, I did my best to shield her from the worst of the press attention, but it was a difficult time. She and I spent a good few months holed up at Wildham Hall where Mel threw herself into a major re-decorating project – stripping, sanding, re-papering and re-painting every room with unswerving gusto. Together we rode out the media storm, and in the process made the big old house our own.

Eventually the story became yesterday's chip paper, people lost interest and life settled into a new kind of normal. I returned to landscaping and now I have my own team of lads to work for me, Olly included of course. Hunt Landscaping is going from strength to strength as word of our garden transformations spread.

When no living heirs could be found, Mel accepted inheritance of the entire Sinclair family's wealth, but she has never been comfortable with it. She has donated large sums to various charities and set up her own independent publishing company, which, though young, is already flourishing.

Mel has become more sociable with time. She is still the headstrong, quirky enigma I fell in love with – sweet and stubborn and still driving me crazy, but in many ways she has integrated into society more easily than I had anticipated. Despite her up-bringing, Mel has successfully rebuilt a relationship with her parents, embraced the role as auntie to my nieces, and befriended all of my mates; Kat and Cally included.

As a group we still support the Wildham Warriors at their matches, and we still meet at The White Bear on Tuesday nights, but for the most part we leave the actual playing to the younger players. Lester retired from playing rugby four years ago – his leg was never the same after his injury – and with my fortieth birthday fast approaching I'm considering giving it up too.

Maintaining the grounds of Wildham Hall is a workout in itself. It's my home now and I enjoy every minute spent here, but it's a never ending job. The first thing Mel and I did after I moved in was reinstate and replant the Édouard Marcel rose garden to his original design. Seven years on, it is maturing nicely and has become such a draw for gardening enthusiasts that two weekends a year we open it to the public to raise money for charity. Visitors come from all over to revel in, and gush over, the abundant perfumed blooms. We're both proud of it, but for Mel it's especially important; a beautiful garden sprung from a weedy quagmire; a public triumph over her unhappy past; a garden that says "look, there is goodness here; the Sinclairs didn't destroy everything; they didn't win; they did not break me." Like a rose cut back hard, Mel has come back stronger than ever.

As I reach the clearing in the trees I spot that the door to Pan's newly-restored grotto garden is open. My wife has the only key.

Barefoot and lost in thought, Mel stands before the reinstated statue of Aphrodite; the goddess of love, beauty and procreation. In her long pale green summer dress and flowery hair-band, Mel looks like a goddess herself; or a nymph of the wood; a spirit of the trees. Sensing my presence she turns and smiles and I take the key from the door, lock it behind me and push through the ferns towards her.

'Everything OK?' I murmur, reluctant to disturb the tranquil, meditative peace of the space.

'It is now,' she says, rising up on her toes, linking her arms up around my neck and pressing her mouth to mine. Every word that passes Mel's lips is precious to me, even after seven years, even when she is upset or angry about something and shouting at me, I am grateful for her voice. 'I knew you'd find me,' she whispers against my cheek.

'I'll always find you.' Dipping my head and breathing her in, I trail kisses down her throat. 'Always.'

She draws back, her pale grey gaze serious and arresting mine. 'There's something I need to tell you.'

'Go on.'

She opens her mouth but no words came out, and after a pause she closes it again, swallowing hard. Worry slithers through me and I touch my fingers to her face. 'What is it?'

327

Stepping back she takes my hand and presses my palm to her abdomen. Wordlessly we stare at each other in silent, intense communication; emotion building inside me as I search her gaze for confirmation.

'Are you...? Are we...? Are you saying we're having a baby...?'

She nods, a smile trembling on her lips, and I kiss her hard, overcome with joy, before abruptly pulling back.

'Wait, are you sure? We only started trying a few weeks ago...' My eyes are brimming with tears and I try to blink them away.

'I'm pregnant,' she says, finding her voice again, 'Don't wimp out on me now, Liam Hunt...'

I laugh, wiping a hand across my face and pull her back into my arms. 'I won't, I promise.'

'You'd better not, I don't know the first thing about being a mother.' I hear the fear in her voice and cup her face in my hand.

'Hey, we've talked about this – you're going to be a wonderful mum – Ferne, Aster, Heath, Daisy, the twins; they all adore you, you know that. You're going to be a natural.'

She pulls my head down to kiss me and as I explore and revel in the sweet familiar taste of her mouth, I lift her up and draw her close. She moans – a delicious sound – as she wraps her legs around my hips and presses herself against where I am already hard for her.

'Make love to me...'

'Here?'

'Yes.'

We undress each other until we are completely naked and lie right there between the ferns at Aphrodite's feet. We make love as if we are the only souls on Earth; as if there is only her and me and the life we are creating between us, until Mel cries out my name and we climax together, euphoric, dazed and breathless. For a long time afterwards we lie in silence just listening to the rustle of the breeze and the birds in the trees above. And then we hear laughter in the distance.

'Oh crap,' she says, a crease appearing between her eyebrows. 'You don't think anyone heard us do you?'

Chuckling I shake my head. 'I think we got away with it.' She strokes her fingers across her smooth stomach and I stare at it, mesmerised. 'I love hearing you scream my name,' I mutter.

She grins. 'I know.'

'I love you, Melanie Hunt; I'll love you forever.'

'Good. I'm holding you to that, Mr Hunt,' she says, returning her lips to mine.

THE END

Grace Lowrie

Having worked as a collage artist, sculptor, prop maker and garden designer, Grace has always been creative, but she is a romantic introvert at heart and writing was, and is, her first love.

A lover of rock music, art nouveau design, blue cheese and grumpy ginger tomcats, Grace is also an avid reader of fiction – preferring coffee and a sinister undercurrent, over tea and chick lit. When not making prop costumes or hanging out with her favourite nephews, she continues to write stories from her Hertfordshire home.

Á

Proudly published by Accent Press

www.accentpress.co.uk